BACK HOME

BETHAN DARWIN

ISIS
LARGE PRINT
Oxford

First published in Great Britain 2009
by
Honno

Published in Large Print 2010 by ISIS Publishing Ltd.,
7 Centremead, Osney Mead, Oxford OX2 0ES
by arrangement with
Honno

British Library Cataloguing in Publication Data
Darwin, Bethan.
    Back home.
    1. Intergenerational relations - - Fiction.
    2. London (England) - - Social life and customs - -
    Fiction.
    3. Wales - - Social life and customs - - Fiction.
    4. Large type books.
    I. Title
    823.9'2–dc22

ISBN 978–0–7531–8568–1 (hb)
ISBN 978–0–7531–8569–8 (pb)

Printed and bound in Great Britain by
T. J. International Ltd., Padstow, Cornwall

This book is dedicated to grandparents who make sure life's edges meet in the middle.

Acknowledgements

Lots of people helped me get this book written and I'd like to say thank you.

To my grandmother, Iris Hopkins, 89 this year, for telling me the story that gave me the idea for the book, and my grandfather-in-law, Alwyn Rowlands, in whose memory with love the character of Trevor is written.

Phil Carradice's books Wales at War and Coming Home: Wales After The War, published by Gomer, for giving me an insight into how life was for Welsh people in the 1940s.

To Pat Clayton, Cressida Downing, Abigail Bosanko and Penny Thomas whose constructive criticism, kindly delivered, made the book better.

To my wonderful family and friends who read early drafts of the book and were encouraging and supportive, with particular thanks to Shelley Murray who was enthusiastic about it when I was not.

To my partners and colleagues in law firm Darwin Gray LLP for their enlightened attitude towards flexible working.

To Helena Earnshaw, Caroline Oakley and everyone at Honno for their hard work.

And finally to my husband, David, and children Caleb and Megan. All the way to Canada and back, you three.

CHAPTER
ONE

For a long time I lived with my mother and grandfather in a tall terraced house in Clapham. I don't remember living anywhere else before that but one summer holiday when I was still in junior school my mother drove me to a leafy street in Balham and pointed out a red brick house, square and squat, and told me how I'd been born there, bursting out of her on the floor of the bathroom. She had gone for a long bath and, soothed by the warm water around her, had not realised that her back ache had turned into full blown labour pains until she'd finally hoisted herself out and discovered that I was already arriving, would be with her before she could even shout to my father to come upstairs and see. My dad rushed up the stairs two at a time to find me flapping and gasping on the bath mat, as if my mother had just landed a fish. The cord that connected us was blue-grey and slippery, coiled like a metal spring and thick and strong as life.

My mother told me how she soaked the bath mat afterwards, left it steeping in a bucket over night. When she washed it, it came up as good as new.

I lived in the red brick house until I was three and my parents decided to get divorced. It was a joint decision apparently, amicably reached, and it did not take long for them to divide up their few possessions and move out. The red brick house was only rented, the only thing they had that was worth anything was me and what was happening with me was not up for discussion. I would be living with my mother but staying with my father every other weekend and that was that. My dad rented another home nearby, a flat this time, with two small bedrooms, one for him and one for me, and my mother and I moved in with my grandfather.

Moving into the house in Clapham is the first thing I remember in life. The memories are just fragments, like bits of a photo that someone has torn up; then thought better of it and tried to fit the pieces back together. They come falling into my head when I least expect them — day dreaming in the kitchen while waiting for the kettle to boil or just before I fall asleep or, oddest of all, during or after sex — they are sudden and don't last long. I try to grasp these flashes when they arrive; see if I can hold onto them a bit longer, inspect them more clearly, but I never can. I have a glimpse of standing outside the house and of my grandfather coming outside to greet us and carrying me in through the front door. I have another one of climbing up a long flight of stairs leading to a big white room, empty except for a single bed, and of feeling lonely and excited when I get there. These memories are blurry and smudged, fuzzy round the edges. Only one memory is in focus, clear and crisp. It is of sitting in the kitchen in Clapham on that first night, eating a boiled egg with a teaspoon. The spoon has an odd metallic taste and I find the egg enormous, so huge that I cannot possibly eat it all, will never reach the bottom of it with my strange-tasting little spoon. My mother and my grandfather watch me as I eat. My first memory is tangy with love and with the sharp taste of silver spoons.

When I left to study English at a university on the south coast I didn't think I would be gone for long. I would be back in the holidays, like all the other students I knew, dragging my dirty washing behind me. I would lounge around in my old bedroom moaning I was bored and getting under the feet of my mother and grandfather. Tap them both up for cash every now and then before raiding the fridge. But it didn't turn out that way. There was always some job or some boy or some country I wanted to visit and the next thing I knew I had graduated and was renting flats of my own, calling somewhere else home. If I'd realised when I closed the door behind me that I was really leaving home I would have paid more attention, would have looked back over my shoulder as I walked away. Paused to feel the weight of the moment. As it is, I don't remember leaving Clapham any better than I do arriving.

I did go back to visit: a series of Sunday lunches and Christmas dinners. Of birthdays and mother's days and bank holidays. I liked being with my mother and grandfather after all. But I rarely stayed over more than a couple of nights. My own life, the real one, was being lived elsewhere and I was keen to get back to it.

Once I'd met Robert, I visited less and less. It wasn't an intentional choice. It was just that Robert took up so much of me there was hardly any room left for anyone else. Even when he wasn't there all I wanted to do was hang around the flat until he came back. To be there waiting for him, with a smile on my face and wearing pretty knickers. Only now Robert wasn't coming back, however long I waited. And, faced with that prospect, I was going home to Clapham.

The day I moved back was a sunny day, one of the first that May. The kind of day that brings with it the promise of a long hot summer ahead and persuades Londoners to leave their suit jackets at home and to start off on their journey to work in shirt sleeves or cotton skirts. In the first precious days of summer, Londoners forget that warm days mean warmer journeys to work and that they will soon tire of the sun and of arriving home at the end of a long day sticky and thirsty, their feet sweating and slipping inside their shoes. On the day I moved home the sun had only just arrived and was still being made welcome by everyone except me, who was too miserable to care.

Cab drivers from north London think south London is located in a distant and altogether alien city and I had to direct the cabbie through the twist of streets to get to the house where I grew up and where I would now be living again. As we turned into the street, I saw that my grandfather, Trevor, was leaning against the iron railings of the tiny front garden waiting for me to arrive. My cab double-parked nonchalantly, ignoring the line of traffic forming a bad mood behind us. I scrambled out of the car but the driver stayed firmly put at the wheel, only just mustering the energy to ping his boot open. The woman in the car behind scowled at me, tapping her fingers frantically on her steering wheel as if her life depended on getting on with her journey. Perhaps it did. I hurled my stuff out on to the pavement and paid the driver hurriedly, tipping with wild abandon rather than have the little traffic jam I'd personally created watch while my change was counted out. There was a time when I could fit my possessions into a couple of rucksacks but now heaped on the pavement was an entire suite of matching bin bags, stuffed with clothes and bed linen and towels. There were boxes of books too and of kitchen utensils: a Gaggia coffee maker, espresso cups from Heals, a Le Creuset casserole dish. A cherry-red leather Gladstone bag.

"You should have ordered a removal van love, not a minicab," the cab driver said as he pulled off.

My grandfather was busy gathering up my bags. He was wearing a cream jumper with beige stripes across the front and cream soft shoes with Velcro straps, like kids' shoes for the elderly. Grandfather clothes. He is a tall man, well built, with a full head of white wavy hair and a nicely rounded belly, due in part to a love of beer and in part to a love of Raspberry Ruffles.

"I'll get those Grandad. They're heavy."

"The cheek of you girl! I'm in pretty good nick for someone over 80 I'll have you know. I'm perfectly capable of helping my granddaughter with a few bags."

And so together we transported my worldly possessions from where they sprawled on the pavement into the safety of the hallway.

When all my stuff was finally inside the house he closed the door behind us and kissed me gently on the forehead. I laid my head against the wide cream expanse of his chest. I hadn't slept much in the past 48 hours and I felt light headed and giddy, the inside of my mouth furry like I had jet lag.

"Thanks Grandad," I mumbled into his shoulder.

My grandfather held me for a while, patting me gently on the back before eventually pulling away.

"Well then, welcome home lovely girl. Your mum said to tell you she's changed the sheets on your bed ready for you and that she'll be getting off work early today. Shall I make us both a nice cup of tea?"

I smiled gratefully at him, tears sliding salt and secret down the back of my throat.

The house in Clapham has big windows and tall ceilings and is always full of light. My grandfather bought it when he moved to London from south Wales, not long after the war ended. When his wife died, suddenly and unexpectedly of TB, he was left all alone with a young baby to look after. He needed a fresh start so he packed up his tiny grieving family and moved to London. He got a job doing maintenance work on the tube and somehow found a way of buying this tall skinny house with four floors although he hardly bothers nowadays with the top three, leaving those to the mercy of my mother and spending most of his time down in the basement.

I've got everything I need down here, is what he says. *I'm out of your mum's way. Got a kitchen, a lav and a door out to my garden. What more could an old man want?*

Trevor's garden is his pride and joy. Long and skinny just like the house and crammed with flowers. Depending on the season he grows old-fashioned tea roses with creamy velvet petals that remind me of old ladies, big brash tarty sun flowers, lavender bushes that tinge the garden purple, lupins and hollyhocks as high as his waist and sweet peas, fragrant and fragile. It's hard to believe when you're out in the garden that the smelly stress of London's traffic is thundering down a busy road just the other side of the house.

The basement hasn't always been Trevor's domain. When he first moved to London he rented this bit of the house out to help pay the mortgage. Families and women with children were offered lower rent if they agreed to help look after his daughter while Trevor was at work and so Trevor and my mother shared their home with a series of other families who had also moved to London to start a new life from places far further away than Wales. The Polish family which lived here last, long before my time, was also the last to decorate and the wallpaper they chose is a deep crimson with enormous psychedelic black swirls. If you stare at it long enough faces appear in the pattern and animal shapes too — an elephant, a fat cat; a dog with its tongue lolling out.

"Mum still hasn't managed to get her hands on your wallpaper then?" I teased gently as I followed Trevor down the stairs to the basement.

"No and she never bloody will if I have anything to do with it. I've told her: I like the wallpaper. Leave it alone!"

I like the wallpaper too. It belongs in the basement and the basement belongs to it. As does the Formica kitchen table I sat at while Trevor made our tea, its pattern of small yellow flowers faded away by years of scrubbing and sunlight.

"There you go love, nice cup of tea," he said, handing me a cup and saucer. "Drink it down now, it'll do you good."

Trevor is a strong believer in the restorative power of tea and is the only person I know who still uses cups and saucers, thin bone china ones, almost transparent. As a child I had to resist the urge to bite down on the cups, imagining how it would feel as the cup cracked and splintered in my mouth, crunching like icing on a wedding cake. Today he gave me the blue Shelley cup. It is my favourite of a precious set of four. There is a yellow one, a pink one and a green one too; they once belonged to Trevor's mother, my great grandmother.

"Getting the posh cups today am I?"

I knew what he would say to this. I was fishing for the comfort of a well worn response.

"No point wasting stuff keeping it for best," he replied. "You can't take it with you."

We sat together for a little while, Trevor and I, sipping our tea and not saying much. I was glad just to be back home with him in this scruffy basement where nothing had changed since I was little and where I knew where everything was without having to look. Trevor's thick, brown-rimmed reading glasses would be on the arm of his chair on top of a neatly folded newspaper and the back door key would be on the windowsill under a ceramic frog I had brought home proudly from a school trip, right next to the giant pot of Vaseline that Trevor rubs into his hands when he's done gardening for the day because it is a truth universally acknowledged that Vaseline is not the same as hand cream — absolutely nothing like it. Just to check that I really was home I got up from my chair to look at the small collection of framed photos on the mantelpiece. There they all were, arranged like I knew they would be, like they had always been. The one of me aged about nine, my hair in big bunches sticking up from my head like the ears of a space hopper, wearing a brown crimplene dress trimmed with bright orange ric rac. The one of my parents on their wedding day, my mother's hair black and bouffant and my father almost unrecognisable with a big droopy moustache and long sideburns. Then came a black and white one of Trevor's mother and father standing at the door of their terraced house, his father in a flat cap and waistcoat and his mother wiping her hands in her apron, two small, serious figures frowning at the camera. The last photograph, also black and white, was of my mother as a baby, sitting on my grandmother's lap, my mother giggling and my grandmother's face turned away from the camera, smiling down at her laughing baby. I had

9

seen these black and white photos hundreds of times but never really looked at them properly. Today I picked them up and stared at the dour glassy faces of my great grandparents, the beautiful line of the cheek and chin of my grandmother.

"Do you ever think about going back, Grandad?"

My grandfather looked up at me in surprise. "Back where?"

"Back home. To Wales."

"Why would I want to do that?"

"You must miss it. I've seen you go all misty eyed whenever you watch Wales play rugby on the telly."

"I do not go all misty eyed as you put it my girl. That's just my eyes getting watery with old age."

"But you must have thought about it sometimes. It's where you're from, your home — like Clapham is my home."

"Clapham is *my* home too Ellie — with your mother and you — has been for a long time. After Laura went there was nothing left for me in Wales. Nothing at all. Everything I need is right here."

My grandfather got up, brushing some invisible crumbs from the front of his trousers.

"Now, if you don't mind it's a sunny day out there and I've got a spot of weeding needs doing. I'll be out the back if you need me. You go upstairs now and have a lie down before your mother comes home. You look shattered."

I sat at the table a little while longer and finished my tea. When I got up and went to the sink to rinse out the Shelley cups carefully, my grandfather was kneeling

10

amongst his strawberry plants. I waved at him but he was hard at work and didn't look up. I went back up to the hallway and started the weary job of getting my stuff upstairs to my room.

CHAPTER
TWO

1944

The end of the war comes early for Trevor. He kept his promise to his mother not to enlist until his nineteenth birthday but before he finishes his training he is called back to the Rhondda valleys. His mother, a widow, is dying and because the war is drawing to a close and he is an only child he is released on compassionate leave.

The people of the Rhondda are closely bound to each other, connected by their history of pit and chapel and choir. By the time of the war these three things are dwindling — hundreds of pits closed before the war even started — and they will dwindle even further in peace time but the close community they have created survives. The women who live in Trevor's steep terraced street of two-up two-down houses are dab hands at coping with death. They have looked after his mother well in his absence, keeping her company, bringing food and keeping the house tidy. They have not attempted to open the draper's shop that she runs from the ground floor of her house but its windows are clean and the square of pavement outside is scrubbed.

His mother had hidden from him how ill she was before he enlisted and when he gets back she lets him know there is not much time left.

"Trevor love," she says, taking his hand and patting it gently, "there's no getting better for me I'm afraid."

He nurses her gently to the end. She does not complain although he knows she must be in pain, her insides eaten away with cancer. He brings her food but she eats very little. Trevor suspects she does this on purpose so that the end will come quicker but he does not force her. It is his mother's body that is sick not her mind and he trusts her judgement.

These last few weeks with her are quiet and dignified. She talks of Trevor's father, handing over her memories for Trevor to keep safe after she has gone, and instructs him how to run the shop.

"Listen love. The coal is coming to an end. There won't be jobs for many a miner when he gets home. But the shop will make you a decent living; provide for you and your family. Your father knew what he was doing when he opened this shop — he had a good head for business he did — and there's a nice little nest egg tucked away for you so you don't have to worry about money. All you've got to do is trust your instincts and not get above yourself. And look after your customers. Trust everybody once and if you can afford to give credit when it is needed then give it, but remember the ones who let you down. You'll find a list of them in the credit book. Mrs Jones in Conley Street is right at the top — she doesn't pay you back that one."

When she is certain that Trevor can manage by himself she closes her eyes and dies as she has lived, neatly and without a fuss.

There are a lot of people at the funeral. Mrs Richards didn't just run a draper's shop. She was also a skilled seamstress who happened to have put by every last bit of left over material that ever crossed her path just in case it came in handy. The Squander Bug had nothing to teach her about avoiding waste and during the long years of rationing she was one of the few who had the means and ability at her disposal to really make do and mend. She was also a woman who took her own advice and looked after her customers, and with her help many a mother learned how to patch and darn, to cut off the worn sleeves of a dress and make a slip over, to let out the generous seams of pre-war clothes and eke out of them another year's wear for growing boys. But it was at wedding dresses that Mrs Richards excelled. It was rare that a girl's coupons could be stretched far enough for a whole new dress but she was always able to find amongst her special stock pile a piece of fabric or lace that would allow a dress to be finished or a second-hand dress to be let out enough to fit a larger, rounder bride.

There have been quite a few weddings organised at short notice over the time of the war. Not always because there was a baby already on the way but sometimes so that a man could go off to fight knowing that if he died he would leave behind a wife with a pension and the proper standing as next of kin from which to mourn, instead of just a fiancée whose grief would be viewed as being of a lesser quality, secondary to that of the mother.

Laura Harris falls into both categories. She married the love of her life, Jack, bloomingly beautiful in ivory silk that just about fits thanks to Mrs Richards' sterling efforts, and had a baby girl four months later. Not long after her daughter was born, Laura received the news that Jack had been killed when Singapore fell to the Japanese in 1942. She became a wife, mother and widow in the space of a year but what Laura is above all these things is sodden with grief. More than two years later she still misses Jack every day of her life and each morning the pain of waking up knowing he is gone is as fresh as the day before and the days before that.

There is only one photo of Laura and Jack on their wedding day. That is how it was for wartime brides — no money for the forests of photographs that couples have today, no difficult decisions about which ones to display in the wedding album — just one single photo of bride and groom and, chop-chop, on with married life. In their photo Laura and Jack look surprised, the photographer's flash having caught them unawares. Laura remembers how she concealed her rounded stomach behind her bouquet, how Jack squeezed her hand tight as the flash went off, kissed her sweetly on the cheek in front of the photographer while secretly pinching her bum at the same time. She remembers the pure undiluted happiness and pride she felt at being pronounced his wife and the fervent urgency of their wedding night, the sweetness of falling asleep together for the first time and the joy of waking up with Jack at

15

her side the next morning. They had five wonderful days and nights before he left for service. When she closes her eyes she can conjure up the moment he had to go, the scratchy, oily wool of his trousers and the press of his thighs hard against her as he kissed her goodbye, the cool cotton of his shirt and the breadth of his shoulders as she slipped her hands beneath his jacket so she could hold him tighter and closer and longer. The desperate leaden sadness of their last drowning kiss. Laura looks at their wedding photograph every day and, each time she does, she runs these memories through her head.

The wedding photograph is the only one she has of Jack to show little Kitty as she grows up. Kitty kisses the photograph good night each night like her mother shows her, leaving little lip marks on the frame that Laura wipes away afterwards with a soft cloth. Laura looks at her wedding dress in the photo every day and over the years Mrs Richards and her shop have become tied up with the memory of her husband. Laura's train of thought when she looks at the photo goes from Jack to her wedding dress to Mrs Richards and so when she goes to the funeral to pay her respects it is to someone she has thought of perhaps more often and more warmly than is merited.

This is how Trevor sees Laura for the first time in years: her eyes are wet with tears as she prays for his mother. She is incredibly beautiful — she has hair as blonde as Betty Grable and a pink mouth with full lips. Her face is the shape of a heart. She is clutching the hand of a small plump girl with brown hair in thick plaits who is altogether bigger boned, than her mother. Kitty takes after her father who was broad shouldered and tall. Trevor remembers Jack and Laura from school — they were older than him, getting ready to leave just as he was starting, and already going steady. The best-looking girl and the handsomest boy.

Trevor watches Laura. It is love at first sight, at least for him.

It takes a lot of time and a lot of effort for Trevor to woo Laura. She is not interested in another relationship, particularly with someone five years younger whom she doesn't remember from school, who hasn't even been to war and who is now running a draper's shop.

But Trevor is patient.

He never quite says that he and Jack were friendly before the war but this is the impression he gives. If Laura were less unhappy she would work out that Trevor was all of sixteen when Jack first enlisted and that it's unlikely they would have been pals, but in any event Trevor doesn't actually say this. What he says is: "I know that Jack would want me to look out for you, give you a hand where I can."

In all probability, from a far-away, shallow, sunny grave, that is exactly what Jack would want. Someone to help look after his wife and daughter in his absence. Trevor doesn't explain why he has taken so long to come forward with this help — after all Kitty is coming up three and Jack has been gone a long time — and Laura doesn't think to ask.

Trevor plays a long game and slowly makes himself indispensable. He closes the shop at 3p.m. on a Saturday and walks to Laura's small, terraced house, bringing bread and beer and scraps of material to make clothes for Kitty's doll. At first his visits are short, just enough for a cup of tea and a chat with Kitty. He figures that if he can get the daughter to like him it will be easier for the mother to follow suit. In fact, Trevor very quickly grows fond of Kitty. She is a sweet-natured, happy girl who has lived her life in the shadow of her mother's grief for a father she has never seen and she enjoys the attention Trevor gives her and the biscuits he brings.

Laura does not care whether Trevor visits or not. She is indifferent. When she opens the door to him she does not smile but she does not frown either.

"Oh it's you," she says, every time she opens the door to him. Trevor wonders whether she remembers his name from week to week. But Kitty does not forget. She comes hurtling to the door.

"Trevor's here! Trevor's here!" she shouts excitedly, rushing up to him, hugging his legs, reaching up furtively to pat the pockets of his jacket where she knows he has hidden the biscuits for her to find.

Laura does not at the beginning seem to notice her daughter's growing affection for Trevor, just shuffles off down the passage back to the kitchen, leaving them to it. Slowly however, she learns to rely on Trevor's visits as being the time on Saturday when she can get on with her chores in peace, leaving Trevor to keep an eye on Kitty. Now when he knocks the door they are often both waiting for him and he stays a little longer every week.

He starts bringing more food with him — a whole loaf of bread, some vegetables, a bit of bacon. He is helped considerably in the task of winning Laura's heart by her weakness for fruit and in particular, strawberries. Although Trevor has dug very hard for Victory he is a keen and skilled gardener and he has a larger-than-usual garden plot at the back of the shop. In amongst Potato Pete, carrots and onions he has grown rhubarb, some blackcurrants and a few precious raspberries and strawberries. Laura's eyes light up the first time Trevor brings her a small bowl of strawberries and, although it is the fruit she is more pleased to see than Trevor, he considers this to be a good start.

CHAPTER
THREE

When I was sixteen and unbearable to live with, my mother cleared out the tiny box room next to my bedroom. She threw out the left-over rolls of wallpaper and the sealed-up tins of paint, the racks of LPs for which we no longer had a record player and a balding silver Christmas tree and she got a plumber to fit a toilet and a shower in there. She installed a Baby Belling in one corner of my bedroom. Finally she got a lock for my bedroom door, gave me a key and told me that my life was my own and that if I was moody all the time that was not her fault.

I was delighted with my little bit of independent space and spent a long time painting the walls magnolia and making long flowing curtains out of white muslin. A lifetime later, when I came back to the beginning to begin again I found I still liked my choice of décor. Although my taste in posters had changed a bit, I was rather proud of my teenage self.

Bin bags covered my bed and the rest of my stuff was piled on the floor but I didn't have the energy to put any of it away. I pushed the bin bags off and collapsed on to the bed. I was still wearing my shoes, a habit that really annoys my mother but I couldn't even stir myself enough to kick them off. I flipped the edges of the duvet round me and lying there, looking at the walls of my old familiar room, I asked myself how come I'd ended up back here after all these years. Robert had never been my type anyway so how had I fallen for him in the first place?

I had met him the September before when I was temping for a firm of solicitors. When I graduated from university I had no idea what sort of job I wanted so I decided to take a year out and did temporary secretarial work in the City until I'd saved up enough to go off and do some travelling. Seven years later, aged 28, my gap year had turned into a gap way of life. I liked the way I lived. Temping was well paid and flexible and so long as I signed up for lots of overtime and lived in cheap, shared houses I could save enough in nine months to go off travelling for three. And temping was very liberating. I could reinvent myself for every new job if I wished. I wore a red beret all day every day during one job and nobody batted an eyelid because I had turned up on the first day wearing it.

City solicitors' offices are the best places to temp. They pay the most, have plush offices with air conditioning and staff fruit bowls and there's always tons of overtime. When my agency rang me and offered me a few weeks work at a firm near St Paul's I jumped at the chance. I'd just got back from a trip to India and I needed to make some serious cash. As I walked to the office that first morning I felt really good about myself. At 5'4" I've got a tendency to plumpness if I don't watch it but thanks to India I was tanned and slimmer than usual and even my hair, lightened by the sun, was looking ok. Ordinarily my hair is my least favourite bit of me. It's thick and curly and the colour of mouse if left to its own devices. I have hair that grows out rather than down and the fact that I've got good clear skin and a heart-shaped face with high cheekbones is generally not much compensation for that. But on this day I was relaxed and loose limbed, happy in my own skin. I felt different from all the other suited and booted people who marched past me to the tune of the seriously employed, tight lipped and tense, focussed on the day ahead. I wore some of the thin silver bangles I'd bought in India and I jangled as I walked. I was just passing through. I certainly didn't expect to fall in love.

I had been taken on to work in the corporate department of the firm, covering for a secretary who was off sick with stress, which didn't surprise me when I met the female partner I was working for. Her job was her life and she was under the impression that, because she had no home life to go to, neither did her secretarial staff. The endless networking events she attended had not been kind to her figure. All her (very expensive) suits were too small for her, the skirts riding up over her thighs and the jackets bunched tight under her armpits so that she looked permanently uncomfortable. She was entirely computer illiterate, even to the point of dictating her personal emails, and thought it was part of a secretary's job to fetch her lunch. She was the most ungracious cow I have ever worked for.

If you want to be a good temp you need to know the rules, the first and foremost of which is that you only really need to say two words out loud. *No problem*. If nothing is ever too much of a problem you are more or less guaranteed a long and successful temping career. So if your boss expects you to go out and buy her lunch every day that is exactly what you do, even if you are not actually going out to buy lunch for yourself because you brought in a ham sandwich from home as part of your effort to save money. Any thoughts of "lazy bitch" must be kept firmly inside your head and not be permitted to slip out under your breath because the second most important rule of temping is to bite your tongue. The fact that you ate your own sandwich at 11a.m. and that going out to queue in Prêt à Manger for her lunch is going to tempt you both to eat again and spend money is not a cause for complaint either.

Other rules of temping include understanding that secretaries are stupid and invisible unless being instructed in matters of work and accepting that your boss may make expensive mistakes such as telling you to send documents to the wrong address, but that it is your typo on the envelope which actually caused the embarrassment and not the address being entirely wrong in the first place.

I followed the temp rules on that job. For a good few weeks I followed them to the letter. Then came the day when my boss screeched at me in reception in front of other staff because I had told a client she was away from her desk.

"I am in a meeting. I am always in a meeting when clients call. You are the stupidest temp I have ever had."

I thought I'd done quite well. I could have told the client the truth which was that she'd gone to the toilet with *The Times* under her arm and, if my experience of the past few weeks was anything to go by, she would be gone for quite a while.

I quickly ran through the options in my head. I could keep to the second rule of temping and bite my tongue. I could apologise. I could even burst into tears. All of these would have been acceptable under the rules of temping but none seemed particularly appropriate or attractive to me at that point. I looked her straight in the eye and said, "And your ego is bigger than your arse." There was a sharp intake of collective breath from the other people in reception and I went to fetch my bag. Times like those were when I most loved being a temp.

When I got to the lift I recognised one of the other partners from the corporate team standing outside. It looked like he was waiting for me.

"Bravo. About time somebody stood up to her," he said. "Do you want to come and work for me for a few weeks instead? My secretary is going on holiday tomorrow and I'm in the middle of a huge deal. My name's Robert. Robert Carmichael."

He stuck his hand out towards me. I shook it, looking at him uncertainly.

"Don't worry," he laughed. "I'll make sure you're out of her range."

"Are you sure? That woman sees everything that goes on around here. You do realise that she can swivel her head 360 degrees like that girl off *The Exorcist?*"

"You'll be perfectly safe with me," he smiled.

Somehow, despite the fact that the ungracious cow with the big ego was seriously ticked off about it, I started work for Robert that afternoon. He was dealing with some highly confidential take over, code named "Project Prawn". I think it had something to do with buying a frozen fish business and involved dozens of legal documents inches thick and so boring I still couldn't tell you who bought what even though I typed most of them.

I fancied him from the off which surprised me. He really was not my type. The kind of blokes I usually went for were traveller types like me — ones with scruffy hair and tatty Tshirts and not much in the way of possessions other than a rucksack and perhaps a guitar. Robert looked like he'd been born to work in the world of big City business. As a partner in a very expensive law firm, he charged hundreds of pounds an hour for his time and he dressed expensively too — Savile Row bespoke suits, double-cuff poplin shirts with cufflinks, heavy silk ties and shiny leather brogues — the kind of clothes that in the past had always signalled unattractive stuffed shirt to me. The only interest I had previously had in men who dressed like Robert was to get them to sign off my time sheets. But even though Robert wore the standard City uniform there was something a bit different about him. He stood out from the other lawyers. His suits may have been pinstripe but his ties were flowered and flamboyant and his cufflinks were chunky and made of silver, not the conservative lozenges of gold the other partners wore. He was not particularly tall, maybe 5′ 10″ at most, and stocky with broad shoulders. His hair was dirty blonde and he was blue eyed, square jawed and had the most fantastic teeth, white and even. Come to think of it, it's not that big a surprise that I fancied him so much.

I wasn't the only one who fancied him. Robert had a reputation for being one of the finest lawyers in the firm, not just clever but a skilled negotiator and dynamic with it. The best junior lawyers in the firm vied with each other for the privilege of working long hours with him. Whenever he talked to you he paid great attention, as if everything you had to say was very important and he somehow made everybody feel special and needed. There were three other lawyers working on that project and two secretaries and I think the whole team, the men included, were all a bit in love with him. When he was out of the office at meetings everyone carried on working just as hard as ever but the atmosphere grew flat and dull. As soon as he was back, striding purposefully down the corridor full of enthusiasm and energy and shouting out instructions, a little of his sparkle rubbed off on us all.

We often didn't get home until the early hours of the morning working on that deal but we'd all be back in the office sharp by 8a.m. the next day. I didn't mind. It was great money and working such long hours meant I didn't even have time to spend what I earned. My bank manager was delighted. Even though Robert was under a lot of pressure, he always made sure that the members of his team were well cared for. If ever we worked past about 8.30p.m. he would tell me to order in pizza or Chinese food for everyone and insisted that everybody take a break to eat. The firm always picked up the bill. If we were still working after 10p.m. everyone was allowed to take a taxi home, paid for on the firm's account, and we didn't even have to combine routes — everyone got a taxi each even if they lived on the way to someone else's house. Robert kept everyone motivated and feeling they were part of something that really mattered. It probably did matter to the others because they were all on steep career paths to huge incomes but I was only doing the job to bring down my overdraft and, even though I knew that at the end of the day it was just one big company buying another, I still willingly put in ridiculous hours without so much as moaning about it.

When the deal was finally signed he took us all out to a wine bar to celebrate, ordering champagne for everybody, effortlessly generous. He was attentive to us all, taking each one of us aside over the course of the evening to thank us for our hard work. When my turn came and he shook my hand it seemed to me his hand lingered in mine just a fraction longer than strictly necessary but then later when I saw him shaking hands with Andrew, one of the male solicitors who had worked on the deal, I realised that was just wishful thinking on my part: Robert must be someone who just shook hands a bit longer than most people. He had rolled his shirtsleeves up and the sight of his forearms, of the tenderness of flesh normally kept hidden away, made him seem even more attractive. I tried not to stare at him too much but can't have done a good job of it because he caught me looking at him more than once. After that, every time I looked at him he appeared to be looking right back at me. As the evening wore on, made bold by more and more champagne, I started to hold his gaze when our eyes met or perhaps it was him holding mine. Excitement and anticipation bubbled up inside me all evening. I just knew that something was going to happen that night, something important. At the end of the evening when everyone else was preoccupied with each other or their drinks he came up to me and whispered.

"Would you like to go somewhere else to have a night cap? Just you and me?"

We left the bar separately in the hope that nobody else would notice and went to another bar a few doors down. Any member of the team would have seen us if they'd walked past but we were drunk and he was euphoric at the conclusion of the deal and the combination led us to believe we were invisible.

"I find you very amusing Ellie Taylor," he told me, pouring me a glass of champagne that I was far too drunk to drink. "I have done ever since I witnessed you being so spectacularly rude to one of my fellow partners. Highly entertaining that was. And these clanking bangles you wear . . ." He paused and ran his finger gently over the thin silver bracelets. "Charming."

28

I blushed. "I think you're charming too," I said and then, realising that it wasn't actually the whole of me he was referring to as charming but just my bangles, I backtracked as deftly as a bottle and a half of champagne would allow and added lamely, "We all think you're charming that is. The whole team."

"The whole team. Is that right? Although I reckon my number one fan is Andrew based on the fact that when I shook his hand earlier he wouldn't let it go and I had to forcibly remove myself from his grasp."

And then he leaned slowly towards me and kissed me. It was a wonderful kiss, gentle and tender, and full of such sexual promise that I felt my stomach flip over.

The next morning I wasn't sure how to conduct myself at work. My heart was hammering hard in my chest when I sat down at my computer and for the first time in my life I realised that being weak at the knees is not just an expression. I had never before felt an attraction and an admiration so strong that it affected me physically — butterflies in the stomach, dry mouth, the lot. My condition wasn't helped by a thick head due to too much champagne and too little sleep. I didn't know what to do with myself and just stared at my screen, trying to look busy. I was edgy with nerves and excitement. It was all I could do not to jump up from my chair and run round the office with my jacket trailing behind me, shouting, *I snogged Robert Carmichael! I snogged Robert Carmichael!*

Robert did not get into the office until after 11 a.m. He said a general good morning to the typing stations and closed the door of his office. I kept staring at my screen, my face clammy and my heart thumping so loudly I could hear the blood banging in my ears. Finally, at 12 p.m. he rang my extension and summoned me in to see him. When I stood up to walk to his office, my knees actually buckled a little. I really had to get a grip.

Thankfully, he looked as nervous as I felt.

"Ellie. About last night. I'm out of practice at this but I would really like to see you again, well, more than see you . . . if you know what I mean?"

I nodded. I knew exactly what he meant.

"Is that something you'd like too?"

The memory of the kiss flashed through my mind and my body, making me tingle.

"Very much so."

"Thank God for that. Will you come to dinner with me on Saturday night?"

I had been hoping for an invite to the pub that same evening and I truly didn't think I would be able to contain myself till Saturday but this man operated differently from the boys I'd been out with before.

"I'd love to come to dinner with you," I said carefully, when what I really wanted to say was, *Can we go straight away? Tonight? Can we? Please, oh please, I want to snog you again.*

"Great," Robert said, "I'll pick you up about 7 p.m."

Later that day, I got a call from HR. I was told that I would no longer be working for Robert as his usual secretary was back from holiday on Monday but that Robert had been very impressed with the work I had done for him and would I like to continue working for a different department of the firm on a temp to permanent basis? I said yes without even bothering to check the hourly rate.

CHAPTER
FOUR

You would have thought that after the physical effort involved in shifting everything I owned across London on the back of almost no sleep for two days I would have fallen into a deep dreamless sleep the minute my head touched the pillow, but once I'd started thinking about how Robert and I got together I couldn't stop. It was a mistake, like starting to watch a film after the ten o'clock news. You know you should already be in bed and that if you carry on watching you'll be fit for nothing in the morning but twenty minutes later there you are somehow rooted to the sofa, sucked in by the story, and you know it's too late and there's no going back — you'll be watching it right through to the end.

I was living in Kennington at the time, sharing a scruffy but cheap fourth floor flat with a bunch of Australian girls. It was really just a place to sleep. My flatmates were all doing two jobs, saving up to do the Australian version of the Grand Tour, and there were five of us sharing a three bed roomed flat which meant that although the rent was low the living space was horribly cramped. Still, they were a cheerful bunch and if we were all in we watched reality TV together and drank cheap red wine. As I got dressed the Saturday night of my date with Robert, I felt like I used to when I was thirteen and getting ready for the youth club disco, applying the cherry lip gloss I'd got free on the front page of *Jackie* and boiling with nerves and hormones at the prospect that Thomas Driscoll might be there and might just ask me for a slow dance.

I didn't want Robert to have to ring the bell and run the risk of getting accosted by my flatmates, who were all keen to check out this City solicitor I had not stopped talking about for weeks, so I watched out for the silver Mercedes he had said he would be driving and ran down quickly to meet him as he parked. He got out of the car with old school chivalry to open the passenger door for me, giving a bird's eye view to the Aussies who were unashamedly hanging out of the windows watching. The girls grinned at me, making exaggerated thumbs-up signs and wolf whistling lasciviously, which made me cringe but which Robert didn't seem to notice. Inside the car the seats were black leather, soft and smooth as butter, and I could smell Robert's aftershave, a lemony, spicy smell.

Robert smiled at me as he swung the big car around.

"I've booked us a table at a restaurant in Battersea. I think you're going to like it there."

I did. The restaurant was right on the river with a lovely view over the water. It was the kind of place I was more used to working in than eating in.

He ordered me a Kir Royale without consulting me first. Ordinarily that would have annoyed me but he was older than me and much more confident in this kind of environment. I quite liked the feeling that I was not required to make a choice: what might have seemed patronising felt like being treated like a lady. I drank most of mine quickly and immediately felt a bit drunk — that lethal combination of bubbles and sweetness.

"Another?" he asked.

I had seen from the menu how much they cost — about the same as I usually spent on food for three days — but then I remembered the size of the bills I had typed in the course of Project Prawn and said why not, airily, as if I drank Kir Royale all the time.

I sipped the second glass while we chose our food. I can't really remember what I ate. It didn't really matter. He told me about the partner I would be starting work for on Monday. I asked what new projects he had on the horizon. I told him a bit about my travels and my family. And then he told me he was married. This information didn't really come as a surprise even though Robert didn't wear a wedding ring and I'd never once, in all the weeks I'd been working with him on Project Prawn, heard him mention a wife or the need to get home to someone. He was in his early forties, handsome and charismatic and at the top of his chosen, well paid profession. Did I really think a man like him wouldn't be married? How could he not be? No, it wasn't the fact that Robert was married that was a surprise to me. It was the fact that I didn't get up there and then and leave the restaurant. Instead I allowed him to explain his situation.

"My marriage has been over for a long time Ellie in everything but name. Children never came our way and we lead almost totally separate lives. I've got a flat in the Barbican and spend most of the week there and then when I do go home to Surrey she has her bedroom and I have mine."

"I bet you tell all your dates that."

Robert looked hurt. "This is not the sort of thing I do on a regular basis. I'm not that kind of man. I don't believe in affairs. Really I don't."

I knocked back some more wine. "So what is this then? Some sort of out-of-hours business meeting? Should I have brought my time sheet with me?"

"Listen Ellie, I'm not explaining this properly. It's not like my wife and I hate each other or anything. Far from it. We actually get on pretty well. She lets me get on with working all hours and while I'm doing that she runs the house and arranges our social life. She picks up my suits from the dry cleaners, she sends flowers to my mother on her birthday, she remembers the names of my sister's kids . . ."

He paused.

"So if you've got all of that and you don't believe in affairs, why are you sitting here with me?" I asked.

"Because last weekend when I got home all I could think about was you and how . . . nervous and excited I get when I see you, how I want to sleep with you so very much —"

He looked me straight in the eye as he said this and while I was hardly surprised at what he had said — in my experience I don't normally get invited to dinner unless the general intention is to get in my pants — I felt as if I had just driven very fast over a steep hill.

". . . and that's emotional infidelity even if you don't want to sleep with me and it's made me face up to things. People shouldn't stay married just because they've got a nice home. Or because they have friends coming round for dinner next week or family coming over for lunch and it would be too embarrassing to cancel. That's just not enough for me any more. I need to end my marriage."

He pushed his plate away and took a long drink from his glass of wine. He looked distraught.

"Wouldn't it be easier just to end it with me? I mean, we haven't really got started."

I said this bravely but I didn't mean it. They way I felt about Robert, he and I were well and truly started, even if he was married.

He smiled at me.

"That would probably be less painful Ellie, and certainly less expensive, but it really isn't an option. You're not the reason my marriage is over — that has nothing to do with you — but you are the reason I'm prepared to acknowledge it. Look, I don't want to scare you off but the way I felt when we kissed the other night . . . well I haven't felt like that for years. And all I've thought about since that night is kissing you again."

It was all I had thought about too and heat rushed to my face and other parts of my body.

Robert leaned over the table and grabbed both my hands in his.

"I want something to happen between you and me, Ellie. Because I haven't wanted something — someone

— as much as this since I can't remember. So I'm going to tell Ann what she knows already. That it's all over. It won't come as a shock. She knows it as well as I do. We haven't had sex for almost two years now. I'm not saying it's going to be easy. It's bound to be painful but I'm going to do it no matter what happens between you and me. Even if you tell me right now that you think it's all too much hassle and you'd rather not see me again I'll still leave her. Because you coming along has reminded me what it's like to really feel again and there's no going back now."

I smiled at him and squeezed his hands. "I do want to carry on seeing you," I said. After the speech Robert had just made I didn't think there was anything more I could usefully add.

"Thank goodness for that! Would you mind if we kept things between you and me for a while? It's going to take a little time to work things out with Ann and I really wouldn't want the other partners or their wives gossiping behind her back, saying that I'm seeing someone else already. Would you be willing to do that for me?"

I nodded.

"Thank you. Have you finished?" and then, without waiting for an answer, "Let's go for a walk."

We drove to the South Bank and parked the car there. We walked along the embankment outside the Festival Hall. It's one of my favourite parts of London, especially at night. The Houses of Parliament to your left, the City to the right and all of it strung with spangles of light. Trains rumbled past on Charing Cross

37

Bridge; I could hear teenagers skateboarding nearby and the sky was that soft navy blue of late summer. Finally he kissed me again, pressing me to him, his lips soft against mine but only for a few seconds. Without saying anything, he turned me round so that we both faced the river and held me close as together we watched the lights and their reflection dancing on the water.

Even though it would technically have been adultery, I had expected, had *wanted*, to end up in bed with Robert that evening but that sweet short kiss on the banks of the river was all I got; that and a quick peck on the cheek good night when he dropped me off at home. However when I got into work on Monday morning there were flowers waiting for me on my desk — the biggest bouquet I had ever seen, wrapped in cellophane and pink tissue paper, heaving with white roses and lilies and pink gerbera wired to stop their heavy heads from flopping. The card said, simply, *Thank you for a wonderful evening. Please will you come out with me again next Friday?* The other secretaries grinned at me when they saw the forest of flowers. "Someone's a lucky girl," they teased. Oh so very lucky I thought.

I had never dated before. With other men I had been out with, things had progressed very quickly, so that by the end of the first week I was either spending just about every evening with them or the whole thing was already off. But then I'd never dated a married man before, not even one that wasn't sleeping with his wife, and I figured the rules were not the same as usual. The firm was a big place and I was working in a different part of the building now but I would make a special detour round the office just so that I could walk past whatever meeting room Robert was in and catch a glimpse of him, his thick, blond hair messy and tousled from where he had run his hands through it while he was concentrating. Even though we didn't speak to each other face to face at work he texted me three or four times a day, telling me how much he was looking forward to Friday and how he couldn't wait to spend time with me again. The ferocity of the feelings I had for him shocked me.

I had plenty of time to plan what I was going to wear on our second date. Normally I was a jeans, little top and fancy flip-flops kind of girl, but in the week leading up to our date I went shopping every lunchtime because I wanted to look as good for Robert as I possibly could. And anyway I'd been too excited to eat for a few weeks so most of my usual clothes were a bit loose on me. I tried on a pair of white trousers so tight that I would never usually have contemplated them but they fitted perfectly and made my bum look smaller if anything. I got a pair of high, wedge-heeled sandals to go with them and a fitted petrol blue T shirt way too expensive to be called a T shirt with a little matching cardigan. That Friday afternoon I left work on the dot and rushed home to get ready, blow drying my hair so that it was curly but not in a bad perm kind of way which is always a distinct risk for me. I applied more mascara than usual and noted with satisfaction that my new T shirt made my eyes look more blue than grey. I left the house with butterflies so bad I felt sick.

This time we were meeting at a pub in Camden Town. It was one of those gastro pubs, more like a restaurant really but nobody objects if you just drink. I was glad I'd made so much effort when I saw Robert waiting at the bar for me. It was the first time I'd seen him in anything other than a suit and just looking at him made my heart swoop. He was wearing beige trousers and a navy linen shirt and his hair was darker blonde than usual, still a little damp from the shower. When he saw me coming towards me he grinned so hard I thought his cheeks would break.

"You look amazing! My little hippy chick all grown up. Wow!" He pulled me towards him, kissed me on the cheek, and whispered in my ear. "I fancy you so very much." Then he took my elbow and steered me to our table.

I felt more at home here than in the fancy restaurant on the river. The wooden tables and chairs were scruffy and did not match but the linen was white and starched and there was an enormous wine list. There were tall glass jars of olives behind the bar, glossy and dark, and sun-dried tomatoes and salted pistachios served in small flat terracotta dishes. The blackboard menu offered things like mushroom risotto and organic chicken with crushed rosemary potatoes and aioli. There was a vase of cornflowers on our table and tea lights twinkled in little glass holders. I remember these details clearly. I remember watching Robert eat, tearing his bread and putting it in his mouth, laughing as he told me that my former boss had got through another two secretaries since me and had now herself been summoned to human resources to discuss her attitude problems. I was enjoying the evening, the food and the conversation but all I really wanted to do was kiss him.

Robert asked me question after question about the department I was working in, what I thought of the partner, the solicitors, the work? What would I do to improve team spirit, to increase communication? When he had finished flattering my intellect he leaned over the table, took hold of both my hands and pulled me towards him.

"You are so beautiful . . . really, really beautiful."

Not the most original of compliments but when he said it he looked right into my eyes, a direct, totally sincere gaze.

This time when he drove me home he kissed me on the lips rather than the cheek — a sweet, tender goodnight kiss — but nothing more. I got into bed feeling incredibly precious but totally disappointed.

After that, the weekend dragged past and although Robert texted me constantly I couldn't wait to get back to work on Monday just so I could actually see him. I had spent all Sunday moping around the flat in Kennington, aching to be with him. It was a beautiful day and I wanted to go for a walk with him, read the paper with him, spend all afternoon in bed with him. I hardly knew him but I felt lonely without him. I tried to remember how my last relationship had started. It was not a fair comparison. Jason and I had met travelling in India and our relationship had been microwaved into two intense months. He was Canadian, tall and healthy and unfailingly happy. We had fallen into bed within a few hours of meeting each other. Sex for Jason was an every day occurrence, just like food and a beer or a new sight-seeing experience. Uncomplicated. We were inseparable during the time we were together and when he returned to Calgary I really missed him — the heft of him next to me in bed, his good nature, his enthusiasm for life — but only for a short while. From the moment I met Jason I got to have my fill of him. I only had to reach out to be able to touch him; so that by the time he left I knew what it was I would be missing. Knowing that made the missing bearable. But Robert had left me hungry and it was not a feeling I was used to coping with.

I got to work early. I stopped first at Robert's floor. I told myself I was only going to see the girls I had worked with on Project Prawn, catch up with them a bit, tell them how I was getting on upstairs. I knew that wasn't true. Robert was in his office as I walked past. He smiled but did not get up from his desk, nor did he make an excuse to come out as I chatted with his secretary Anita. Like a schoolgirl I asked her how Robert was, now that Project Prawn was over.

"Same as always," she said sniffily, "working on the next big deal. Nothing much changes round here."

I was irrationally disappointed. I had hoped she would say that he was acting strangely, smiling like the cat that got the cream. I made my way to my own desk and ploughed my way through piles of dictation in an effort to distract myself.

Robert finally called me the end of that day.

"Doing anything tomorrow?"

I didn't even bother to play it cool.

"No."

"Fancy going to the theatre? There's an Alan Bleasdale play on at the Barbican that I would really like to see."

"Sure."

"Great. I'll meet you at the bar in the theatre about 7 p.m. And Ellie?"

"Yes?"

"We could have a coffee back at the flat afterwards if you like."

My insides went liquid when he said this.

I can't remember anything about the play. I presume it was funny because the people sitting around me, including Robert, all laughed. I did too in that instinctive herd way that people do in a crowd. All I could think about was getting back to his flat afterwards and being alone with him.

I have never liked the Barbican. I think it is a depressing place, all concrete and dark and sealed off, not unlike a prison and about as welcoming. Inside Robert's flat was a different story. It was like something out of a magazine, with cream carpets and leather furniture. A few paintings, a Bang and Olufsen stereo that looked incredibly expensive, a sleek coffee table with absolutely nothing on it save for a single, very beautiful, deep glass bowl. Not a pizza flyer in sight.

Robert offered me coffee or red wine. I chose red wine. I felt I needed it, to take the edge off my nervousness. He presented me with a glass goblet from the same expensive school of design as the bowl. The wine was at perfect room temperature, velvety and smooth. I perched myself on the slippery leather sofa, trying not to sink down in an unattractive way and concentrated on not spilling wine on the thick pile of the cream carpet. He asked me what music I liked. For some reason I always find this a difficult question and every artist that I like with any sort of street cred promptly disappears from my mind and I find myself saying something really naff like Ronan Keating or Girls Aloud (and I do like them, truth be told, just not only them).

"Oh, all sorts. You choose."

"Tell you what. I've got some great stuff on my iPod. I'll put it on shuffle and let's see what comes up."

Before I could recover from the shock of Robert having an iPod whereas I had never progressed beyond a Sony Discman, the sound of James Blunt's voice — full of sorrow and yearning — rose up from some hidden but powerful speakers and tugged gently at my heart. And then finally, finally, Robert sat down next to me and pulled me towards him. It was not the most comfortable place to kiss. The obvious choice was to lie on the sofa and kiss horizontally but that felt too forward, too much of an invitation. So we sat sideways, me grasping the end of the cushions to avoid sliding off the leather sofa altogether, which was awkward and a bit distracting. He kissed my neck, my throat, the corners of my mouth. Light little breathy kisses. At last he ran his tongue gently over my lower lip and opened his mouth. It was the most powerful kiss I have ever experienced. He sighed and in that one sigh managed to conjure up a huge sexual hunger. We kissed for ages and he touched me like I was precious, beautiful, perfect. And when I was hollow with desire he jumped up, tapped me on the knee and said, "Come on. I'll take you home. We've both got work tomorrow."

CHAPTER
FIVE

At this point in the Robert movie I finally fell asleep, wrapped up in my duvet like a hotdog in a bun, a sleep so heavy that when I woke up my arms and legs ached. My mother was tapping on the door of my bedroom. She picked her way over the boxes and bags and sat on the edge of the bed, setting a tray down gently on the bedside table. She had made me hot chocolate like she used to if I was ill when I was little. I struggled to sit up and she handed me the mug carefully.

"Mind now, it's hot."

She watched me as I sipped. The chocolate was sweet and comforting. She patted my arm, looking at me worriedly.

"Do you want to talk about it Ellie?"

"There's nothing to talk about Mum. It's over that's all."

"Well all right. If you don't want to talk about it right now, that's just fine."

I wished I was small again and could crawl into my mother's lap and have her rock me gently, stroke my hair and whisper in my ear *I've got you baby. I've got you. Everything is going to be ok*. I think my mother wished it too. Instead she handed me a plate of crumpets. I bit into one hungrily, suddenly realising I hadn't eaten for two days, and melted butter oozed greasily down my wrist. I licked it up quickly to stop it dripping onto the sheets.

"Is it ok for me to stay here for a while?" I asked.

"Sweetheart, you always have a home with me and your grandfather. Always. You know that. Now, I left the water on all day today so you can have a really hot bath — that'll be nice, won't it? A good long soak always makes me feel better anyway. But before I go run that for you how about I make a start on putting some of these things away? You really should have let me come and help you move you know. I told you when you phoned that I would have taken the day off."

My mother has a very developed work ethic. Her idea of a day well lived is a long list of jobs and objectives all ticked off by end of play. She likes phone calls made and bills paid. She buys her Christmas presents in the January sales. It's not in her nature to sit around and she can't even watch telly without knitting constantly. One of the Polish tenants taught her when she was a little girl — even though my grandfather was a pretty impressive single parent, his skills didn't quite run to knitting lessons — and the constant clack of her needles was one of the soundtracks to my childhood. While I sat up in bed like a recovering invalid, eating crumpets and sipping my hot chocolate, she set to unpacking my stuff.

"I'll put your kitchen equipment over here next to the Baby Belling shall I? What a heavy coffee machine. There's plenty of room on the bookshelves for all your

47

books. And most of the hangers are still in your clothes so I can have them hung up in your wardrobe in no time. There. That looks better already doesn't it? Do these bedclothes need washing do you think? Looks like it to me. I'll just put them here by the door and I'll pop them in the washer when I go back downstairs. Oh what lovely leather on this bag . . . and such a gorgeous colour red.."

I jumped up out of bed and took the bag from her, trying not to snatch. "I'll sort that one out later Mum."

"Oh, ok — right you are — I'll go down now and run you that bath. Be ready in about fifteen minutes."

My mother bundled up the sheets and pillowcases I'd stripped from the bed in my flat that morning and left me on my own.

The bag was indeed beautiful — a modern twist on a Gladstone, made of red cherry leather and lined inside with red cherry silk. It was the first present Robert ever gave me, although not the last. He loved bringing me presents — a Hermes silk scarf, rich and slippery with colour, that had come in a beautiful burnt-orange box tied with black ribbon, a box almost as beautiful as the scarf itself and far too lovely to put in the bin, an antique bracelet made of rose gold, Penhaligon's lily of the valley soaps, beautiful cream stationery, thick as card and bottle after bottle of Jo Malone perfume and bath bubbles. Each gift was luxurious and expensive and almost all of them were now stuffed into that red bag. I had shoved them in there as I packed, half meaning to leave the bag behind on the doorstep of the flat as I left but I hadn't been able to do it. Not yet anyway. There was too much of me folded away in there.

Robert gave me the bag when he took me away to make love to me for the first time. We had been dating for a month by then — four incredible weeks during which we went to some of the most famous and glamorous restaurants in London, when flowers were delivered to me every Friday and when each day in the internal post at work I received some funny or romantic message from him — my horoscope ripped from the *Evening Standard* with a reference to falling in love highlighted in pink marker, a post card of love poetry from the tube, heart-shaped post it notes, a plastic smiley face. Every time we met he hugged me so tight I could feel his heart beating fast against my own. I felt more special and more wanted than I'd ever felt before in my life but for one thing. All the kissing and hugging and touching we were doing had not yet developed into actual sex. Finally, when I was just starting to get a little worried, Robert suggested a night away together in Brighton.

"I want our first time together to be special. An occasion. I've arranged a client meeting down there as a bit of a cover up but it shouldn't take too long and then we can have the rest of the day together and stay overnight. I'll book somewhere really nice."

I was bowled over by this romantic gesture. I had not been able to imagine Robert staying over at my place in Kennington, queuing up in the morning for the bathroom with the Aussie girls, and although his flat in the Barbican would have been ok, I loved the idea of going out of London to christen our relationship.

"We'll take my fun car for the run down," Robert said.

The fun car turned out to be an Audi TT convertible.

"Sun's shining. Let's get the roof off shall we?" Robert clapped his hands together enthusiastically.

I didn't dare point out that it was eight o'clock in the morning in the middle of October and that despite the autumn sunshine it was really rather nippy.

It was the first time I had travelled in a convertible and I was surprised at how uncomfortable the journey was. The wind whipped my hair around my face and into my mouth in an unglamorous way and I was freezing within ten minutes. It was noisy without a roof and impossible to talk, but Robert seemed to be really enjoying it so I crouched down into my seat as far as I could, turning the collar of my coat up and shoving my hands between my thighs for warmth. Thankfully Robert was a very fast driver and just before my entire body turned numb we arrived in Brighton and our wonderful hotel, all retro modern chic with a famous restaurant and bar and little boutique shops in the foyer. Our room had a huge, kingsized bed and a bath big enough for two with the taps in the middle. It had mood lighting which meant you could swivel a dial and turn the room pink or lime green or blue to suit your mood.

We were checked in by 11 a.m. Robert's meeting was not until lunch time and I had thought we might do the deed before he went but sex pre client meeting was clearly not on Robert's agenda. He set about unpacking his stuff when we got into the room, putting his capacious black leather wash bag in the bathroom, hanging up a shirt and a spare suit in the wardrobe, even putting those wooden things into his spare shoes. I had only brought a tiny rucksack with me — big enough for a pair of clean knickers, my toothbrush, a book and some vanilla tea lights.

"Right," he said, "make yourself comfortable and I'll be back as soon as I can. Should be done by about 5ish at latest. Going to have to take the clients for a quick drink after the meeting but that shouldn't take too long."

"Can't I come with you for a drink with the clients?"

Robert laughed gently.

"I'm sorry sweetheart. That wouldn't really be appropriate. These guys know I'm married and I don't think they need to know that I'm getting divorced and have got myself a beautiful new girlfriend. Not just yet at least."

I was disappointed but I could see sense in what he said. It was perhaps a little premature for me to play the corporate wife when we hadn't even slept together. Robert went off to his meeting and I filled time, walking around Brighton, window shopping in the Lanes and sitting shivering on the deserted beach, reading my book and reflecting smugly on the fact that I was Robert's girlfriend. At about three I went back to the hotel, had a long bath in the cavernous bathroom, put on the fluffy bathrobe and helped myself to a gin and tonic from the mini bar. At 7.30p.m. Robert sent a short text — *meeting running on, sorry, there as soon as I can* — and so I had another gin and tonic while I watched the rest of Coronation Street and ate some peanuts. I was trying hard not to be miffed. I knew from experience how lawyers' meetings tended to run on forever, probably something to do with the fact that they charged by the hour, but this trip wasn't meant to be about Robert's job. It was meant to be about me and him at last, after more than a month, getting down to more than just kissing. At 10p.m. when I finally heard him knock quietly on the door of the room I was a bit tipsy, very hungry and in an almighty huff.

The huff disappeared the second I opened the door. Robert was standing there with a wilting tulip in his mouth, his tie undone and his shirt unbuttoned to his belly button revealing that his chest hair was also dark blonde. The red Gladstone bag was slung over his shoulder.

"I would have preferred a rose," he mumbled apologetically through the flower in his teeth, "but there weren't any of those in the vase on the front desk. I'm really sorry I've ruined our evening Ellie. Really, really sorry. The meeting ran on and on and then it took ages to get away from the clients. I know it's too late to go out for dinner so I ordered us some room service instead."

He stepped aside to reveal a trolley. There was an ice bucket with a bottle of Bollinger nestling in it. Robert lifted a big silver cloche to reveal enormous toasted club sandwiches. There were strawberries too, arranged in a big pile.

"And I brought you a present too — thought you could pack this next time we go away instead of that tatty little backpack." He handed me the beautiful bag, put on a hang dog look, cocking his head to one side. "Am I forgiven?"

I didn't bother to answer, just grabbed hold of his shirt and yanked him towards me, kissing him full and hard on the lips and then steering him firmly towards the bed. I wriggled out of the fluffy bathrobe and helped him strip off his suit. He pulled his shirt off over his head in a fluid movement involving only one hand and I saw that his skin was very white but that across the top of his arms he had pale freckles the colour of tea. He had wide, muscular thighs and his dark blond chest hair narrowed to a thin line leading down his midriff.

After a month of anticipation we were both of us already at slow-rolling boiling point and I could have come the minute Robert pushed inside me but he made sure we took it slowly and when we did come — at almost exactly the same time — he kept my gaze throughout.

"That was amazing," he said as we lay on the bed together afterwards sipping champagne. "I was really worried about it. It's been a long time since I . . . well since I last did this . . . I wasn't certain if I'd remember how."

"You remembered all right," I grinned at him popping a strawberry into each of our glasses.

"Yes I did, didn't I?" he said proudly. "Tell you something though. I don't remember it being as good as that before. Not ever."

We talked for a long time afterwards. He was very excited about the meeting he had just had.

"It's very hush hush Ellie but they are planning a hostile take over of one of their major competitors. It's a huge amount of work and a huge fee in the offing. If I land this one, I'll be the biggest biller in the firm this year. The meeting went excellently — I really think this one is in the bag."

I was watching him talk more than actually listening to what he said, taking in the shape of his cheekbones, the thickness of his hair, his beautiful blue eyes. It was bliss to be there, lying naked next to him and to be able to look at him for as long as I liked. Just stare at him. I had never in my life enjoyed looking at someone so much. My Indian tan was all but gone, but when I laid my arm across the pale skin of his it looked like we were two different races of people.

"Hey," he said, suddenly propping himself up on one elbow, "I've just had a thought. How about I help you find somewhere else to live rather than that flat in Kennington, somewhere a bit better you can have all to yourself."

"Kennington's not that bad. A bit of a squeeze but it's fun. And cheap."

"But wouldn't you like to have a place where I can come visit you, spend some time with you?"

"Of course I would."

"Well, we'll find you somewhere then."

"OK great, but let's remember when we're out flat hunting that I'm on a temp secretary's wage, eh?"

He nodded, pulled me towards him and started to kiss me some more. It shouldn't be possible to fall in love with someone in a matter of weeks. Something so very important, so significant, should not be capable of being given away lightly or quickly. But the truth was that I had started falling in love with Robert from the very first time he kissed me, and by the time we were lying in that bed together in Brighton I was done for.

When my grandfather came up to my room to pass on my mother's message that the bath was ready, he found me sitting on the end of the bed clutching the red bag to my chest. He didn't say anything, just gently took the bag from me and put his arms round me and hugged me tight. When I was a little girl he would hold me high above his head and spin me round and round and, although this made me scream in joyful terror, I was never once frightened that he would drop me. As he comforted me I knew that, even though I'd been too big to pick up for years, he would still never let me fall.

CHAPTER
SIX

1944

Trevor bides his time and eventually his patience starts to pay dividends. One evening Laura invites Trevor to join her and Kitty for their tea, most of which Trevor has brought. It is not a romantic proposition.

"There's plenty for three. Would you like some too?"

Funny that, how there is enough for three.

Trevor is careful with his acceptance. He replies coolly, casually, as if he has not been hoping for this for weeks.

"That would be nice. Ta."

They eat at 5.30p.m., about the time most families sit down together for tea. Trevor has been placed at one end of the small square table, Laura at the other. Laura pulls Kitty's chair up tight next to her, helps her to cut up her food, tells her to keep her mouth closed while she eats. She puts enough distance between their huddle of two and Trevor, so that he could be a total stranger, as if they were at the Bracchi's café with not enough tables to go round and Trevor had just asked politely whether they would mind if he sat at the end of theirs. And, just like at the Bracchi's, Trevor respects their privacy, does not intrude into this small family's meal time, but keeps to his end of the table and eats his own tea in silence, taking great care to keep his mouth shut while he eats too. Trevor knows that he will not be invited to stay for another cup of tea after Kitty is put to bed. Not this time anyway.

It is not as if Trevor has ever been short of female attention. Like Jack he too is tall and broad shouldered which is unusual for the Rhondda whose men tend to be of shorter build. And again just like Jack he is handsome, with jet black hair and dark eyes. The girls like him anyway and a number of them have passed through his arms. It has been wartime for a long time — at least as long as Trevor has been interested in girls — and most people have had the shadow of loss cross over their lives — brothers and fathers and lovers who went away to fight and will not return. Even those lucky enough not to have lost in this terrible way have endured years of a dreary diet and the captivity of black outs. It has always seemed entirely natural to Trevor that girls should want to grab hold of the few pleasures still readily available in life and to spend time with him ever so quietly in the Anderson shelter to which, after the first few air-raid warnings, his mother simply refuses to go, even after a bomb was dropped on Cwmparc killing 27 people. *If I have to be killed it'll be in my own home*, she says, *next to a good fire*. In the weeks before he went off to training camp he spent his evenings with a girl from school called Margaret Lewis who had brown curls, smiling eyes and a big bust that she would press against Trevor and whisper in his ear, "You're brown as a Spaniard you are Trevor Richards and handsome with it and I'll be waiting right here for you when you get back."

But Trevor hasn't given poor, eager little Margaret Lewis a single thought since he laid eyes on Laura at his mother's funeral, of the sweet joy Margaret hinted they would share together if he got home safe and sound. That is not what he wants to do with Laura, or at least it is not the only thing he wants to do with Laura. With Laura he also wants to mend her, fix her so that she doesn't hurt anymore and then fold her up and place her safely next to his heart where she will be warm and comfy.

It is a summer evening, still warm and sunny, and Trevor and Kitty are out the back in Laura's tiny garden, where Trevor has been making a start on clearing the weeds that have been bothering him for weeks now. Laura comes out with a laundry basket full of wet sheets.

"I know I should really have waited till Monday to do this lot," she says, "but who decided Monday should be wash day anyway? Sunny days are wash days in my book."

She shakes each sheet before pegging it out tightly on the line so that it will dry nice and smooth, cutting down on the ironing afterwards. The sheets make a damp cracking noise when she shakes them. They are heavily darned in places but white like ice having been soaked all afternoon in Dolly Blue. The late sunshine shines through the material of Laura's dress so that Trevor catches a brief glimpse of the narrowness of her waist and the outline of her legs beneath. He wants to hold her so much he feels dizzy, takes a sharp intake of breath to steady himself. Laura bends to pick up another sheet from the basket, looks straight at him and smiles.

Kitty bounces over to her mother, dodging the sheets sailing on the line,

"Can Trevor stay for his tea again Mam?"

"I was hoping he might like to," Laura says, pegging out the last sheet, the biggest of them all.

"Hurrah! Did you hear that Trevor? You can stay for your tea so we've got time to finish the weeding," and Kitty hurtles her strong, sturdy little self straight at Trevor who catches her.

Tiny baby steps are how Trevor makes his way to Laura. This late summer night is not the night he arrives at his destination but it is the night on which his journey finally gets underway. When they sit down for their tea, Kitty places her chair smack bang in the middle between Laura and Trevor. They are close enough that she can touch them both from where she sits.

Trevor waits for permission from Laura. He thinks he understands by now how she ticks and hopes that when she is ready he will know. Each night after Kitty is in bed, he and Laura sit together in the kitchen drinking more tea than either of them wants. Laura talks to Trevor of Jack — how handsome he was, how witty, how much she misses him. Trevor lets her do this, knows instinctively that it is better for Laura to wear her sorrow openly and not try to hide it away. Only in this way will she heal enough to love him a little. He waits and he watches and he listens. One evening at tea time, she puts her hand on his shoulder when she is serving him potatoes. It is the slightest and swiftest of touches and is bestowed in the safety of Kitty's presence but it is a touch nevertheless. A few nights later she does it again and this time her hand lingers a little longer. Trevor knows that the time has come. He lifts his own hand to his shoulder and touches her fingers ever so gently and just for a moment.

That night, when Laura comes downstairs after putting Kitty to bed, Trevor is not sitting at the kitchen table with a pot of tea at the ready. Instead he is standing at the back door, looking out over the garden and the tiny patch of lawn that he has now weeded and watered, at the slim frill of flower beds around it that he has planted out with late geraniums taken from his own garden for a last little bit of colour before autumn. He does not turn around to look at her, does not say anything, just moves over a bit so there is a little space in the doorway for her to come and stand by his side and look out at the garden too if she wants. Which she does. Trevor still does not say anything, just reaches out his hand. Laura does not take it immediately but eventually, very slowly, she puts her hand in his and Trevor rubs his thumb ever so gently across the back of it.

"Trevor, I . . ."

"I know Laura. I know how you felt the last time you kissed a man. I know you think a kiss can never feel like that again but it will. Trust me."

When Trevor finally turns towards Laura, he finds she is already holding her beautiful face up to him.

Laura keeps herself nice. It is not so much that she is vain — although Trevor often catches her looking at herself in the mirror or at her reflection in the kitchen window while she is doing the dishes, turning her head ever so slightly from side to side, pursing her lips and licking her front teeth — but more that looking after herself gave her something other than Kitty to focus on after Jack had gone. She takes a long time each week doing her hair in the Victory Roll style. It is a complicated process, involving dampening her long, blonde hair with sugar water and curling it at the front into rolls, three fat ones perched high above her brow. Trevor loves to watch her doing this, the curve of her smooth white arms lifted over the top of her head, her long, slim fingers moving quickly and skilfully over her hair as she backcombs it and then pins it up with Kirby grips. She applies rouge and mascara every morning and three or four times a day she re-anoints her beautiful mouth, always the same shade of pink. She takes great care when she does this not to get lipstick on her front teeth which cross over each other ever so slightly.

"First thing I do every day is put on my make up," she tells Trevor. "I could never go out without it."

Trevor understands why Laura makes her face bright and slick and shiny. The colours she paints on helped her from disappearing altogether in Jack's absence, made it appear to Kitty that Laura was still alive. But

Trevor likes it best when Laura's lips are pale and bare, when he has kissed all the sticky, spiky pink right off her mouth and he can see her properly. The real Laura is younger and softer and Trevor knows he will never get bored of lying next to her in bed and just looking at her. Filling himself up with her.

He has been bowled over by the strength of Laura's passion for him. He had not expected their first attempt at love making to be so glidingly easy, so sweetly successful. He had thought that the first time after Jack would have been difficult for Laura, have rendered her tearful and guilty. He had not been without concerns about his own performance, his previous encounters having been quick and fumbled experiences during which both participants were more or less fully clothed. Trevor had never before seen a real live woman totally naked and he was worried that all things taken into consideration he might not be man enough for the job. He need not have worried. Laura had missed physical contact, someone to hold her tight and stroke her cheek and tell her she is beautiful. Sex seems to set her free, make her more confident and relaxed than she ever is during the day. She is not in the least bit self conscious about her body or the thin silvery lines that cross her belly, like the shimmering slug trails in his garden. There are lots of these trails. Kitty, taking after her father as she does, was an enormous baby who had stretched and pulled Laura's tiny frame fit to burst.

"Honestly," Laura laughs as they lie in bed and Trevor presses his lips to her stomach, "by the end I was so crammed full of baby I felt like she would pop right out of my mouth if only I could yawn widely enough."

When Trevor makes love to Laura she is calm and happy and her skin flushes a rosy pink so that she becomes even more beautiful. When she falls asleep afterwards, which she does as quickly and suddenly as stepping off a cliff, Trevor stays awake for as long as he possibly can so that he can watch over her for a while.

Laura's second wedding is organised as quickly as her first and for the same reason. Laura is pregnant. There is no need for a fuss or a big do. After all, Laura has done it once already and Trevor is an only child whose parents are both dead. A quick visit to the register office and the job is done. They don't even take Kitty with them. Laura says it will just confuse her and heaven knows her life is about to be turned upside down enough as it is with a new baby taking up her mother's attention.

Laura knows she does not love Trevor in the same way as she loved Jack but she does love him. He has swept away the dirtiest, darkest corners of her grief and filled her with so much love that she has enough spilling over the top to give some of it back to him. She does not doubt how much he cares for Kitty, will care for the baby she is carrying. She relies on his strength, his company, his wages and the caring, selfless way he takes her to bed, smoothing her soft skin for a long time before he touches her in any other way. When the weight of his body covers hers, she is no longer empty and dry, like she might just blow away on the wind like seed from a dandelion clock. She is anchored by the certainty of him. In bed, she closes her eyes and reaches up to run her hands slowly across the width of Trevor's shoulders, and although it is Jack that she thinks of when she does this, Trevor does not know it.

1945

Pregnancy suits Laura. It makes her slow and languorous, forces her to sit down more, do less. Kitty grabs at the chance to spend more time with her mother and they sit together on the settee for hours at a time, reading and chanting nursery rhymes. Laura is full of baby again and when she does move she does so slowly and gracefully, gliding around the house with a small secret smile on her face. Her face is fuller, almost plump, and she has stopped wearing make up altogether. She doesn't curl or pin up her hair any more and now Trevor is allowed to touch it, to lift it gently so that he can kiss the back of his wife's neck. He treats her even more carefully during this time, cherishing her and the precious cargo she is carrying. He comes home from the shop at lunchtime to make sure she takes a nap, whisking Kitty away to the garden to give her some peace. Peace is something that Laura no longer seems to lack. They are careful with each other in bed, slow and gentle, but Laura will not hear of them stopping while they wait for the baby. They lie facing each other and she cups his face in both her hands and kisses him, each eye, each cheek and finally his mouth. They lie so close Trevor can hear the sound of her eyelashes brushing against her pillow. The bump of Laura's belly presses against his flat stomach and he feels their baby press and knead his own skin. They lie in bed and cradle between them the life they have made together. It is a baby girl they have. After a fast and furious labour, Laura delivers a perfect, plump daughter with a round face and fat dimpled arms and thighs.

Laura giggles at the size of her robust newborn.

"She takes after her dad all right. Got your legs she has Trevor."

"I hope for her sake it's your looks she gets then!"

Trevor turns to Kitty.

"What do you think of your baby sister then Kit? Isn't she gorgeous? Just like you."

He picks Kitty up in a swoop, holding her high above his head in one big hand, spinning her gently in celebration of this day, this life. Kitty screams with delight, shouts, "Again Dad again".

"OK but not here. Your mother and sister are tired and need to get some sleep. We'll go play in the garden for a while shall we? Leave them to it."

Trevor takes one last look at his wife and daughter before he goes. They are asleep already; Laura's hair is matted to her forehead, spiky with sweat, the baby lying flat out in her cot, her brand new hands splayed like stars. Kitty takes Trevor firmly by the hand and leads him out the bedroom. He shuts the door behind them very quietly.

CHAPTER
SEVEN

The first morning I woke up back home in Clapham, in my old bed, I had forgotten where I was and why. The sun was shining for the second day in a row and those long muslin curtains from my teenage years were doing a poor job at keeping the light out. I thought of the curtains in the flat, so thick and lined they let you sleep in till lunchtime if you wanted, and then I remembered and an enormous boulder of sadness suddenly appeared and perched right on the middle of my chest. Eventually I struggled out from beneath it and, still in my pyjamas, I walked out on to the narrow landing outside my room and lifted the sash window wide open. I perched myself on the windowsill, swinging my legs over and resting my feet on the flat roof beneath. As I expected, Trevor was already up and working hard on his garden. He looked up at me.

"Are you having a cigarette, young lady?"

That was one of the main reasons I spent a lot of time sitting out on the windowsill when I lived at home. To have a sneaky fag.

"I don't do that so much any more," I said, "Robert hated smoking."

"I loved smoking," Trevor said wistfully. It's true. Trevor really did love smoking but he gave it up when he retired. He said that without the routine of work he would smoke himself to an early grave and so the morning after his last day of work he gave up, just like that. He says that if he gets to ninety he will start again because by then his grave won't be that far away anyway.

The felt of the flat roof was warm and scratchy under my feet. I watched Trevor move around his garden: touching growing things, pulling up weeds.

"Ellie? You're not sitting on that roof again are you? You know it's not safe."

I felt a sudden hot spurt of Pavlovian guilt gush through me at the sound of my mother's voice, as if I was sixteen again and she had just caught me smoking, red handed.

"Not sitting on it Mum, just resting my feet on it. Nothing dangerous."

Like my grandfather, my mother is an early riser. Not even 7a.m. on a Wednesday morning and yet here she was, already showered and dressed and dusting the skirting boards before she went to work, a damp cloth wrapped tight round her index finger.

"You know I don't even like you resting your feet on it Ellie. Those roofs weren't meant to be weight bearing."

"Hey, are you saying I'm fat?" I was only half teasing. My mother has never been backwards at coming forwards if she thinks I've put on weight.

"I'm saying nothing of the sort. You're looking very slim nowadays. All I'm saying is that roof's not safe to stand on. Now please," her voice became harsher, shorter tempered, "will you get off that window sill? You're making me nervous."

I managed to contain the surge of mutinous teenager rising up in me and quickly changed the subject.

"You look good Mum. That new hairdo really suits you."

"Thanks very much!" My mother looked pleased, patted her hair self consciously. She deserved the compliment. She looks better now than she did ten years ago. She has found a style of dressing in later life that works for her — wide-legged linen trousers and shirts with loafers in the summer and charcoal wool trousers and soft, slash-necked jumpers in the winter. She started to go grey very young and until recently she dyed her hair dark brown which made her look a bit Dot Cotton. Then, a few months after she turned sixty, she announced she was finally old enough to merit being full-on grey. She stopped colouring her hair and let her own colour come through which turned out to be a fabulous steely grey that she then got cut in a short, choppy style.

"I was thinking of getting off to work when I'm finished up here Ellie. Will you be all right with your grandfather until I get home? I could take the day off instead if you'd like me to?"

"Mum! I'm a grown woman. I don't need you to stay home to look after me. Go to work!"

"Well all right then, if you're sure you'll be ok." She dropped a kiss on my head as she made her way down the stairs. "You know, everything always comes out in the wash eventually Ellie."

The first few days back home were long and heavy with time. I counted hours through my fingers like the beads of a rosary. When I looked at my watch, lumpy, leaden and miserable, I was disappointed that only a few hours had passed and all that lay ahead of me were endless, Robert-less days. Being miserable — really miserable — is like being ill. It saps your strength to carry unhappiness around with you, especially an unhappiness so big it stretches to fill up every bit of your body. Every morning, sunlight leaked through my flimsy curtains and splashed around my room but I wished it was winter, cold and dark. I yearned for brushed cotton sheets and flannelette pyjamas so that I could lie in bed, stuck to my sheets like fuzzy felt, with a big heavy duvet to pull over my head and hide under. I wanted to sleep for a very long time and not wake up until I didn't hurt any more, but every morning the sun chased me out of bed earlier and earlier.

Trevor was always up before me. Once I'd dragged my sadness downstairs he would make tea and we would go out to the garden and sit on the wooden bench together to drink it. At this, the very beginning of each new day, it was quiet and calm, the air fresh and cool. The rest of London lay sleeping and Trevor and I had a little bit of day all to ourselves that no-one else was using yet. Neither of us spoiled it by talking.

There was a regular pattern to my mother and Trevor's days and I fell into step with them because I found the steady order soothing and because I had nothing better to do. After my mother had gone off to work, Trevor worked in his garden and I tried listlessly to read. At 12p.m. we went inside to listen to the news on the radio and eat a sandwich and then we went shopping. Trevor has a rule that he only buys what will get eaten within the next 24 hours which makes shopping a daily event. He dislikes supermarkets and buys his meat at the butchers, his bread from the bakers and his fruit and vegetables at the local market stalls. I listened to him banter with the shop owners as he stashed his purchases in his tatty canvas shopping bag, refusing the flimsy, pink-and-white-striped plastic bags the shop keepers offered. In his own small way, Trevor is quite the eco warrior, recycling furiously and saving all fruit and vegetable peelings for his organic compost. After shopping there was just enough time for a sit down with a cup of tea and the crossword before Trevor set to making the evening meal. He's a pretty good cook although he doesn't make anything fancy: cottage pie, lamb chops, grilled fish, and dinner — or tea as we call it — was always ready the minute my mother got through the door. We ate together, sitting round the kitchen table. Once the dishes were done, Trevor walked down to the working men's club for two pints — never more — and was back home by 10p.m. for the news.

While Trevor was out of the way my mother settled herself in front of the telly and got on with some knitting. This was done for my benefit — my mother is usually out in the evening, her diary crammed with evening classes and good deed doing — but because I was home she stayed home too. At some point around 8p.m. she would fish two bars of Dairy Milk out of her handbag and try gently to steer me round to talking about Robert.

"How was your day love? Did you speak to anyone?"

"Just Grandad."

"And are you feeling ok?"

"I'm fine Mum, honest. I really like this next programme. Shall we watch it together?" At which point my mother would give up and the evening would pass in a chocolaty clack of needles and the sudsy swish of soap operas.

In fact I was far from fine. Even though I didn't want to talk about Robert, in my head all I did was think about him: about our life together and about the flat. Because Robert didn't just find me somewhere a bit better than the flat in Kennington.

He found me the best place ever.

"You're going to absolutely love it," he said excitedly when he picked me up to go to view it. "It's just come on the market this month, been renovated top to bottom to a very high specification, and I've got the keys right here in my pocket."

I did love it. Anyone would. It was in Primrose Hill for a start, on the top floor of a gracious Victorian house. It was small, only just big enough for one person or a couple, and had a tiny bathroom, a small kitchen, one bedroom and a living room. All the rooms were freshly painted in a rich cream colour and everything in it was high quality — shiny chrome kitchen fittings, power shower, corner bath.

"You like it then?" Robert grinned at me, taking in the look of wonder on my face.

"I think it's wonderful. But you know I can't afford a place like this Robert. It's in Primrose Hill! It would cost an absolute fortune in rent."

"There's no need to worry about the rent. I'm going to sort all that out for you."

"I can't have you doing that. What do you mean you're going to sort all that out for me? Are you planning on leaving the money on the bedside table when you leave in the morning?"

"Don't be like that Ellie. You make it sound so sordid. It's just that it's too soon for us to move in together or anything — while I'm still finalising arrangements with Ann — but I'd like you to live somewhere that's as lovely as you are while all that is happening. Somewhere I can come and join you eventually."

"Well — I could pay what I pay now in Kennington — or pay half or something."

"Ellie . . . you know us fat-cat lawyers earn far too much money. So will you let me sort out the rent for you? Please?"

When he put it like that the answer was easy. "Yes of course."

"Good, because I've already signed the paperwork and you can move in whenever you're ready."

After years of living in grotty, shared flats, I enjoyed playing house. I bought a raspberry-pink throw and cushions for the sofa, white Egyptian cotton sheets for the bed and a Gaggia coffee maker for the kitchen. I put fresh flowers in the window, lit lots of candles when it got dark. Sunlight shone through the tall windows of my living room and dappled the floor. If I wanted to go out, there were dozens of trendy shops and restaurants to choose from and always some celebrity to watch having a double mocha chocolate whip or a double vodka. I could be walking on Primrose Hill within just a few minutes of leaving the flat. I could stand on the top with all the courting couples and the perfect families with children and dogs and look down on London. It felt like living in the pages of the Sunday supplements.

When Robert came round we usually went out to eat because he was quite a foodie and always read the restaurant reviews in the papers and I wasn't that interested in cooking. Don't get me wrong I certainly liked eating well enough, as my figure showed when I was not newly thin from a trip to India, but I mostly survived on beans and toast or baked potatoes and cheese and a lot of chocolate — food that was cheap and quick and easy to make.

It amused Robert to check out what was in my fridge and poke fun at me.

"Is this all you've got — pasta and ready-made tomato sauce? Where's the rocket? The parmesan?"

"I happen to like pasta and tomato sauce," I said, trying to grab the jar out of his hand. "It does the job and doesn't involve much washing up."

"You're a bit old to be eating like a student aren't you?" he teased, holding the jar above his head out of my reach. "What are you trying to do? Hold on to your youth?"

"Ha bloody ha," I made a face at him. "I suppose your fridge is full of home-baked treats?"

"Well, Ann does like to cook," he said, almost wistfully.

"What sort of things does Ann like to cook?" I asked, trying not to sound hurt because I had actually been referring to his fridge in the Barbican, not the one back in his marital home at Surrey.

"Oh all sorts . . . but I don't want to talk about Ann."

"No — go on. Now that you've started."

"She makes lots of things . . . goat's cheese tart, beef Wellington, herbed chicken with gruyere —"

He was almost salivating at this point. I conjured up an image of his dowdy little wife moving around her enormous kitchen, whipping up gourmet treats as she waited for her husband to come home, humming gently to herself amongst her shiny copper pans and gleaming surfaces.

"Anybody can cook. You've only got to be able to read to cook. It's hardly brain surgery."

"I didn't say it was," he grinned "but I think it's a bit more difficult than just reading a recipe."

"Bet you I could make you a dinner every bit as good as your wife."

"There's no need for you to do that."

"Yes there is. How about next Wednesday?"

74

"All right then, I'll look forward to it."

I rushed out that weekend and bought two Delia Smith cookbooks. "How difficult can it be?" I thought to myself as I pored over them.

Only it was difficult. When people talk about how they like to cook, they seem to leave out the fact that to cook you have to shop first. I had decided on a starter of Thai prawns in lime and ginger, followed by a beef-in-Guinness casserole with dauphinoise potatoes and steamed broccoli followed by a lemon syllabub. To make these seemingly simple recipes I had to buy an enormous list of ingredients — lemon grass, ginger, bay leaves, limes — things I didn't normally keep in my cupboard alongside my tins of beans and jars of pasta sauce. Plus I had to buy cooking utensils — a pestle and mortar, a citrus fruit grater, even a casserole dish, one of those unfeasibly heavy Le Creuset ones that figure so much in the pictures in cook books. I had been shopping for two days before I even started to cook and was thoroughly fed up with lugging big bags up the three flights of stairs to my flat.

I went to Leadenhall Market during my lunch hour on Wednesday to buy the final few fresh ingredients I needed. Leadenhall Market always comes as a bit of a surprise — one minute you are walking down a busy city street, bristling with concrete and glass offices and the next you turn off and are in the cool gloom of a cobbled market. Steel and chrome seem to have bypassed Leadenhall; it can't have changed much since the turn of the century. It has a distinct feel of the Harry Potter about it. The shops are small with old-fashioned, wooden-framed windows and doors painted dark red or British racing green. They don't quite have signs above them that say "Ye Olde Quaint Provision shop" but you get the gist. There are wonderful butchers and fish shops and tiny sandwich shops where people queue out of the door to buy sandwiches that are made up there and then from a bewildering choice of fillings and handed to you wrapped up in greaseproof paper rather than ready-made in a triangular plastic box. There's also The Lamb pub, outside of which an inordinate amount of city workers stand, gaily ignoring health guidelines to drink less and eat five selections of fruit and vegetables a day, choosing instead to spend their lunch hour getting on the outside of a few pints. You can buy anything a Victorian gentleman might need in Leadenhall Market, from a well hung pheasant right through to a saddle for your horse. I bought my prawns and my best British beef, queuing behind city shoppers far more seasoned than me, who produced special insulated bags to keep their purchases cool back at the office. I had to make do with a plastic bag.

I knocked off work a bit early, pleading a headache. I didn't look a bit sick and, as I had returned from lunch festooned with carrier bags, it was pretty obvious that I had plans for the evening. I don't think the solicitors I worked for believed me for one minute when I said I was poorly but I hadn't been sick once since starting work and they let it go.

Once back at the flat I started on the cooking. About half an hour in I realised that I had badly underestimated the amount of time my three-course menu was going to take. Why had nobody warned me how long it takes to peel and chop lemon grass or grate ginger? Why hadn't I practised the dishes first rather than cook them on the day that Robert was coming?

A sense of panic began to build in my chest which grew greater the longer I grappled with my ingredients. I was dying for a wee but didn't dare take time to go until I had at least got my casserole in the oven, only increasing my agitation. I had been planning on having a shower before Robert arrived, and to waft around my flat smelling of the Jo Malone lime blossom cologne he liked so much whilst drinking a glass of perfectly chilled Chablis, before I serenely served up a wonderful meal. Instead I was sticky with sweat and dread and had somehow managed to get ginger in my fringe as I wiped my brow mid-grate. I hadn't even started on the syllabub when Robert let himself in.

"How's it going then Nigella?" he asked, trying to stifle a smile.

"Wonderful," I lied. "Everything's under control. Would you like a drink? Oh bugger I forgot to put the wine in the fridge. I meant to put it in earlier but the fridge was too full of food."

"Not a problem," Robert said, producing a bottle of Bollinger champagne with a flourish. I had acquired quite a taste for Bolly being with Robert. "I bought this ready chilled. I'll find the glasses shall I?"

"Marvellous. Make mine a double. I'll just put this casserole in the oven and then I'm popping to the bathroom."

Strangely, I was very conscious about going to the toilet when Robert was with me. The flat was tiny and you could hear everything that went on in the bathroom from the living room. I shoved handfuls of toilet roll in the bowl before I sat down, hoping this would muffle the noise.

As I came out Robert said, "Golly. You needed to go!"

I blushed from the roots of my hair down to my chest.

"Hmm, yes, well . . . where's my champagne? Here it is. Lovely." And I downed my glass in three big gulps.

"You needed that too," Robert laughed. "When are we eating? I'm ravenous."

"The starter is ready right now and the main course will be ready in about . . . ooh —"

I consulted the recipe. It said two and a half hours but I'd fried the meat before I put it in the casserole. How long could it take for a bit of beef to cook?

". . . about 45 minutes. I'll finish off the pud — I mean dessert — while we wait for the main course."

This was a lie too as I hadn't even started preparing the syllabub but I figured if Robert kept up with me on the champagne he wouldn't notice the wait.

I dished up the prawns. Even though the preparation for the meal had been so frenetic and I didn't feel at all relaxed when we sat down, they were really rather good. The flavours reminded me of the meals I had eaten in Thailand and I had spent a lot of money in Leadenhall Market on the prawns, which were big and meaty.

Robert enjoyed them too and since I was by now halfway through my second glass of champagne I began to relax.

I gathered up the plates and went out into the kitchen. I scanned the recipe hurriedly. Bother, it called for more grating of citrus fruits — lemon this time and whipping of cream and I didn't have a food processor, just a whisk. I set to whipping very determinedly. I figured if I whipped very fast it wouldn't take that long. My arm soon began to ache but I worked through the burn in a way that would have made Jane Fonda proud and was gratified when my cream began to stiffen into peaks. Almost there. Just a few more whips. Only after a few more whips my formerly stiff peaks had collapsed and there at the bottom of the bowl was what looked like watery cottage cheese.

"Fuck, fuck, fuck," I said under my breath so Robert wouldn't hear me. I stuck my finger in the bowl. It tasted pretty good. Perhaps it was meant to be like that. I hoped so because it was just going to have to do. I bunged in the lemon juice and grated the rind, whipped the stuff round the bowl one more time, scraped it into two sundae dishes and shoved it into the fridge before serving up the main course.

The beef was tough as old boots. Robert valiantly chewed his way through a few mouthfuls and then put his knife and fork down and told me what I knew already.

"Sweetheart, I don't think this is quite cooked," he said gently.

"I think that's a bit of an understatement," I said glumly. "As my grandfather might say, a good vet could get this back on its feet."

"It tastes nice," Robert said politely, "why don't you put it all back in the oven and we'll go down the pub for the next three hours or so."

"No, no need for that. I've got us a lovely pudding. We'll just move straight to that and have another glass of champagne."

"That's fine by me. I'm always up for more champagne."

I served up the watery, lemon-flavoured cottage cheese with a flourish.

"Ta da!" I said as I handed him his sundae dish. "I've never seen curds and whey but I reckon this is what it looks like."

Robert stuck his spoon into his dish and then put it back down carefully.

"Little Miss Tuffet," he said, as he looked at me ruefully, reaching over the table to cup my face between the palms of his hands, "I think you've whipped the cream for too long and it's separated. It was a good effort but I think I'd rather we just went to bed now."

Good effort sounded like something they used to say to me at school but he was dead right. I had efforted for three days but, except for the prawns, I had failed miserably.

"Ok," I said. "At least that's something I can do."

Robert gathered up our glasses and escorted me to the bedroom.

80

What I could not match in the kitchen I figured I could match in the sack. I kissed Robert from head to toe, tiny butterfly kisses from his neck right down to his feet and back again. When I had finished, Robert kissed me all over in the same way, telling me he loved me all the while. Afterwards he curled himself around me and held me tight.

"You really are a domestic goddess you know. Just not one that cooks. And if I needed cooking I would have stayed with Ann."

CHAPTER
EIGHT

By Saturday afternoon my mother's patience was exhausted.

"Why don't you ring Gina?" she suggested. "Go out for a drink with her or something. Gina will know how to cheer you up."

I bottled it and instead of ringing Gina I sent her a text. Not a very truthful one. *Home to visit Mum and Trevor. Fancy a drink tonight?* I got a text back almost in return. *In pub already. Come join us stranger.*

I didn't need to ask Gina which pub she meant. When we say the pub we mean only one place: the scruffy, ugly local that is our own very dear scruffy, ugly local just up the road from Trevor's house.

When I got there, I spotted Gina sitting outside in the concrete area that pretends to be a beer garden. Beth was there too, and her brother Paul. I felt a slosh of nerves and guilt in my stomach as I walked over to join them. I had once been very much part of this gang — one of the people included in any arrangements for Saturday nights out or Sunday lunches in — but I had dropped off the scene while I was with Robert and deserved some pointed comments about my absence.

"Hey babe," was all Gina said. "Come sit here next to me." She budged Paul unceremoniously along the bench to make room for me and patted the space next to her eagerly.

It was quite a squeeze. Paul was clearly reluctant to give up his position next to Gina, and to sit down I had to wedge myself tightly between them so that we sat thigh jammed against thigh. Gina put her arm round my shoulder, hugged me to her in a cramped sideways clasp and planted a big, sloppy, lager-fragranced kiss on my cheek.

"Boy, Ellie have I missed you," she grinned at me. "Now then, the reason we're here today is to help console Paul. He's been dumped. Again."

I was grateful to her for the easy way she brought me back into the group, made me feel included.

"I'll get a round in shall I? Try to catch up with you lot. What do you want to drink?" I eased myself back out of the row of thighs, noticing that Paul immediately stretched out to fill the gap I'd left.

"Our friend Stella," they chorused.

I turned to look back at them over my shoulder as I walked to the bar.

"She's not our friend really," I shouted.

It took me about a pint and a half to catch up with them. One of the good things about Stella is that she works quickly. It was mean of me but I was relieved that there was a crisis at hand and that Paul had called upon his first two loves — his sister and Gina — to help drown his sorrows. The end of Paul's latest relationship meant I could postpone telling anyone about the end of mine. I didn't have to contribute a great deal to the conversation, just a few "plenty more fish in the sea" and "more fool her" type comments. The years of shared life behind us all anchored me to them and smoothed over my recent months of neglect.

There are dozens of people on my Christmas card list and loads of numbers stored in my mobile phone but there are just a few people in my life I could call upon if I was in trouble and Gina is one of those. If I were stranded in the middle of nowhere Gina would come and get me, however long the journey. If I was broke she would share her money with me, without me even having to ask. And even if I hadn't seen her for a while she would still make room for me on the bench. Sometimes in birthday cards and texts I sign off with "Luv". When I do that, I am referring to a different kind of emotion from love; something less, a little lighter. Perhaps that's the definition of "luv". Luv is liking someone a lot. But Gina? Gina always gets the full fat spelling.

I met her on the very first day of secondary school. She happened to have the desk next to mine. Even then Gina was more exotic than the rest of us — her father is Iranian (or Persian as she likes to say because she thinks it sounds more romantic) and her mother is a Londoner and a red head, and they gave Gina the best bits of both of them. She is olive-skinned with big green eyes and dark red hair and even then, when she was only eleven, people turned round for a second look at her and smiled. Gina is so used to the privilege of being pretty that she doesn't even notice that people are always pleased to see her. Smiling faces are part of the birthright of the beautiful and Gina is well aware that she is a looker which can get annoying at times, but people forgive her for being a bit vain because wherever Gina is, that's where the party is and whichever table she is sitting at, that's the fun table. It's fair to say that I am well and truly in Gina's shadow when it comes to looks but so were most of the girls at school so I didn't get too much of a complex about it. There was a degree of kudos in being her best friend and, as a result, always having a seat at the fun table too.

Life is so random. I could have sat next to someone else that first day of school and my life would have taken a different path but it was Gina who was sitting next to me on that first day and it was Gina who sat next to me for much of the next seven years. I used to say to her when we went to concerts that somewhere in that huge crowd of people could be the love of our life, the person we were meant to spend the rest of our lives with and that we might just have passed him on the way to the toilet without realising that we had sailed straight past our soulmate. Gina disagreed with me on that — she said it was all down to fate and that soul mates would find each other out somehow, however big the crowd. My soul mate would be the person behind me in the queue for the bar and I'd turn round and slosh lager from a plastic cup all over him and that would be it — the first step on the path to true love.

Paul and Gina were each other's soulmates once, a long time ago when she and I were in the fifth form and considered it the height of glamour to bag ourselves a boyfriend from amongst the lofty ranks of the sixth formers, older, taller and more aloof than the boys in our own year. Paul was widely regarded as being not only one of the best-looking boys but also the coolest because he played electric guitar in the school band and wore sunglasses just like Bono's, but Gina and I kept our admiration for him to ourselves because he was Beth's brother and it freaked her out when the other girls told her how gorgeous they thought he was. Gina started off her love life much as it has continued ever since and got the pick of the crop without even trying. One break time, Beth announced that Paul had promised her twenty pounds if she could persuade Gina to go out with him. Beth got her twenty pounds and I went with her on her trip to Top Shop the following Saturday to spend it while Paul and Gina were at the pictures on their first date. They were inseparable for the next two years until the point Paul left school, gave up on the guitar and became a trainee at a local bank which is when Gina decided he'd become boring and dumped him. Paul was devastated at the time but with hindsight he should be rather proud of himself. He still holds the record for the person Gina has been out with the longest.

Unusually for schoolyard sweethearts, Gina and Paul have stayed good friends and over the years Paul has established a pattern of calling on Gina and Beth to drink with him to mourn the end of his subsequent relationships. Some of those relationships have been long standing, some have lasted only months. The one thing they all have in common is the fact they come to

86

an end and that Gina and Beth (and me too a lot of the time) have been there at the finish, just as we were that day, with a pint of Stella in our hands.

Once she was confident that Paul was sufficiently supplied with lager, Gina turned her attention to me.

"Robert not with you?"

I paused before I answered. "Nah. He's away at some legal conference this weekend."

Gina gave me a sharp look and I knew that the pause had been too long and that she was thinking, *There's more to that answer than meets the eye and I'm going to tackle you about that very soon, just not today because today is about Paul's issues.* I was relieved she was willing to let the moment pass. I knew I had it coming but that afternoon I needed just to be with my friends, one of whom had recuperated enough from his broken heart to start listing his ex's faults. I was surprised how innocuous they were. Her main vices appeared to be eating McDonald's chips in a particularly aggressive manner, jabbing them into her mouth without stopping, and never having anything in her fridge other than vodka and nail varnish.

Three pints after I arrived, Beth said she would have to get going.

"I'm going to be in such trouble with Tony. I don't think he's ever had to look after both kids on his own for so long. He'll be going spare."

"Don't go Beth," I pleaded, "I haven't seen you in ages."

"I'd like to stay out Ellie but I said I'd only be gone an hour and it's been . . ." she squinted at her watch for a while and then gave up ". . . way too many drinks for me to be able to tell the time anymore. I'm drunk and I'm tired and I need to get home. I must look a state."

"You look great," I lied.

Beth didn't just look tired. She looked absolutely knackered. There were big bags under her eyes and she was still carrying a lot of baby weight. She caught me looking at her, smiled, and tugged her shirt down over her belly.

"Can I come and see you and the kids soon?" I asked.

Beth put her hand over mine. "We'd like that Ellie, we really would."

I watched her as she staggered out of the pub, weaving her way unsteadily through the tables. Perhaps I should have offered to walk her home but she only lived round the corner and might not have appreciated the suggestion that she was incapable of walking a few hundred yards on her own. I turned to Gina and Paul to ask them if they thought I should go with her but they were in deep, drunken conversation.

"You were the first person I ever loved, Gina, and I'll always have a soft spot for you, you know that don't you?"

"I didn't think it was just a *soft* spot you'd always have for me Paul."

There was no room for three people in that sort of conversation so I wandered into the pub to see if anybody would give me a game of pool. Living so close to the pub meant I learned to play pool at a young age and I'm good enough to put my money down on the table without too much huffing and puffing from the men waiting to play. There was nobody around except Clive, our next-door neighbour, who indulged me by playing three games, all of which he won. I would have said goodbye to Gina and Paul before I left but they looked pretty engrossed in each other.

I realised as I walked home that I too was drunk and tired. Even though it was still early Trevor was already in bed and my mother was out, clearly glad of the opportunity provided by my absence to resume her own social life. I got into bed without even cleaning my teeth. The last thing I saw as I closed my eyes was a jug of flowers that my grandfather had placed on my bedside table.

1946

Trevor finally persuades Laura that the four of them should move out of the terrace she rented while she waited for Jack to come home, and live above the draper's shop.

Laura sets about cleaning and redecorating, putting her own stamp on the place. There is not much money but there is enough for a lick of paint. She empties all the kitchen cupboards and scrubs out the drawers, lining them all with fresh, clean paper. Her hands hover over the tins and packets bought by Trevor's mother. She wants to throw them out, make a clean start, but with food in such short supply this would be more than foolish. There are a few tins of Spam here and one of

Golden Syrup, some twists of tea, a bag of flour and half a bag of precious sugar. Laura knows she can make good use of these and contents herself with just wiping down the tins. The house smells damply of soap for Laura has washed every towel and sheet and pillow case she can find. She plans on working her way through the contents of Trevor's mother's wardrobe just as soon as she can find time, but her new daughter is a hungry girl and Laura must interrupt her work frequently to sit down to feed her baby.

"You know love," Trevor says as he walks into their front room at the end of his working day, "there's no need to rush through all this work. It'll be right there waiting for you tomorrow and the day after and the day after that."

Laura smiles up at him from where she is pinned to the settee by the baby who has fallen asleep after a feed, sprawled across Laura's lap, her belly tight with milk. She motions to him with the tips of her fingers and Trevor bends down to receive her kiss. She knows he is right. This is already a comfortable, happy home and she need not fuss so much. Trevor's love is steadfast and he holds his family safe in the palm of his hand. Other families are finding it far more difficult to adjust after the end of the war. So many soldiers have not made the journey home and many of those who have are grey-faced and damaged. The collieries don't need as many men as they did and there is not enough work even for those still fit enough to go underground. These men have been institutionalised by war and find that everything has changed since they went away; their children are strangers and resent these tired men who take up their mothers' time and look nothing like the daddy in the photo. Their wives have changed too, grown independent, used to looking after themselves. The men drink too much and earn too little.

Laura is lucky — she has a new husband who is whole and healthy, good with business and good with children. Her life holds hope and promise again.

With the long, terrible war in Europe finally over, Trevor has big plans for the shop. People will want to start getting on with life. There are going to be lots of new homes, new marriages, new children. Trevor foresees a sharp upturn in demand for the goods he has available to sell. He does not have anywhere near the full range of items that were sold pre-war but the things he does have, people have need of. People want to make cushions and hem curtains for their new, peace-time lives. Business is going to be good and Trevor wants to make sure he is ready for it.

He spends long hours at night working out figures, considering catalogues, making lists. He thinks of his mother from time to time but he does not miss her as much as he might. With Laura and the two girls in his life now, there is too much living to do for that.

The baby is finally weaned and Laura has time to help Trevor in the shop. She enjoys it, likes the quiet orderliness of the shop's cupboards and drawers, everything in its place and a place for everything. She enjoys the ritual of helping customers, of packing up their purchases and taking their money. The ring of the till and the sing of the change, the small talk. Trevor has just taken delivery of a tiny amount of new ribbons and trimmings and Laura particularly loves arranging these, smoothing the satiny ribbon between her finger and thumb. Eventually Trevor feels confident enough to leave Laura in charge of the shop for a few hours in the afternoon, so that he can nip out back to the garden and pay some attention to the potatoes and peas and beans that will help feed his family later in the year. Laura likes being left in this way. She likes standing behind the counter, her baby sleeping peacefully in her crib at the back of the shop and Kitty playing beside her, sorting piles of buttons and scraps of fabric.

It is on an afternoon like this that the shop bell clangs loudly and Jack's brother comes barging through the door, out of breath and panting.

"Laura, Laura — come quick. Jack's just got home. He's not dead Laura — not dead at all. He's sitting in my Mam's kitchen, asking for you."

CHAPTER
NINE

I was out of practice at drinking Stella and I woke up even earlier on Sunday morning but this time with a thick head, desperate for a drink of water and a wee. Hearing me move around upstairs, my mother bustled into my bedroom with a cup of tea.

"I'm glad you're up. I'm making a big Sunday dinner. Teresa's coming round and Joan and Cliff too. Your grandfather's got a huge leg of lamb in. I thought you might like to invite Gina to join us. We'll be eating about 2 p.m."

I knew better than to argue with my mother when she was in Sunday dinner mode. Gina was delighted with her invitation.

"Bloody brilliant," she said when I phoned her. "I've got a filthy hangover and a cooked dinner is just what I need to sort me out. That and a glass of wine. Is it ok if I come round straight away? I could murder a cup of tea and there's no milk in the flat."

She turned up while I was still in the shower. By the time I was dressed she and Trevor were sitting in the kitchen having tea and buttered toast and discussing gardening. Trevor has always liked Gina, he says she is irreverent and a bit wicked which means that Gina can tell him what she gets up to and he finds it amusing, whereas if I were to tell him stuff like that he would worry his granddaughter was loose. But ever since Gina got into gardening they have had an extra bond. I blame Trevor entirely for Gina's gardening fetish. She had never shown the slightest interest in horticulture until Trevor gave her some terracotta pots one Christmas, already planted out with spring bulbs. At the time Gina had been none too impressed with her Christmas gift and had moaned non stop that she had spilled compost in the boot of her beloved Nissan Figaro when taking the pots home. She slung them unceremoniously out onto her tiny balcony and forgot all about them. However in spring when the bulbs started to come out Gina had been absolutely delighted with the process, marvelling at the way the waxy green shoots had pushed themselves hesitantly out of the dark crumbly soil before finally exploding into joyful daffodils and tulips. After that she had been a total convert, badgering Trevor into showing her how to take cuttings and choose seeds and soon her balcony was stuffed full of plants. It was after she'd managed to grow a small crop of tomatoes from a grobag that Trevor suggested she put her name down for an allotment and she had been waiting impatiently ever since, a stack of seed catalogues on her kitchen table where once there had been fashion magazines, covered with sticky yellow labels flagging up the things she planned to grow. She visited the allotments regularly in the hope that her devotion to her cause would persuade the committee to push her up the list a few places, and was semi-stalking one fellow whom she believed was unfairly cultivating three separate plots. She even knew the technical word for people with allotments — allotmenteers.

She was remarkably chirpy that morning considering how much she had had to drink the night before. She was wearing combat trousers and a white, cap-sleeved T shirt, which on a short arse like me would have looked butch but on Gina looked fit and sexy. To add to her already good looks, and throwing everyone even further into her shadow, she grew a fantastic pair of boobs when we were about thirteen and she now has a figure that goes out, in and out again in all the right places. The white cotton of her T shirt was stretched tight over her breasts, accentuating her narrow waist, and this, together with the combat trousers, gave her a decided Lara Croft look.

"Hey you," she said brightly.

"Hey yourself. Did you have a good time last night?"

She blushed ever so slightly. "Tell you about it later. Thought we could go for a walk up to the Common. I could do with some fresh air before lunch."

We walked up Clapham High Street, checking out all the new restaurants and bars. Clapham had become an awful lot trendier since I'd left home but I was glad to see that some of the dingy shops of my youth were surviving the lifestyle onslaught. The children's clothes shop that sells velour-padded babygros and frilly christening dresses was still there. It still covered its windows with yellow plastic to stop the sun fading the wares and had a half day on a Wednesday. The junk shop selling ends of china and rolls of bin bags had survived too, and the greengrocer's, defiantly selling bananas by the pound. At the fringes of the common we stopped at the estate agents and looked at the glossy pictures of houses we'd walked past on our way to school for years, now fitted with Agas and French windows, wall-to-wall wooden floors and Farrow & Ball, and priced way beyond Clapham girls like Gina and me.

"Do you fancy a coffee?" I asked when we reached a coffee shop.

Gina took a quick peek inside.

"You can't move in there for Boden and Bugaboos. Let's go get a cup of tea on the Common instead."

"Is that just an excuse to go to the allotments and do a spot of patrolling?"

"Maybe."

We ordered tea to go from the outdoor café on the Common. It came in flimsy polystyrene cups and was bright orange, stewed and lukewarm. I would have preferred a frothy coffee from Costa Lot but Gina had adopted the role of true Londoner that morning, outraged by the influence of America on our way of life.

"Every high street in the world is the same," she complained, "Gap, McDonald's, Blockbusters. Dull, dull, dull. You could be anywhere in the world and Gap would be there before you."

I thought of all the places in the world I had visited where there was no Gap — no high street even — but Gina was on a rant and I let her get on with it.

"Do you know that companies like Costa Lot keep their prices down until the independents go out of business and then, when the competition finally folds, they charge what they like?"

I did know that, sort of, but I also liked being able to buy a good cup of coffee.

"I'm a firm believer in supporting small local business me," Gina went on, sipping her tea. "Trouble is this stuff tastes like shite. Come on! Let's go to the allotments."

I made a face at her.

"Not for long. Just half an hour. Please."

"It'll take almost as long as that to walk there."

"Stop being such a City shandy girl will you? It'll build up your appetite for your roast lamb."

Gina almost jogged the last five minutes of the walk to the allotments in her eagerness to get there.

"You really love coming here don't you?" I asked in wonder as we walked through the tall, iron-mesh gates.

"What's not to love? Look at them. Don't they look wonderful?" She spread her arms out wide, as if gathering the expanse of allotments towards her in an embrace.

Even I had to acknowledge they looked pretty. Each little patch staked out with rows of bamboo canes, already laden with frothy green fronds that would soon turn into runner beans and sweet peas and strung with CDs that glinted and sparkled in the early summer sunshine and kept the birds off the seeds. All around us there were people hard at work, pushing wheelbarrows round and poking their compost heaps but mostly digging. Lots of digging.

"Go on then. Show me which one you want."

"It's just down here, that really big one there. See it? All overgrown."

"Overgrown?! Sleeping Beauty could be asleep behind that lot and not even the Prince could get at her."

"Ah, that's where Gabriel comes in."

"Who's he? The Archangel of brambles?"

"He's the bloke who's got the allotment next door. He's got a rotovator. Says he can get rid of those brambles in no time. I bet you he's working on his allotment right now. Let's go over and say hello."

Hidden behind the thicket of thorns that was Gina's heart's desire, there was another allotment, complete with the obligatory bamboo canes and CDs flashing in the wind, and a tall, dark-haired man digging it.

He raised his hand when he saw Gina and me approaching.

"Good morning Gina, come to check over your land have you?"

"I wish Gabriel, I wish. It's so obvious it's been abandoned I don't know why the committee won't let me have it."

"Because there's other people on the list ahead of you Gina, that's why, and the committee have to check with them first in case they still want it."

"Most probably all died waiting by now," Gina muttered. "Gabriel — I'd like you to meet my friend Ellie."

"Nice to meet you Ellie. I'd shake hands but mine are dirty."

They were. Absolutely filthy. As were his wellies and the knees of his faded jeans.

"Nice to meet you too. Gina tells me you've got a rotovator." I said this like I knew what a rotovator was. I hadn't a clue.

"I do indeed. Very nice one it is too. Red. Open top." Gabriel grinned cheekily at me.

"It's brilliant Ellie," Gina said enthusiastically, "I can't wait to see it in action on my allotment." She was smiling flirtatiously at Gabriel through her fringe and I could see why. Gabriel was good looking. Even through the mists of my longing for Robert I could see that. Tall and tanned, with his dark hair cropped very short.

"Ellie and I fancy a quick glass of wine over in Battersea Rise. Want to join us?"

"I would have liked that, but soon as I've finished up here I'm going to do a job in Stockwell." Gabriel looked at me and smiled. "Don't worry, I'm a landscape gardener. Not a bank robber."

"That's a pity," Gina said. "Another time then."

"Another time would be great. Have fun ladies." Gabriel went back to his digging.

"Isn't he handsome?" Gina whispered as we walked away.

"I guess so, if you like your men grubby and wearing wellies. Are you going to give him a run out?"

"Perhaps. Not till I've got my allotment though and he's got rid of those brambles for me. Don't want to fall out with him before then."

We walked back across the Common to a wine bar at the top of Battersea Rise. It was another trendy place, full of young people all wearing the same kind of clothes — cropped trousers with toggles at the hem, T shirts that talked of billabongs and kangaroos, suede surf shoes that would more than likely leak if you actually tried to surf in them. There were a few people dressed in matching his and hers pastel Ralph Lauren shirts and chinos, aspirational types who were no doubt living in the houses we could never afford and setting themselves five-year life plans right there and then over their coffee and croissants: how to treble house prices in Clapham and then get the hell out and move to Sloane Square where they belonged. I could almost see the word "Pah" rising up in a bubble above Gina's head. We agreed on a bottle of Sauvignon Blanc (third cheapest bottle on the list) and headed to the back of the bar.

"I suppose you want to know if I copped off with Paul?" was the first thing she said after she had poured the wine. "I'll put you out of your misery. Of course I did. I do every time he gets dumped."

This was news to me. I thought Gina and Paul had been nothing but good friends for years.

"Don't look so surprised. Sleeping with old boyfriends doesn't count in my book. And it doesn't add to your numbers. It's quite interesting really — I like to see if he has learnt anything since the last time."

"And had he?"

"No, not really. Do you remember that Becky girl he went out with a few years back?"

"Sort of."

"Well she taught him to talk dirty which was bizarre. He never made a sound before that. And he wasn't very good at it. The talking bit that is — the rest of it he's always been rather good at. He had a sort of pre-prepared speech and it detracted from the main event if you know what I mean. Thank God he didn't do it last night. Mind you he was rather drunk — perhaps he'd forgotten his lines."

"I take it he was back on form then?"

"You bet. But enough about my sex life. How about yours? What's going on with you and Robert?"

I took a big gulp of my wine. "It's over between us, that's all. Really over. And . . ." I could feel my chin dimpling as I tried hard not to cry. "And the thing is . . . I can't face talking about it right now. Do you think you could distract me and tell me some more about your sex life instead?"

Gina believes in living life to the full and as fast as possible. Her philosophy on sex is that you regret the men you don't do, not the ones you do. She says she doesn't want to be eighty years of age and in an armchair in the old people's home, thinking about how tidy her airing cupboard was. She says when she is old she wants to think back on all the hot sex she had. From what she told me over our bottle of Sauvignon she shouldn't have too much difficulty.

By the time we got back to the house, our cheeks flushed pink from the wine and ready for our dinner, my mother was not best pleased.

"You're late," she said crossly. "Now your grandfather has gone and given Cliff another gin and Dubonnet and he was already a bit worse for wear when he got here."

"Been doing a spot of work on his car had he?" I grinned.

Joan would not under any circumstances allow liquor in her house. Cliff abided dutifully by this prohibition but on the fairly regular occasions he fancied a drink at home, he simply went out into the street and climbed under his car where he pretended to be doing maintenance. What he was actually doing was drinking rum from a hip flask, well out of sight of Joan.

"Just hurry up in there would you, so I can serve up." my mum said curtly. "He'll sober up just as soon as he's got some dinner inside him."

Everyone was seated expectantly at the dining table when Gina and I walked in — Trevor, Teresa, Joan and Cliff — all four of them beaming benevolently at us. I felt like I did when I was a little girl and my mother would present me to her dinner party guests to say goodnight before I went to bed.

"Will you look at the two of you, pretty as a picture." Joan struggled to her feet to hug me, grabbing hold of the back of my head and clutching me to her so powerfully that my cheek scratched against the squeaky acrylic wool of her yellow cardigan. Gina got away lightly with a kiss on the cheek. Cliff, looking decidedly sozzled, just raised a hand and waved wordlessly in our general direction.

102

Although devoted to each other, Joan and Cliff were an unlikely couple. Both in their seventies, Joan was a stout Irish woman with arms as wide as hocks of ham and a line of fat around her wrists so pronounced it looked like she had an elastic band wound round them. She wore her hair in tight grey curls and had a reputation for speaking her mind. Cliff on the other hand was Jamaican, a slight man who couldn't have weighed more than eight stone and was pretty much bald, who wore big, gold-framed spectacles he must have had since the seventies. They had thick lenses with a greyish tinge which magnified his eyes so much they made him look constantly surprised, like a bush baby.

They had apparently caused something of a stir when they moved into the street at a time when mixed race couples were very rare. It was the second marriage for them both and when I was younger Joan would tell me stories about how Cliff had saved her from her first husband. She talked in rather veiled terms but I eventually figured out that her first husband drank (which explained her dislike of keeping drink in the house) and used to beat her. It was difficult to imagine a time when Joan needed saving from anybody, least of all by someone as gentle as Cliff.

Although they had a child each from their first marriages, these children did not come with them when they moved to Clapham, and visited only occasionally. Cliff shrugged off the absence of his daughter — she was back in Jamaica with her mother and had an excuse for not being able to visit — but Joan's son, Graham, was only in Norfolk and the lack of him weighed heavily on her heart. With little in the way of family themselves, Joan and Cliff had been adopted into mine.

"Got any gossip for us Joan?" Gina asked, helping herself to roast potatoes.

For years Joan had cleaned for local people to make ends meet and even now she took in a lot of ironing. Her job provided her with seriously good inside information on our neighbours.

"Let me think. Them at number 29 got themselves a new telly, huge thing it is with an electricity bill to match. Must be like going to the pictures to watch it. And the Crawfords are having another baby. A fourth. In this day and age. Can you believe it? Those two are either rowing the live-long day or making babies."

Gina shook her head in mock horror, her mouth full of roast potato.

Once Joan got going about the fecund Crawfords, she was difficult to stop so I changed the subject swiftly.

"And how are you Teresa. Quaffers still keeping you busy?"

Quaffers is the local wine-tasting club my mum joined after her divorce from my dad, when she decided she had better get out more and join some social clubs. She joined quite a few but Quaffers proved to be by far the best for meeting men, and over the years has supplied my mother with a steady stream of male companions — some serious, some not. I tease her that Quaffers is just a singles club where everyone has an excuse to get tiddly but she assures me it is much more cultured than that; that they have proper speakers and take notes on the wines and everything. Teresa joined the club at about the same time and has made her way steadily through every position on the committee before finally reaching the heady ranks of Club Secretary. This is no mean feat. Quaffers is a hot bed of political ambition and committee positions are only obtained after contested elections.

"Very busy thank you. I'm arranging for us to go on a coach trip to the Bordeaux vineyards next Easter and it's taking quite some organisation."

I can see why Teresa and my mum get on so well. She's another one who would give her kingdom for a list. They are both capable by nature, the kind of women that if ever marooned on a desert island could whip up a decent meal while building a shelter from driftwood. Teresa has never been married and sometimes I think her affection for my Mum goes a little further than just friendship. I did ask my mother once about that but she just laughed. Wearing sensible shoes and blouses from the Marks and Spencer Classic Range doesn't make someone a lesbian she said, but it wouldn't make any difference to our friendship even if she were.

After the roast lamb we had apple crumble and custard. I was so full that my belly was as tight as cling film stretched over a trifle dish, and Joan and Cliff were both looking very sleepy.

"Lovely dinner that love," my grandfather said. "Done us proud you have. Now, if you're ready Joan and Cliff, I'll walk you home and I'll pop into the club to see the boys on the way back."

It made me smile, watching my grandfather help Joan on with her coat and find Cliff's hat for him. They were both at least ten years younger than him. That's how Trevor is. He says he likes to help the old people out and I tease him by asking what counts as old given that he himself is in his eighties. He is always in demand with the widows in our street being handy and capable of fixing leaks and of plumbing in washing machines. Even though he's an old man, my grandfather is still handsome and strong. A gentleman.

CHAPTER
TEN

1946

His message delivered, Jack's brother bangs straight back out of the door again. The bell clangs loudly, just like it did a few moments earlier. Only in the space of those moments Laura's life has changed for ever for a second time. She does nothing for a long while, stands at the counter, staring straight ahead of her, pushing her fingers down so hard on the counter that the tips go white and numb. Eventually she turns to Kitty.

"You stay there a minute. I'm just going to take the baby out to Trevor."

She almost runs down the garden to Trevor who throws his spade to the ground the second he sees the look on her face.

"What on earth's the matter Laura love?" he asks worriedly. "Do you feel sick? You look awful pale. Let's get you inside and sat down and I'll fetch you a drink of water."

She hands the baby to Trevor wordlessly. He takes her, shifts his daughter's weight on to his hip in one natural fluid movement. At the same time he puts his hand in the small of Laura's back, tries to steer her gently into the house where he can take better care of her. She turns to face him, looks him straight in the eye.

"I have to go."

"What do you mean you have to go? Go where?"

"To be with Jack," she says.

She runs away from him, back into the shop. Trevor follows close behind her. "Laura? Laura. Stop! What the hell is going on?"

Laura ignores him. "Get your coat!" she calls to Kitty. "We're going out."

Kitty looks up from her little pile of scraps and buttons, surprised.

"Where are we going Mam?" she asks Laura doesn't answer, just grabs Kitty's hand, almost drags her out of the door.

After they have gone Trevor stands in the middle of the shop holding his baby daughter in his arms. He can't move, feels like his feet are stuck to the floor and all he can hear is the sound of his heart thumping. Eventually the baby starts to cry. He takes his daughter upstairs, feeds her, baths her, puts her to bed. He waits.

Laura does not come back until the following morning. Kitty is not with her. She doesn't use her key to let herself in but rings the bell instead.

Trevor doesn't know what to say as he opens the door, holds out his arms to her, tries to say with his body what words cannot. Laura just pushes past him, runs up the stairs. When he eventually follows her up the stairs he finds her packing her things.

"What's going on Laura? What's happening?"

There is panic in Trevor's voice but Laura answers him calmly, coolly, in the low steady voice she uses when she catches Kitty doing something dangerous like feeding the fire or poking the baby. "Jack wasn't killed in Singapore. He was taken prisoner there by the Japanese and kept in a camp. There was some mix up with his identity documents apparently and so I was told he was dead when actually some other man was. He can't weigh much more than Kitty and he's covered in these horrible oozing sores and ulcers and I think he must have malaria too but he's alive. Barely. It's taken him this long lying alone in some hospital just to remember who he is. Who his wife is."

All the air in Trevor's lungs is suddenly and viciously squeezed out of him, as if he'd jumped into the river on a hot summer's day and ice cold water was gripping his chest like an iron band. He breathes in, as deep as he can. "We can help him Laura. You and me. We can find a way. I know we can . . ." He tries to take Laura's hand in his but she snatches it away.

"I'm sorry Trevor. I've got to be with Jack. He was the one I loved first."

She doesn't say it but Trevor knows that in her head she adds the words *and the most*.

"And he needs me. Me and Kitty. I'm sorry. I just don't know what else to do."

"And what about Sarah? Your other daughter. *Our* daughter. What about her?"

"She's your daughter Trevor. You keep her. You'll take good care of her I know you will."

Laura finishes packing. She goes into the living room where Sarah, who has only just learned to sit up, is playing quietly. Laura picks up her daughter, hugs her to her fiercely, rubs her cheek against Sarah's soft, innocent baby skin one last time and then hands her over to Trevor.

"Goodbye Trevor."

As Laura walks away she does not once look back.

Trevor waits. He waits for three long days. He keeps the shop open so that when Laura and Kitty come back everything will seem normal and he and Sarah will be right there ready to greet them both. He ignores his accounts and his order books and sits on the floor with Sarah, reading stories and singing to her. He makes sure his baby is well fed but does not eat himself and at night when Sarah is asleep in bed Trevor stands at the back door looking out over the garden and waits for his wife to come back home.

On the fourth day he closes the shop and puts Sarah in her pram. It takes him a little while to find the brake for it is Laura who takes the girls out for a walk every day while he stays behind in the shop. The handle of the pram is too low for him and he has to hunch down to steer it properly. People in the street look at him curiously as he passes by because it isn't often you see a man out and about pushing a pram. He walks the mile or so to the house where Jack's mother lives.

Jack's brother comes to the door when Trevor knocks. When he sees that it is Trevor he quickly steps out into the street.

"Laura said you would probably be calling by."

"I'd like to talk to her please," Trevor says calmly.

"I'm sorry but she doesn't want to talk to you."

"Could you please let my wife know that I'm here with her daughter and that I'd like to talk to her please?"

"Look, Laura and me and my Mam, we've agreed what we need to do now. Laura's going to be with Jack again and everybody round here is going to pretend like you and your little girl never existed. Because otherwise Jack will die all over again. Do you understand?"

"I'd like to hear that from my wife please."

"You're starting to get on my nerves now butty boy. She's not your wife, she's Jack's wife, and she's already been round and told you that's the way it's going to be."

"Then I'd like her please to tell me again. Because as far as I'm concerned she's my wife and the mother of my daughter and I love her enough for us all to get through this."

Laura's voice comes from behind the front door. Trevor cannot see her but he hears her very clearly. "Go away now Trevor and take Sarah with you. I don't want to see either of you ever again."

Trevor visits another draper who runs a shop higher up the valley. When Trevor tells him the price at which he is willing to sell his shop and its entire contents the other man agrees quickly, before Trevor can come to his senses and change his mind.

There are two more visits Trevor needs to make. He goes to the cemetery to say goodbye to his mother and he calls on Margaret Lewis.

The stony expression on Margaret's face when she comes to the door doesn't last long when she hears what Trevor has to say.

"I've got an apology to make to you Margaret. I should have had the courtesy to call on you when I got back home, should have explained to you in person about me and Laura."

"Yes Trevor you should have done that. You really should have."

"I know and I'm sorry. Very sorry. Because you didn't deserve to be treated like that. Not at all."

"Well, it's a little late for apologies now." Margaret gestures at the pram where Sarah lies sleeping but her tone is not unkind. "You and Laura are married and you've got this little one and that's the end of that."

"It is the end Margaret but not the end I'd expected. Thing is — Laura's husband, her first one that is, Jack — turns out he wasn't dead, just sick, and now he's back and Laura . . . well Laura wants to be with him not me."

Margaret's jaw drops in amazement and she clutches her hands to her ample chest.

"Oh Trevor, you poor thing! That's terrible. Well not terrible for Jack I suppose, for him it's a good thing, but it's terrible for you. And terrible for Laura too. You're not just going to give her up are you? Not just like that? Not without a fight?"

112

Trevor looks down at the pram and at his sleeping baby. "Jack's the one who did the fighting Meg, not me. And Laura's made it very clear that she doesn't want me and she doesn't want Sarah either."

When Trevor looks up again there are tears in Margaret's eyes and when he sees the look she gives him — of pity and affection, mixed in with the tiniest amount of hope — he knows he is making the right decision. The only honourable decision.

"So me and Sarah are going away tomorrow. Just the two of us. We're going to London where no-one knows us, so we can start again, and Laura and Jack and Kitty can carry on here as if nothing had changed and me and Sarah won't have to watch them doing it. And even though I've absolutely no right to do so, I want to ask you to do something for me please?"

Margaret fishes a handkerchief from the sleeve of her cardigan and dabbing at her eyes she smiles at him just a little bit.

"You're not going to ask me to marry you or anything now are you?"

Trevor smiles just a little bit back. "I can't do that Margaret love. Thing is see I'm married already."

By the time Margaret's first letter arrives, Trevor and Sarah have been living in the house in Clapham for almost six months. The first of many families is safely installed in the basement quarters of the tall skinny house and Trevor has found a good job with the Underground. Sarah can walk now — a good four or five yards without falling over once — and she spends a lot of time with Trevor outside in the back yard, watching him collect wheelbarrow after wheelbarrow of bricks and rubble and other debris as he slowly uncovers the damp London clay beneath. Margaret's letter has been forwarded from the boarding house in Paddington where Trevor and Sarah lived when they first got to London and must have lain on the mahogany sideboard in the hallway for a good long while before the landlady bothered to forward it, because the news within is already some weeks old. Margaret's writing is dutifully tucked up neat right into the margin of the paper even though the war is over and there is no longer any need to save paper for munitions.

Dear Trevor
I hope this letter finds you well. I am doing as you asked and have kept an eye out for what is happening with Laura and Jack and little Kitty. From what I can gather, which is not much, all is well. Kitty has started school now and by all accounts she is a happy, placid little girl who has plenty of friends and enjoys her learning. You don't have anything to worry about there Trevor. Laura and Jack keep themselves to themselves. They are all still living with Jack's mother at present and Jack rarely leaves the house. Laura we see at chapel about once a month and to be honest with you Trevor I think she did you a favour. She keeps herself ever so, made up to the nines like she thinks she's a film star or something, and with a

look on her face like she smelled something bad. Everyone knows the truth about her and knows she's no right to be so la-di-da but nobody says much about it, well not to me anyway. Jack's brother and his Mam have had words round and about, told people they'd appreciate it if there was no gossip, what with Jack being so sick and everything. So many people never came home at all and even those that did seem to have things they'd rather not talk about, so people round here are keeping shtum about all sorts. What with your Mam's shop now belonging to Mr Drake — he's put up a new sign over the door he has that says Drake's the Drapers — it's hard even for me sometimes to remember you ever lived round here. Mr Drake's prices are a lot dearer than your Mam's ever were and he's done away with getting things on tick — that's long gone that has — but guess what? A great big Woolworths has opened now on the main square — went up almost overnight it did — and even though you can't get everything for sixpence or less anymore it's still a lot cheaper than Drake's. I'd say he's losing a lot of business to Woolworths so there's another favour that Laura did for you.

All is well here for me. Do you remember Tommy Davies from school? He was in the same class as you and me and he's been courting me now for a good few months. He made it back from the war all in one piece and while he may not be as big and handsome as you he's a really good laugh and he

likes me every bit as much as I like him which is more than I could ever say for you! I hope your little girl is keeping well. It can't be easy bringing her up without a mother but at least she's got you. Bye for now then and best wishes
from
Margaret

CHAPTER
ELEVEN

My mother and I stood shoulder to shoulder at the steps of our front door and waved off my grandfather and Joan and Cliff. We kept waving until they disappeared round the corner, watching as Joan placed her meaty arm in the crook of Cliff's spindly little one and my grandfather tried unsuccessfully to slow his pace down to theirs, like a border collie rounding up a pair of very sedate, elderly sheep. When they were all finally out of sight, mum clapped her hands together in a business-like way.

"Right, time to tackle the clearing up," she announced enthusiastically.

Gina was, as ever, quick to dodge out of the household chores.

"Thanks for a lovely dinner Sarah but I've got to be off now. I've got a gig tonight in Pizza on the Park. You can come with me if you want Ellie."

Gina is a singer. She's not a pop star or famous or anything — she gave up hoping for that years ago — but she does earn her living from singing in jazz clubs and fancy restaurants and at big corporate events. She loves what she does — says she gets paid for doing something she would gladly do for free — which is more than most of us can say about our jobs, and her odd working hours only add to Gina's aura of being different from everyone else.

"Another time. I'm going to help Mum and Teresa wash up and then I think I'll get an early night."

"OK Ellie fish face. Give me a call soon. Ciao bella." And she bounced out of the door.

My mother and Teresa are professional washer uppers with asbestos hands capable of plunging into water so hot it would scald the skin off mere mortals. We had the dishes done in no time but before I'd even hung my tea towel up to dry, my mother was on at me again.

"Are you planning on visiting your father some time soon Ellie? I saw Sandra at the shops the other day and she said they hadn't seen you in a while."

I'm one of that rare group of people whose parents' divorce was amicable. Because I was so young when it happened, it has always seemed entirely normal to me to have parents who live in different houses. When I was little I spent a lot of time with Dad. He's a teacher and I stayed at his flat in Balham most school holidays, just hanging out with him. We were spared the awkwardness of those soulless every other weekend visits to the zoo and to McDonald's endured by many divorced fathers and their kids under the guise of "quality time". Dad and I had enough time together to be able to fall out and sulk and not even talk to each other if we felt like it. The luxury of normal, ordinary time that parents who live with their kids take for granted.

Mum says she got on even better with him once they'd split up and I didn't realise until I was much older how lucky I was to have parents who not only still speak to each other but regularly meet up for a coffee, even now. We even spent Christmas day together for years so that they could both be with me when I opened my presents and Dad always came to all my birthday parties.

I never thought either of my parents would get married again. Thanks to Quaffers Mum had a fairly active social life and there were one or two men that she brought home to meet me and Trevor but nothing that lasted more than a few years at most. Dad on the other hand didn't go out with anyone for years and then all of a sudden all he was talking about was the new art teacher at his school and how wonderful she was and the next thing I knew they were getting married. I was eleven at the time and thought it incredibly romantic. I almost burst with excitement when I got to dress up for their wedding at Lambeth town hall in a turquoise bridesmaid's dress with little pumps dyed to match in exactly the same shade and a basket of flowers to carry over my arm. I tripped down the short aisle at the town hall feeling like Cinderella on my way to the ball and was only miffed that they hadn't got married in church so that the aisle could have been longer with more flowers.

Getting married at all was a concession on the part of Sandra. She's a bit of an old hippy with armfuls of clanking silver bracelets and her hair still long and coloured bright orange with henna. She would probably have preferred to whisk my dad away in her camper van and have a pagan friendship ceremony on a beach somewhere but my dad is a bit more old school and wanted to do things properly. She was way too hip to want to parent me and from the moment she arrived in Dad's life she let him get on with the father stuff and adopted the role of good older friend to me. We had the odd cross word at the beginning while I got used to sharing dad but she was good about that too and would go off to art exhibitions on her own at weekends to make sure Dad and I still had plenty of time when it was just the two of us. My life has been altogether richer for having Sandra in it but at that precise moment in time I couldn't face seeing her or my Dad.

"I'll give them a ring in the week," I said guiltily. "I don't think I can cope with their happiness ever after right now."

That's the one annoying thing about dad and Sandra. They are incredibly loved up which is fine when you are too but deeply irritating if you're not.

"Yes," Teresa said. "I imagine the last thing you need is to watch your father and his wife rubbing each other's feet while they listen to folk music."

"Teresa!" my mother scolded.

Teresa ignored her. "Tell me? Is Sandra still wearing those ridiculously low cut tunic tops, the ones that show far too much cleavage?"

"Sandra suits those tops," my mother was teasing now, "they're very sexy."

"Make her look like mutton dressed as mutton if you ask me," Teresa snorted. "She should dress her age."

"Well I like them," I said coming to Sandra's defence, "and Dad certainly does."

"Yes well," Teresa sniffed. "I suppose they're all right if you're the type of person who listens to Bob Dylan all day long and rolls her own cigarettes."

"That's enough Teresa," my mother said trying to stifle a giggle. "Now come on and finish your tea. We're due at Violet's in half an hour."

My mother and Teresa are religious people who don't believe in God. Or christians with a small c. Or just good people. They spend at least part of each weekend doing good works. I had no idea who Violet was but was pretty sure she had recently been bereaved or her house had flooded or some equivalent disaster.

"I'm only going to be gone a few hours Ellie. Will you still be up when I get back?"

I shook my head.

"I'm pretty tired Mum."

"Well you get an early night and I'll see you in the morning."

I kissed her goodnight before going upstairs. My mum's cheeks are soft and smooth and slightly saggy. She smells of Pond's cream and soap. She smells like love.

Every night when I went upstairs to my old bedroom I promised myself I wouldn't go to sleep thinking about Robert. Most nights I failed. I've got a good memory sadly and I could remember some of our conversations word for word.

"She's absolutely devastated," Robert would say whenever I plucked up the courage to ask how things were going with Ann. "Keeps asking me whether I've met someone else and what she can do to fix it. I feel so dreadfully guilty Ellie. I really want her to be happy, just not happy with me."

I felt guilty too, even though Robert kept assuring me that their marriage had been over long before he took up with me. I tried to make things easier for him.

"I don't think you should tell her about us yet. You both need to deal with the end of your marriage first. Give her the time she needs. See if you can help her through this. There'll be plenty of time for us ahead. Let's keep you and me secret for a while longer."

I meant it when I said this, but it was taking Robert's wife a lot longer to come to terms with the end of her marriage than I would have liked. It was months since I'd moved into the flat in Primrose Hill but he was still dealing with phone calls from her late at night or during the early hours of the morning, long phone calls during which he told me she would sob her heart out and beg him to come back, to work things out. Sometimes she phoned when Robert was with me and he would scurry out of the flat or whatever wine bar we were in and go out into the street to take the call with a stricken look on his face. I hated seeing him hunched secretively around his phone, glancing guiltily over his shoulder at me.

"Is everything ok?" I would ask when he returned.

"Fine," he would reply flatly, his voice weary, making it clear he didn't want to discuss it and for a while after one of these calls he would be quiet and sad.

It was me who suggested that, since we'd decided Robert should not tell Ann about me just yet, it would be better if he slept at the flat in the Barbican most of the time so that if his wife called or turned up on the doorstep as she had threatened to do, she wouldn't find out the truth.

"It *will* get better Ellie, I promise you. She'll accept the situation in the end and then you and I can go public. I love you so very much."

And I believed him. I really believed him. And even though I hated all the lurking in the shadows I thought the end result would be worth it because there was nothing in the world I wanted more than to be with Robert and if that meant waiting patiently until he'd sorted things out as best he could with his wife, then that was what I was willing to do. The last thing I wanted was to give Robert the same sort of grief he was getting from Ann. What I wanted was for the time Robert spent with me to be full of light and fun and sex and totally separate from the sadness and guilt he felt about making his wife unhappy. But of course with him working ridiculously long hours, I could never be certain what night I was going to see him. And so, to make sure I would be free on whatever nights Robert was free, I put my social life on hold and I stopped going out. I spent hours at home in the flat, lying on my bed reading and waiting and watching the clock. Even though I knew Robert wouldn't come round if he hadn't got to the flat by 10p.m. I would still be hoping for a call as I turned off my bedside light at 11.30p.m. And at 6a.m. I would be awake again, hoping he might call in for breakfast on his way to work as he sometimes did. Some evenings I even stood at the window of my flat, willing him to walk round the corner, wishing that, if I only wanted to enough, I could conjure him up out of thin air. Even though I knew I was being pathetic, I preferred to spend my evenings on my own than miss the chance of being with him and I consoled myself with the knowledge that this phase would be over very soon. And when he did turn up, a big grin on his face as I opened the door and a pleased-to-see-me in his pocket, it made all the waiting worthwhile.

Best of all were the precious nights that Robert knew his wife had another social engagement, with her sister or her friends, when he could count on not receiving a sobbing phone call in the middle of the night and could stay overnight with me at Primrose Hill. On those nights we would have a few glasses of wine in one of the local bars and Robert would tell me all about the progress on his deal. He liked talking to me about work stuff, explaining to me why documents had to be drafted in a certain way, why somebody selling a business had to disclose all the bad stuff about their business as well as the good. I was a fast learner and soon got my head around some of the basics of corporate law and it delighted Robert that I could actually have a decent conversation with him about his job.

124

"You know Ellie, if you wanted to, you could go to law school and become a solicitor. You'd be excellent at it."

I had absolutely no interest in becoming a solicitor but I loved the fact that he had confidence in me, valued my views enough to ask my opinion. Sometimes I made suggestions on how I thought he should handle a meeting or a difficult issue in negotiations and it tickled Robert to report back to me that he had done exactly as I had said and that it had worked like a dream. I never had the heart to tell him that I had learned most of my negotiation tactics from watching re-runs of *This Life* on telly.

Afterwards we would walk home to the flat, arm in arm, and fall tipsily into bed. Only once Robert had switched off his mobile phone would he finally relax enough to have sex. He told me his wife had never been particularly bothered about sex and when they did sleep together she would always insist on the light being off. Apparently she would only ever have sex in the missionary position. Consequently it was not difficult to keep Robert entertained in bed. What I liked best of all was the feeling of intimacy afterwards when we would lie skin against skin in the big warm bed and talk not about the world of corporate transactions but about our families and our childhoods and Robert would ask me lots of questions about the places I had travelled.

"So," he'd say, propping his head up on his elbow to look at me and hooking one of his legs over mine, "if I was going to pack my job in tomorrow and take some time out where would we go? Of all the places you've been to in the world where would you want to take me?"

"That's easy. All of them. I'd like to go to everywhere I've ever been again, only this time with you."

"Yes but if you could choose only one which would it be? I'm the boring one, the one who's spent all his life passing exams and then being a lawyer, I'd need you to lead the way. If I was going to step away from that world where would you take me?"

"Ok first things first — what sort of budget have we got?"

"Limitless. We've just won the lottery."

"And how long have we got?"

"As long as we like. We've just won the lottery remember."

So we'd lie there together in bed and I would describe for him the trips we'd take to the temples of Thailand or the mountains of Peru and Robert would smile and sigh.

"I've only ever been to boring middle-class places like gites in France and skiing in the Alps. You, Ellie, have sand in your suitcase from places I've never even heard of."

And then he'd reach for me again and there was nowhere in the world either of us would rather be.

CHAPTER
TWELVE

Maybe it was the early night or maybe it was the belly full of crumble and Sauvignon but the next morning I was up before Trevor had even finished making the tea. As we sat drinking it together on the bench I heard a faint clip-clopping sound coming from the back lane.

"That sounds just like a horse," I said.

"That's because it is," Trevor laughed. "It's the old rag and bone man. He retired a few years back now but he's still got his horses. He'll be taking them up to the Common to get some exercise before anyone else is up and about."

"What? You mean someone keeps horses right here in the middle of gridlocked SW9?"

"Yes. Where do you think I get all my manure from? Come see."

We rushed across to the lane door, popping and spilling shiny spheres of dew beneath our feet as we crossed our tiny spangled lawn, and when Trevor unlocked it I saw, coming towards us and framed by the fuzzy sunlight of early morning, two old horses. One looked me straight in the eye, blew a big windy breath through his nostril and blinked, as if he were winking at me. The rag and bone man who was no longer a rag and bone man lifted his hand in a wave and all three of them clip clopped past me. The sight of those horses, grey at the muzzle, sneaking out joyfully onto the Common for their morning exercise while the rest of the city slept, made me feel like I'd been let in on a special secret, as if I'd just discovered fairies living at the bottom of our garden.

I felt cheered enough to go and visit Beth later that morning. I took presents for the children, a pink music box for Janey that played "Claire de Lune", something so girly I was surprised by the fierceness of my desire to buy it when I saw it in the toy shop on the High Street. For William there was a plastic sword and shield which I knew was not a politically correct gift for a four year old but which I calculated would earn me instant popularity with him at least.

Beth and Tony live just a few streets away, in a small terraced house they got for a good price because the old lady who had it before them had lived there for forty years or more and the house was very run down with a lot of work to be done. Tony and Beth worked on it every weekend for years, renovating it in stages whenever they managed to save up another bit of money, cheerfully living with maroon carpets and an avocado green bathroom suite in the meantime. They were the first of my friends to get married, to have a house of their own, to have children. They have been together since they were sixteen and have only ever slept with each other. Some people think that you miss out if you only ever have sex with one person but I envy Tony and Beth the certainty of their relationship and the fact that they have no skeletons in their closets. They don't lie in the dark afterwards, wondering if they are as good as the last person. Or the wife.

Beth looked pleased to see me when she opened the door although I saw a shadow of concern flit over her face at the same time as her smile.

"Come in Ellie, great to see you. House is a bit upside down though, I'm sorry."

Will, who was still in his pyjamas, looked at her quizzically and then rushed to the window to look out.

"No, it isn't Mum!" he said disappointedly.

"What *are* you talking about?" Beth asked him, looking confused.

"The house Mum. It isn't upside down at all. It's the way it's always been."

"Sorry Will. That's just something that grown ups say. It doesn't mean the house is really upside down. Just that it's a bit messy, that's all."

The house wasn't that messy. Yes there were breakfast dishes piled in the sink and dirty clothes stacked up next to the washing machine but those were just the jobs of the day. Beth and Tony had stripped and varnished the original floorboards since the last time I was there and the kitchen walls were decorated cheerfully with Will's paintings; their house was now a pretty family home.

"Here Ellie, take Janey while I make some coffee."

Beth removed her baby from her hip and passed her to me. Janey had filled out since the last time I saw her. Then she was just a few days old, a newborn scrap of a person with eyes tight shut. Now she had big round eyes and chubby cheeks and she smiled at me as I took her in my arms, a huge, heart-warming smile that revealed two tiny, sharp, bottom teeth and made me laugh out loud with delight. This made Janey smile even more.

"She's lovely Beth, a real smiler."

"Isn't she just? I can't believe such a happy little person grew inside me."

We sat down to drink coffee and I gave William his gift of weapons. He was very impressed with them and looked at me with new-found respect.

"Say thank you Will," urged Beth.

"Wow, thanks Lady, these are cool." He ran off to the living room to practise killing.

Beth looked at me, embarrassed.

"I'm sorry Ellie, I should have reminded him who you are."

"That's ok. It's me that's at fault for being such a stranger. I'm the one who should be sorry, shouldn't I Janey?" I looked at Janey as I said this in a high-pitched cheerful voice, holding her plump little hands in mine and waving them about in an effort to disguise how upset I was. I kissed Janey's sweet little face and sat her on the table opposite me, blocking the end of the table with my arms so that she couldn't fall off.

"I suppose you heard that Robert and I are finished."

Beth took Janey from me, put her down on the floor in a rubber ring affair, and sat down next to me.

"Gina sent me a text last night. I'm sorry Ellie. How are you feeling?"

130

"Bloody terrible but I'm hoping your beautiful kids will be able to cheer me up a bit."

"We're always here for you Ellie. You know that. You must come round for dinner one evening soon so that Tony can see you too. It'll be fun. Assuming Tony gets home from work on time because he's hardly home nowadays."

Beth swallowed a sob as she said this, looking at me with tears in her eyes.

"In fact Ellie, I think he's having an affair."

I went cold. I didn't say *He's not — you must be mistaken — don't be silly* and reassure her like I wanted to because I had not seen Tony for months and for all I knew he could well be having an affair. Instead I asked carefully, "What makes you say that Beth?"

"We haven't had sex in weeks," she cried. "That's unheard of for me and Tony — all the time we've been together we've always fancied each other, even when I was pregnant, and now he's just not interested. I know I'm fat — haven't shifted any pregnancy weight — that's never bothered Tony before but now he turns his back on me in bed and pretends to go straight to sleep. And he works all the time — he's never here. Doesn't even eat at home, says he'll get something in the canteen, so I just eat chocolate biscuits for dinner and get even fatter."

Beth was sobbing by now and my heart turned over for her and, selfishly, for me too, because Tony and Beth are the only couple I knew with a real live marriage, one that has passed through the other side of romance and passion and become true love and when I was with Robert and dared to imagine us being married some day, it was a marriage like Tony and Beth's that I wanted. Suddenly another thought curled tight round my heart, this time a guilty one. Was the way that Beth was feeling now the same way Ann had felt for all those months? I tried to push the thought away but all it did was tighten its grip.

"Have you talked to him about it?" I asked.

"I haven't had a chance. He's never here. I've suggested sex a few times but he says he's too tired and I vowed last time he said no that I would say no to him the next time he asked me, to get him back. But he hasn't asked since."

"It's not all about sex Beth. How is everything else in your lives?"

"I know it's not all about sex but I read somewhere that 27 per cent of divorcees state the reason for their divorce was lack of sex. And everything else in our lives is pretty crap too. He works all day. I work all day with the kids. He thinks we live in a house with magic drawers and I get pissed off with him for being taken for granted. Is it too early to have a glass of wine?"

I looked at my watch. It was 11.45 a.m.

"Yes. Way too early. What do you mean magic drawers?"

"Oh you know drawers that fill themselves with clean ironed clothes, paid bills, birthday presents for his family, food. As if by magic."

"Oh, that kind of magic."

"And because he doesn't see all the work that goes into filling those drawers he thinks I don't do anything all day. The other night I hadn't got round to picking up his suits from the dry cleaners and he asked me what exactly did I do all day."

"That's not fair. Have you told him?"

"I made a list after that comment of everything I do throughout the week."

"And?"

"And he asked me how come I was overweight, if I did that much stuff every day I should weigh nine stone two."

"Ouch. Anyway, you're not fat. Just a bit cuddly."

Beth looked at me witheringly.

"I was cuddly before I had babies. Now I'm plain fat. Remind me if I'm ever tempted to have a baby again that it's not a good idea to combat morning sickness with cheese and onion pasties and that what you put in your mouth while you're pregnant doesn't come out at the end with the baby. I should go for another scan because I'm convinced that my arse is pregnant now. Look at it! It's that big there must be another baby in there. And I have a pouch instead of a belly."

I smiled at this. Beth did too but it was a sad smile.

"It's not funny really Ellie. I've gone past joking about it, really I have. Do you know what? I'm ashamed to admit this but the tops of my thighs rub together when I walk and they hurt. How bad is that? My legs are so fat they chafe."

She dropped her head in what I could see was real shame. I shook my head, made tutting noises to show that I disagreed with her and that things couldn't be all that bad but the truth was Beth was fatter than she had ever been. Her small frame looked burdened by the extra weight even though she was still pretty, with curly blonde hair and big blue eyes.

"And I'm so tired all the time. I'm still feeding Janey myself and she wakes up twice a night. My head feels like it's packed with cotton wool and I'm not even enjoying being with the kids — I just feel like they're one big tidal wave of work that I can never get on top of, however hard I swim. Yesterday there were no clean boxers for Tony so I fished a pair out of the laundry, sprayed them with Febreze and put them back in his drawer. And I haven't had time to wash my hair for three days. No wonder he's gone off me."

The look on Beth's face was one of total defeat. She rested her head in her hands, tears dripping through her fingers and plopping on to the table. I got up, rubbed her shoulders and cuddled her tight. I could feel the bones of her spine and collar bone even through her extra flesh.

"Have you tried formula?"

"Yes of course," Beth wailed, "but Janey just refuses the bottle when I give it to her so I give up in the end and feed her myself. I'd ask Tony to do it but he's never here."

I went upstairs, in this house that had changed so much but which was still so familiar, and ran a deep bath. There was no bubble bath so I used baby shampoo instead.

"Beth — go take a bath and then have a lie down, I'll look after the kids, feed Janey. Go on."

Beth wanted to argue with me but she was too tired for that too. She smiled at me, went upstairs wordlessly.

Making bottles is a palaver. They don't mention how complicated a process it is in the adverts on the telly. All they ever show is a couple of tins and some smiling babies. They don't show you on the telly how you've got to sterilise the bottles (once you've managed to actually locate some bottles in the first place that is) and boil water (fresh, not previously boiled) and then let the water cool down to warm before adding the right number of scoops of powder. It was harder than most of the stuff I'd done for chemistry GCSE. But it was worth it because while I was helping my friend who was worried her husband was being unfaithful, I could push out of my mind the growing realisation that people can only be unfaithful if there is someone out there for them to be unfaithful with. When the bottles were finally ready, Janey took one from me without complaining, probably because she'd been screaming her head off starving for 20 minutes before the bottle cooled down enough for her to drink. Will sat next to me watching television while I fed her, worn out after an extended bout of sword fighting. When Janey was done he patted me gently on the arm.

"You've got to burp her now," he said.

"How exactly do I do that?"

"Mum just jiggles her about on her shoulder and then she burps; real big loud ones."

I lifted Janey to my shoulder and jiggled her about as instructed and sure enough within a minute or so she belched loudly and satisfyingly.

When Will's programme was finished, I somehow managed to strap Janey into her pram and the three of us walked to McDonald's where Will and I both had happy meals. Graciously I gave him my toy too. From there we went up to the common and Janey slept in the pram next to me while I pushed Will on the swings. On the way back we stopped at Sainsbury's where I bought fresh bread, olives, hummus, tomatoes on the vine, grapes and peaches and a bottle of unoaked chardonnay.

When we got back, I shouted up the stairs to Beth.

"Get down here will you and help me drink this wine. It's not too early to have a drink any more."

CHAPTER
THIRTEEN

I knew there was no way on earth I would get away with telling Gina that Robert and I were finished and leaving it at that. Gina is not the type to be fobbed off easily. When I had not called her by Wednesday night she called me.

"Get round to my flat right now. I've got plenty of wine in. Come on."

I hesitated. I didn't think I was strong enough for a full confession.

"If you don't come round this minute I'll ring Paul and Beth and Tony and we'll all come round and cart you off to the pub instead."

I went round.

Gina has lived in the same flat since she left home at eighteen. She put her name down with the council for a hard-to-let flat, claiming that her parents had ordered her to leave home when she left school which was wholly untrue because her mum and dad both worship her. Gina is a convincing actress and the council fell for her story, allocating her a two-bedroom duplex flat in a massive tower block at a very low rent.

There was a reason why the flat was classed as hard to rent. It was on the sixteenth floor of the tower block and the lifts hardly ever worked and when they did they stank of pee. The block was grey concrete, dark and miserable, and it seemed a lot of unhappy people lived there because there was always lots of shouting and wailing in the corridors. Gina ignored all this because once you were in through the door of her flat it was light and airy with a big kitchen/dining room and a large living room and fantastic views over south London.

It was in a terrible state when Gina moved in — absolutely filthy with damp carpets, mould all over the bathroom and toilet and at least an inch of grease and grey fluff on the cooker. Even this did not put Gina off. She ripped out the carpets and scrubbed the place from top to bottom using vats of bleach in the process. Once it was clean she painted the whole of the flat white to maximise the light and she's kept it painted white ever since. She could not afford new carpets so laid plain white lino down instead and the whole place has a kind of futuristic, space age look. I have spent many happy hours in Gina's flat but very few nights. It is not that Gina is inhospitable — she loves having people round for cheese and wine (because it involves no cooking and hardly any washing up) — and she's not exactly what you'd call house proud either being more than happy to allow a few days' dishes to pile up in the sink and for dust balls to form under the settee. It is just that she likes living alone and has always made it very clear to everyone, including boyfriends, that she does not want a flat-mate.

"I couldn't possibly live with anyone," she says. "I just couldn't. And besides singing means I work such unsociable hours it wouldn't be fair."

She doesn't even have a spare bed. Her second bedroom is her music room. "I need the space for singing practice," is how she puts it. But really it's because she doesn't want overnight visitors. The rare nights I've stayed over with her have been because I've fallen asleep drunk on the sofa and she hasn't quite had the nerve to wake me up and throw me out. Even when I've returned home from travelling, absolutely skint and with nowhere to live I have known better than to ask Gina if I can doss down at hers for a week or so.

Gina opened the door with her head swathed in yards of cling film.

"What?" she said, when I looked at her curiously, "I've just finished putting a colour on and this'll stop the dye leaking everywhere while you tell me what the hell is going on with you."

Gina changes the colour of her hair regularly so she can be a different person every few months. Sometimes she is a brunette, sometimes glossy black, this time she was going for a chestnut red, close to her natural colour but more vibrant, the colour of a red setter. She always does her eyebrows to match and has different clothes for each colour hair — her black hair has a vampy wardrobe, her brunette a sporty one. The chestnut red is more demure, wears summer frocks and lacy camisoles, but still manages to look sexy, as if she might not be wearing knickers under those floaty skirts which, knowing Gina, is highly likely. She never dyes her hair

139

blonde but she is blonde most often of all because Gina's singing persona is blonde. She uses wigs for that, wigs so outrageous they don't pretend to look like hair and she has a wide variety of them — a Farrah Fawcett curly long one, a Dusty Springfield bouffant bob, a long, straight Cher one. She likes the contrast between her olive skin and the blonde wigs and the plastic, false way they make her look. She also only ever wears evening frocks to sing in — long and glittery, cut low at the back and front, which show off her ample cleavage and her long strong back. She sings songs by Ella Fitzgerald, Billie Holiday, Etta James. Gina sings the blues.

She handed me a glass of wine and ushered me into the living room

"Go on then. Sit down and spill them."

"Thing is Gina, what I never got round to telling you was that Robert was married and he didn't actually live with me in the flat in Primrose Hill."

"Figured that one out for myself," Gina said smugly.

"Did you?" I was surprised. "How?"

"Ellie, you've been half way round the world and back dozens of times and wherever you've been you've sent me loads of postcards and tons of texts, telling me exactly what you were seeing and who you were seeing it with. And then you took up with Robert and were living a few miles across London and I didn't hear from you for months. I knew we hadn't fallen out so I figured there was stuff you weren't telling me. I didn't realise your pants were quite so much on fire though. You didn't need to lie to me you know."

I hung my head, adopting an exaggerated ashamed posture. There was nothing I could say to excuse myself. Gina was right.

"And you never asked any of us round to your swanky flat on the hill even though you know I love Jude Law and you never brought him round to the pub or to visit your mum and Trevor — Robert that is, not Jude Law. I only met him a few times — in that fancy restaurant you took us to for your birthday and once or twice in a wine bar — but I always thought he looked sort of married, what with the polished shoes and that jumper tied round the neck thing going on and checking his phone every two seconds."

"I'm sorry Gina. I shouldn't have lied. But Robert told me it was all over with his wife and that they were getting divorced and I believed him."

Gina lifted one eyebrow, looked at me quizzically.

"Don't look at me like that. I did believe him. Really I did."

"So why didn't you just tell us the truth then. That he was separated and getting divorced?"

"I guess I didn't tell anyone he was married because I didn't want you to think badly of him — or of me — and anyway the way I saw things he wasn't going to be married much longer, so it wasn't really lying. More like telling a premature truth. And the reason I took you to that restaurant for my birthday was because I thought it was more of a treat than a takeaway round the flat."

This sounded lame when I said it out loud but at the same time it was the truth. I had felt so proud being

141

able to invite mum and Trevor and Teresa and Gina to the fancy restaurant in Battersea that Robert had taken me to on our first date, enjoyed the way in which he took charge and ordered lovely wine for everybody, paid the bill so discreetly. It was Robert who suggested we do that and at the time I was thrilled with his thoughtfulness and generosity but now it just seemed like shameless showing off.

"Oldest line in the book that," Gina said, "telling your new girlfriend you're in the process of getting divorced. Did he also tell you that his wife didn't understand him and that they didn't sleep together?"

"Actually he kept telling me that his wife did understand him and that they were like best friends but yes, he did tell me that he didn't sleep with his wife."

"Bollocks he didn't."

"Why do you say that?"

"I've hardly been whiter than white when it comes to matters of the heart have I? Remember Herb from New York — he was married and I was quite happy to chase him round the bedroom every time he was in London. Never gave one thought to his wife back in the Bronx or wherever she was."

"Was he the one with a quiff like Elvis and a huge . . .?"

"That's him. *Enormous*."

"He always told me that he didn't sleep with his wife. And then I heard him on the phone one evening telling her how much he missed her and exactly what he was planning to do to her in bed when he got home. Trust me — every married man I've slept with claimed he didn't sleep with his wife. Look, put it like this — if the bloke in your life suddenly stopped wanting to sleep with you what would you do?"

"I don't think it happens suddenly. I think people just have sex less regularly and over time it just gets less and less and then it stops altogether."

"Okay, if the bloke in your life *gradually* stopped wanting to sleep with you what would you do?"

"I'd feel miserable and rejected and eventually one night I'd have a few drinks too many and ask him what the hell was going on."

"Exactly. I mean I know people have less how's your father over time and that's perfectly natural but none at all? Ever? And yet all these married men would have us believe that their wives are quite happy with the situation. More bollocks. Listen Ellie, I'm not in a position to judge — I'm not exactly the faithful type — but years of being a bad girl mean I know how these things work."

"I wouldn't call you a *bad* girl Gina, just a busy one."

"Oh come on Ellie. I am bad. What about the time I left Herb in that bar? Some younger, better-looking bloke gives me the come on and I turn on my heel and leave with him. Didn't even bother to tell Herb I was going, just left him sitting there!"

"Was that before or after you heard him on the phone to his wife?"

"Before!"

"Hmm, in that case that was a pretty horrible thing to do. But Herb was playing away from home so he could hardly complain."

"OK, what about Steve and Brian then? I was seeing the two of them at the same time and neither of them had a clue. I left Brian in my bed one Sunday morning, went over to Steve's for brunch and had sex with him and then had sex with Brian again when I got home. Didn't even bother to shower in between. How bad is that?"

I winced. "Pretty bad I have to admit. But even if you are a bad girl Gina, you're a good friend."

"Wrong again Ellie. I'm not a good friend. I'm a *great* one. I put up with you disappearing off the face of the earth for months just because you'd taken up with a married smoothie-chops and I didn't even grind your ass about it when you finally turned up again, just greeted you with a smile on my face."

I hung my head again.

"Ok, ok, fair point. You're a bad girl, great friend. Hey, what happened to Steve and Brian in the end?"

"I dumped them both. All that juggling was doing my head in. And all the eating out. Going out for meals with two different men is way too fattening. And then there was the double sex. It all got just too knackering. I couldn't decide which one I liked most so I got rid of them both."

Gina illustrated her point by wringing her hands together: washing them clean of both boyfriends.

"Anyway," she said, "there was another bloke from the jazz club that I fancied more than either of them so I took up with him next. Now, will you stop trying to put off telling me? What happened?"

So, finally, I told her.

CHAPTER
FOURTEEN

Just ten days ago, the Saturday before last, Robert promised me that he would be at the flat by mid-afternoon.

"I've got to go down to Surrey to fetch some more of my stuff and chat through some financial issues with Ann, but after that we can have the rest of the weekend together. I love you so much my darling," he had said.

It wasn't often that I got to spend the weekend with Robert and I couldn't wait. What I wanted more than anything was to spend normal, ordinary time with him. Not going out to Michelin-starred restaurants or struggling to make fancy meals at home to impress him. I wanted to eat tea and toast together in bed, lie on the sofa reading the paper, order pizza delivery for dinner and watch a DVD with a glass of red wine each. Normal, ordinary couple time: the sort of weekend that might be mundane for other people but for me would be a treat from start to finish. And this weekend I was going to get it.

Finally it was Saturday. I took a long time getting ready, to fill in the time waiting for Robert to arrive. I took a long bath, shaved my legs and underarms, applied a face pack, exfoliated and moisturised myself all over. I painted my nails a pearly pink — three coats — and put on my very best matching bra and knickers. Robert liked underwear and had bought me a lot. He expected me to wear it when I was with him.

I had been surprised the first time he presented me with a La Senza bag full of puffs of black and cream and oyster silk.

"How did you know my size?"

"I looked in your knicker drawer when you were in the shower. Honestly Ellie some of the stuff you've got isn't fit to be used for dusters!"

The underwear I chose to wear for Robert that day was my favourite, made of cream silk with tiny embroidered pink rosebuds. The bra was padded and plunging, creating a cleavage that gave even Gina a run for her money and there were knickers to match, high legged and flattering. Plucked and oiled like an oven-ready chicken I killed time waiting for Robert, moving magazines around and fiddling with cushions so that the flat would look perfect when he arrived. I planned to open the door to him wearing only my bra and knickers and a pair of neck-breakingly high shoes which I would never have worn outside the flat but which I knew Robert would appreciate. My stomach was flipping over in anticipation of the sex when he arrived and the time dragged, however often I looked at my watch, wandering through the rooms of my tiny flat.

Only Robert didn't arrive. I waited and waited, not wanting to phone his mobile as he was with his wife. Eventually I sent him a text asking where he was, and another an hour later. By this time I had changed into a vest-top and jogging bottoms and had picked off my nail varnish. The remains lay on the coffee table next to me in a small pile, like glossy pink sea shells. Finally at 7p.m. I got a text back saying that something had come up and that he would not be able to see me that weekend after all.

I cried like a child at this point, throwing myself on to the floor, lying full length on the carpet. I cried so hard that the people living downstairs must surely have heard me, sobbing through the floor boards. There was fluff in my mouth and snot and tears in the carpet. I was disappointed, angry and frustrated. Even as I lay there wailing a part of me, the more mature part, detached itself and hovered somewhere in the top corner of the room, watching me cry as if I were in a movie, panning in for a close up on the unworn vampy shoes like a symbol of my rejection. Eventually, worn out by so much crying, I fell asleep.

I must have slept for an hour or more because when I woke up I was stiff and there were creases in my face from sleeping on the carpet. I went to the local 24-hour shop and bought a bottle of wine and two packs of Marlboro Lights. It had been ages since I'd had a fag because Robert hated it so much. I only smoked two or three a day but Robert swore he could smell it on me and so I stopped to please him, just like I started to wear suits to work because he said it looked sexy and had my curly hair straightened because he liked that too. I smoked half a pack of cigarettes and drank most of the wine. The world was spinning when I went to bed and when I woke in the morning my throat ached from dehydration and smoking and my head throbbed.

I heard nothing from Robert on Sunday. I tried one more text — a pitiful request that he call me — but he didn't.

I got into the office by 8a.m. on the Monday. I didn't start work until 9.30a.m. but I knew Robert was usually in early and I wanted to talk to him. Part of me wanted to shout and scream and ask him what the hell was going on and part of me was so hurt at the loss of my weekend that I wanted him to hold me and stroke me and make it better. I knew that both of those were impossible in the office but I did hope to find out exactly what the problem was.

I made my way straight to Robert's floor, but there was someone with him in his room. A woman. A pretty woman with blonde hair in a neat bob. They were talking animatedly, laughing and joking. She walked over to the table in the corner of Robert's room, poured herself some mineral water. She looked to be at ease, very comfortable in Robert's presence and in his room.

"I've got some documents I need Robert to sign," I said to Anita, Robert's secretary. "Is he likely to be long in there?"

Anita had never much liked me. She knew there was something going on between Robert and me and didn't approve.

"Not that long," she said. "They're due to be going out for breakfast. That's his wife. She's pregnant — after years of trying with no success they've finally done it. Isn't that great news? And after he'd bought her an

Audi TT for her fortieth to make up for not having a baby. Bless."

There was a ringing in my ears and I felt that everything had gone into slow motion, like in the *Six Million Dollar Man* when I was a kid. There must be some mistake I thought. That can't be Robert's wife — Robert's wife wears A-line navy skirts and American tan tights and doesn't shave her legs, she's not that tall elegant blonde in there. And it can't be Robert's baby, Robert has sex with me, not his wife. And even with that lot rolling around in my head like a bag of marbles I still had time to clock that the Audi TT he took to Brighton that first time we made love was not his fun car at all but his wife's car. As I looked again into Robert's room, I caught Robert's eye: the look he gave me confirmed that this was indeed his wife, his baby to be.

Anita looked at me witheringly.

"Don't tell me you thought you were the one Ellie. You were just the latest in a long line sweetheart."

I left the office and, not knowing what else to do with myself, I turned in the general direction of Primrose Hill and started walking, just putting one foot after the other, and every step I took I asked myself the same question. *How could I have been so stupid? So bloody, bloody stupid?* I didn't answer my mobile even though it rang several times and I could see it was Robert ringing. I just kept on walking; the physical activity was calming, reassuring, and I was relieved that all that weeping into the carpet at the weekend meant that I had no tears left. It started to rain and as the pavement got wet it released a smell of dust and pollution, the tang of grubby London.

When I got to the flat Robert was waiting outside for me.

"I gather Anita told you." He was defiant, almost aggressive.

"Is it true?"

"It's true that my wife is up the duff, yes."

Even though I had already been told this by Anita, hearing it again from Robert and his choice of phrase was just as shocking as if I were learning it for the first time. I gathered the energy to be cool and collected.

"Forgive me for asking but how can that happen? You told me you don't sleep with your wife."

"That *is* what I told you and it was true, really it was. But when I told her it was over between us and that I wanted to move on she was so wretched, so miserable — she threatened to kill herself. I found her in the guest bathroom with a Waitrose bag full of paracetamol and I picked her up, carried her away from there and comforted her while she cried and somehow or other we ended up sleeping with each other for old time's sake."

"Oh your guest bathroom was it? I take it there's a guest bedroom to go with your guest bathroom? And a Waitrose bag was it? Ann's too posh to buy her paracetamol at Superdrug like the rest of us, is she?"

"What's that got to do with anything?" Robert asked, bemused.

"Nothing," I said dejectedly. "So what happened then?"

150

"Well, she got pregnant."

"Are you honestly trying to tell me that after just one shag she got pregnant?"

He looked shocked, visibly flinched when I said the word shag, as if I had offended his sensibilities. "That's exactly what I am trying to tell you because it's true."

"What? That was the only time you slept with her for months before me and the only time after and you hit lucky?" My voice wobbled at this, high pitched and whiny.

"It's the truth. It was the only time we had sex since I met you. I'm sorry Ellie but that's the truth."

He was so convincing I almost believed him.

"And you told me your wife was plain."

"I didn't say that — I wouldn't have said that because it wouldn't have been true."

I realised that I'd never actually asked Robert what his wife looked like, that I had drawn my own picture of her based on how he described her life.

"Why didn't you tell me before?"

"I was scared to. I knew you'd be angry — rightly so — and I didn't know what to do."

"How pregnant is she?"

"Five months."

I gasped. "Five months! How long have you known?"

"About three."

"You've known for three months that your wife is pregnant but carried on sleeping with me, acting as if nothing had changed —"

Even Robert managed to look ashamed at this; he tried to take my hands in his.

"Nothing has changed the way I feel about you Ellie. I just didn't know how to tell you."

I snatched my hands away.

"*You* didn't even tell me in the end. I had to find it out from Anita. So when exactly *were* you planning to tell me?"

"I kept meaning to. But you were always so happy to see me and so loving — every time I came round I was going to tell you but the time was never right."

"That's pathetic Robert. Truly pathetic. You should have told me straight away — in fact, you should have told me that the two of you had had sex. That way I might not have been around to have to listen to this."

"I was going to tell you this weekend I swear but —"

"But what?"

"Ann wanted us to go to buy furniture for the nursery and I just couldn't think of an excuse not to go."

I was stunned. While I had been crying into my carpet he had been out shopping for cots. I felt like I'd been punched in the stomach.

"And what's going to happen now?" I asked. I knew what he was going to say but I wanted to make him say it.

"I'm sorry Ellie but I can't leave her now, can't walk out on her while she's pregnant. I can't do that. But we can carry on seeing each other if you'd like."

I looked at him in disbelief.

"You think you can just tumble through all this and come out the other end unscathed don't you Robert?

You think you can just betray the people who love you, even those that haven't even been born yet?"

Then, with all the eloquence that a woman with a degree in English literature can muster, I looked him straight in the eye and said: "So. Just. Fuck. Right. Off."

Finally and for good measure I added: "Fucker."

That was the last night I ever spent in the flat in Primrose Hill. I hurt so much I could barely breathe, couldn't even cry. I wanted to shake off my skin, peel the flesh from my bones so that I could escape myself. Pick myself clean and bare and step out of my body so that I could get away from how stupid and ashamed and embarrassed I felt. Had Robert ever meant to leave his wife or had he been stringing me along the whole time? Had he been sleeping with us both the whole time? Had he ever loved me even? And then I remembered the way he looked into my eyes when he made love to me and how afterwards he'd hug me tight to his chest, wrapping his legs round mine so that I was all wrapped up in his body, and tell me over and over how much he loved me, and I knew that the answer to the last question at least was yes. And then, finally, a feeling stronger than disappointment or shame or embarrassment flooded through me and that feeling was anger.

I had a vision of tearing through the flat with a sharp knife. I imagined the ripping noise as I plunged the knife into my mattress, how the pillows would make a satisfying pop and fill the room with feathers, how foam would spill like blood out of the leather settee as I sliced neatly through the seats. I was far too strung out to go to bed. Instead I packed up everything I owned and cleaned the flat from top to bottom. I defrosted the fridge, scrubbed the bath and shower, wiped out the cutlery drawer. For as long as I kept working, kept swilling and rinsing and rubbing, the chemical smell of lemon Cif sharp in my nostrils and my fingers red and swollen from squeezing out J-cloths, I could hold it all together. At last, when it was already growing light and I was crouched on my hands and knees washing the kitchen floor, I let the tears come again.

In the calm that comes after a good cry, I rang the temping agency and left a message on their answerphone to say that I would not be working at the firm any longer. I didn't explain why. I suppose I could have said that one of the firm's senior partners had dumped me and I was suffering from a broken heart but frankly that was none of their business. I wondered idly when someone would go through my desk and throw away my collection of Cup-a-Soups and my spare pair of tights. Only once I had no home and no job did I phone my mother and, for the first time since I was eighteen, ask her if I could please move back home for a while.

Gina rushed to me, wrapped her arms tight around me.

"I'm sorry Ellie. I'm so sorry. Do you want me to go round his house right now? Because I will. I'll wrap it in toilet paper and when his wife comes out and asks what I'm doing I'll tell her what an out-and-out shit her husband is. Shall I do that?"

I smiled weakly. "There's no need Gina. I'm better off without him. It's just going to take a little while before I actually *feel* better off without him."

Gina handed me an enormous glass of wine.

"Get that down you. You know the mistake you made Ellie fish face?"

"Going out with a married man maybe?"

"It wasn't the going out bit you got wrong. It was the falling in love with him bit you did afterwards. If you go in for adultery Ellie you need to be a whole lot smarter than that."

CHAPTER
FIFTEEN

1947

A second letter arrives from Margaret. Trevor rips it open, his hands shaking, hoping there will be some scrap of news in there, however tiny, that will give him the excuse to do what he has been thinking of every day of the life he has lived so far in London. To go back home to Laura and Kitty. But there is no hope.

Dear Trevor

Thank you for sending me your new address and telling me how you and Sarah are getting on up there in London. Clapham sounds an interesting place to live. You'd better be careful not to pick up a Cockney accent. The evacuee girls we had living with us during the war sounded common as anything. Mind, after a couple of years at home with us in the Rhondda they went back with lovely Welsh accents and roses in their cheeks too!
I hope all is well with you and Sarah. Everything here is wonderful. Tommy and I are engaged. Who would have thought! We get married next spring and I can't wait. I'm getting myself all organised and Mam and me have started putting things by

for my bottom drawer. I've already embroidered six pillowcases with a lovely floral pattern: lupins and hollyhocks just like you had in your back garden at the shop, but I haven't got as much done as I would have liked these past two weeks as I've had a horrible cough and not been able to shake it off. Tommy says I need to get myself out for a walk up the mountain with him and then I'll be right as rain.

Laura and Jack seem to be doing just fine Trevor. Laura's as hoity toity as ever and by all accounts Jack is coming along, gaining weight and starting to get back to normal. Kitty's becoming a right little chatterbox at school apparently and doing well there. You asked me to let you know if they moved and last month they got themselves their own house, just a few streets away from his mother. I'll put the address on the bottom of this letter so that you have it should you need it.

I would invite you to our wedding Trevor but I guess you wouldn't come even if I did. To be honest I don't think Tommy would be best pleased if you were there anyway.

Best wishes

Margaret Lewis (soon to be Davies)

Trevor reads the letter twice very quickly and then, more slowly, a third time. He wonders what news can come from the Rhondda now that can possibly make him happy. If Jack should die of the illnesses he suffered serving his country? If Laura was missing him so badly she could not cope with the choice she made? If Kitty was miserable and not doing well at school? He folds the letter in half and places it in the back of the cupboard where he keeps his seeds. Later, when Sarah is in bed and the house is quiet, he writes back to Margaret. Thanks her for her letter, congratulates her on her engagement and encloses some hollyhock seeds, carefully sealed in a sturdy brown envelope on which he has also written instructions on how to plant them and look after the seedlings. When he has finished that letter he writes another, much more difficult letter, this time to Laura.

Dear Laura

I thought you might like to know how Sarah is doing. She is eighteen months old now and has been walking since she turned one. She is steady on her feet and not at all clumsy like other children. She likes to help me garden which is just as well because as you know I like to garden.

We live in Clapham in South London. I have managed to get myself a job and have engaged the services of a married lady to help with Sarah while I am at work. The arrangement works well for us all and Sarah is very happy and content. She has settled well into life in London and so have I. There is much rebuilding required here after the Blitz but the work has already started and soon it will be as if the war never happened.

I plan to write to you once a year about the time of Sarah's birthday to let you know how she is doing.

Our daughter is a joy Laura. I hope some day soon you will want to see that for yourself, and when you do, you need only write to me and I will bring Sarah to you.
Trevor

My mother stepped up her nagging campaign and finally I went to visit dad and Sandra. I took the bus to Balham. I enjoy travelling by bus outside of peak hours. I like the lumbering pace and the slow swagger, the whole stop, start, stop-again pro . I sat in one of the front seats on the upper deck, u ones that children always choose. When the bus drove p st tall trees, leaves brushed and squeaked against the windows, pushing against the glass like the branches might just burst through at any moment. I liked the vantage point my seat gave me to stare out of the window and watch the houses and office and people go by.

Whenever I am not working in a nine-to-five job, it always takes me a little while to readjust to all the life that goes on daily while office workers are behind their desks. High up on the top deck of that bus I watched all sorts of people getting on and off — a bloke in black tie carrying an enormous music case that looked like it contained a tuba or something; a tired mother with three small children and a baby whose buggy was weighed down with plastic shopping bags and festooned with balloons; a little old lady struggling with one of those tartan shopping trolleys in which she was carrying a small black Scottie dog. I don't know why I should think all these people are not out there living their lives just because I'm at work and not around to watch them doing it. It's not as if London drains of people during the working day, but sometimes that is how it feels.

I found the sway of the bus journey very calming and I climbed the stairs to Dad's flat in a bit of a trance. He and Sandra live at the top of a well kept 1930s' mansion house block. All the residents take great pride in keeping the hallway and the stairs clean and well maintained and they all put out window boxes dripping with geraniums and lobelia. It is a cheerful place to live even if, as Trevor always points out, there are no gardens.

Sandra's taste is the direct opposite to my mother's. Sandra, my mother says, abhors a vacuum and if there is a blank space on a wall or an empty corner in a room she likes to fill it. She thrives on clutter and colour. When she moved in with dad she stuffed the flat full of paintings and postcards, crammed the side tables with coloured glass bottles, hung fringed scarves over the mantelpieces. I like the busy feel of the flat — there is always something new or unusual to look at — and she puts it all together with great flair. My mother on the other hand hates clutter — she likes white walls, plain carpets, no knick knacks, clean surfaces. I like the tastes of both my dad's wives.

Sandra flung the door open when I rang their bell.

"Ellie — what a surprise to see you. Come in!"

She enfolded me in an over-enthusiastic hug, holding me against her bosom and giving me one extra sympathy squeeze before she finally released me. It is just as well Sandra teaches art and not drama because she is a hopeless actress. It was quite clear that she already knew and I figured Mum must have phoned ahead and warned them I was coming. Winded slightly from the force of her embrace I followed her unsteadily into the living room where Dad was waiting, ostensibly reading the paper but actually gearing himself up to act surprised.

My dad dresses like a geography teacher primarily because he is a geography teacher. He wears brown jumbo corduroy trousers and shirts with small green and brown checked patterns, the collars of which are tucked neatly into the turtle necks of his bottle green pullovers. Unlike Trevor, who has hair as thick and white and bouncy as Blake Carrington's, my dad is more or less bald. He used to go for the comb-over look before he met Sandra but she had the courage I lacked and told him that it just made him look more bald, before taking a pair of clippers to his head. He has a little bit of a pot belly but not too much and he has a habit of wiping his hands on the seat of his trousers when he is nervous, which is exactly what he was doing as he stood up to kiss me.

"Well, well, well," he said stagily, rocking gently backwards and forwards on his heels, "Look who it is."

I went along with the pretence, resisting the urge to point out that they had laid the tea tray for three.

I let Sandra fuss with the teapot and mugs for a while before putting them out of their misery. She and Dad made exaggerated faces of surprise when I told them that I was back in my old room at Clapham. I didn't give any more details than I'd given my mother — just that Robert had ended it and I was pretty upset about it.

"His loss sweetheart," my dad said matter of factly. "I know you hurt right now but you'll get over him soon enough. And it's nice for your mum to have you back at home for a while."

"And anyway," Sandra said, "you're far too young to be settling down. You've got more of the world to visit yet and more men to try out. You need to be at least forty to find the right man. And if you're lucky like me, that's when you'll find the one that'll last you a lifetime."

She snuggled up to my dad as she said this, kissing his ear in a lustful sort of way that made me feel slightly queasy.

"It's not just your mum who's glad to have you at home," my dad carried on. "I hope we'll get to see a bit more of you nowadays. You have seemed to be incredibly busy of late, when we call. Perhaps you'll be free now to come round more often."

I groaned inwardly. I knew what that meant. They'd be throwing one of their famous dinner parties any Saturday now with the sole intention of introducing me to some of their interesting friends or, worse still, suggesting one of their walks round London with the same interesting friends, visiting sites of historical importance. Actually the walks could be quite fun but I wasn't up to being paraded as their newly single daughter with lots of free time on her hands and no home of her own.

"That would be great Dad. I'd like that very much. Just as soon as I feel up to socialising again I'll let you know."

"Leave the girl alone Roy. She'll come again to visit when she's good and ready." Sandra took my elbow and steered me into the kitchen away from Dad, before presenting me stealthily with a plastic bag containing four, expertly rolled cigarettes.

"That's good of you Sandra but actually when I smoke I prefer a Marlboro Light."

Sandra looked at me quizzically.

"Tobacco alone is not strong enough to help mend a broken heart girl. These are premium-quality, freshly rolled spliffs. In case of emergency. Now put them away quick before Roy sees them."

"Where did you get it?" I asked, stuffing them into my bag and trying not to let out the smile that was curling around the edges of my mouth.

"I can't tell you that. Girl's got to protect her sources. Suffice to say it's really good stuff and entirely organic. Now shall I put the kettle on again while we're here and we can have another cup of tea? I've also made you some artery-clogging almond cake, loaded with butter and eggs."

You've got to hand it to Sandra. She does know how to take the knees out from under misery.

CHAPTER
SIXTEEN

Living at home in Clapham with Mum and Trevor was cheap but I still needed to make some money, especially if I was to keep up with Gina who had expensive tastes in Sauvignon Blanc.

I dusted off my dictionaries and got in touch with the word puzzle people. Throughout university I'd made good beer money compiling crossword puzzles and word games for magazines and competitions. My particular speciality was dogs. For a long time I was on a retainer with one of the major dog food manufacturers to produce crossword puzzles for their quarterly magazine competition. I have never owned a dog but I do own some hefty dog encyclopaedias and can work out clues, the answer to which is Miniature Schnauzer or Dalmatian, as quickly as you can say Best in Show at Crufts. I got in touch with Maisy, the editor of the magazine.

"Ellie! How are you? Thought you'd got lost in Kathmandu or wherever it is you went."

"Not Kathmandu, EC2." I said.

"Eh?"

"I've been temping in the City for a while but I'm fed up of that now, wondered if there is any work going?"

"Oh, I should think so. Our readers love your crossword puzzles. How about you do me a few to start off with and we'll take it from there."

Maisy was offering less than a week's work but at least it was a start. I thanked her and got down to business. I set up my laptop. I worked for a while on a crossword, glad of the comfort of a familiar, time-consuming task. I tried to resist the urge to check my emails but eventually gave in. I had about sixty, most of which were spam offering me last minute trips abroad or cheap Viagra. There was just one from Robert, sent a few days earlier. It said:

Ellie
I loved you more than you'll ever know. I'm sorry.
I hope you got the cheque.
Robert

Love? The bastard didn't know the meaning of the word, or loyalty or truth. And what did he mean a cheque? He must have thought I really was some sort of prostitute, something he could pay for, like a hotel bill or a bar tab.

I tried to return to my puzzle but Robert's email kept niggling at me. I rehearsed over and over in my head what I wanted to say back to him, drafted several emails in response, none of which I sent. I couldn't help wondering what sort of price Robert had put on me, on our relationship. He probably didn't know I'd moved back to Clapham, would think I was still living in the flat. I decided I would go there, pick up my post and see what he had sent.

I was outside the Primrose Hill flat an hour later. I fumbled around in my bag for my keys, let myself in through the shared front door, climbed up the three flights of stairs to the flat that had been mine. As I went to open the door of my flat I heard voices inside. My heart began to pound, thinking perhaps Robert was in there, but when I knocked on the door it was opened by a slim girl in her early twenties, a mobile phone clamped to her head. She was wearing a dark trouser suit, high-heeled black boots and thick-framed black spectacles.

"I'll call you back," she muttered into the phone and then to me, "Can I help you?"

"I'm Ellie Taylor. I used to live here."

"Oh hello. Yes, I picked up some post for you from downstairs." She handed it to me.

I looked at her, a little confused.

"I'm the estate agent," she explained, "I've been showing people round the flat. Probably best if you get a re-direct for your post. Someone else is moving in here soon."

"Already?"

"Yes. Isn't that lucky? We found another tenant within days of you moving out. Just as well because the landlord of these flats is a solicitor and very demanding."

Realisation dawned on me.

"Yes, Robert Carmichael, isn't it? I've met him a few times coming to check on things."

"That's him. I didn't know he came here himself to check on things — thought he used us for all of that."

"I didn't know he owned all the flats. I thought it was just mine."

"He bought the whole house a while back as an investment, converted it into executive flats. Did a lovely job."

"He did indeed."

"Best be getting on. The couple taking this flat are arriving any minute to sign up the documents and get the keys. That's a point. You shouldn't still have a set — could I have them back please?"

Wordlessly, I started to fish the keys off my key ring, easing them over the silver heart from Tiffany's that Robert gave me when I moved in. Then I thought better of it and handed the whole key ring to the agent.

"What about the lovely key ring? It looks expensive."

"Oh that belongs to the landlord. It came with the keys. Give that set to the new tenants — a little house-warming present."

The bastard had just got more bastardly.

When I was back outside on the street and my heart had finally stopped thumping around in my chest, I opened the letter from him that was among the mail the agent had handed me. It was dated the day after I had learned of Ann's pregnancy.

Dear Ellie,
Now that our relationship is over I think it best that you move out of the flat. I will give notice to

the agents to start looking for another tenant and perhaps you could be out within two weeks. I know that I have hurt you and I am sorry for that. I also know that you have stopped working at the firm and that money will therefore be tight, particularly as you need to find somewhere else to live. I hope you will not take this the wrong way but I enclose a cheque. Money can't make what I have done right but it can make the next few months a bit easier for you.
Robert

The cheque was for £10,000. I gasped when I unfolded it. Robert had written the cheque with his favourite Mont Blanc pen, thick-nibbed and generous, using his trademark royal blue ink. The sight of his familiar handwriting made me immediately yearn with longing for him even through my anger.

Ten thousand pounds was the price that Robert put on me. About half what I calculated he earned a month. About four months' rent on the Primrose Hill flat. Which I was glad I had moved out of before I was told to.

1948

The next letter from Wales to arrive in Clapham is not from Margaret or from Laura either but from Tommy Davies.

Dear Trevor

Margaret said I was to write to you. Sadly she passed away two months ago. She had a bad cough for ages but it was only when she started coughing up blood that we realised it was tuberculosis she had. We managed to get her a place in a sanatorium all the way over in Swansea and she had six months of total rest, fresh sea air and good food but she never managed to beat it. She was cheerful all the way through, always seeing the positive side of everything, and she was the heart and soul of that sanatorium keeping everyone's spirits up and smiling the live long day. Doctors collapsed one of her lungs in the end but that didn't work and she died suddenly a few days later. This was about a month before we should have been wed. Now all I read about is a miracle cure called streptomycin but it didn't come fast enough for my Meg. I wouldn't bother coming back here Trevor if I were you. The collieries are laying people off and there's not much work about. Laura and Jack and Kitty are doing just fine. It would be better for all concerned if you just stayed away.

Respectfully yours

Thomas Davies

Trevor adds this letter to the others in the back of his seed cupboard. He grieves for little Margaret Lewis in a way he has not been able to grieve for Laura. He digs over a corner of his garden in memory of Meg and

169

plants there lupins and hollyhocks but also roses and delphiniums and lots and lots of cheerful smiling daisies. With Margaret gone and no-one to tell him what is going on back home comes an acceptance that his life from now on is in London. The next pretty single lady who smiles at him gets asked out to the Saturday dance in the Labour Club. And the one after that and the one after that. He hopes that love will one day hit him again with the same force but when it does not he parts company courteously with each lady lest she gets hurt. Whenever he is asked what happened to his wife it seems natural to say that she died of TB in a sanatorium high up on a hill overlooking the sea, where even in illness she kept people smiling. He tells Sarah the same thing when she is old enough to ask.

CHAPTER
SEVENTEEN

After that first visit to see Beth, I started calling round most days. It gave me something more constructive to do than trail around aimlessly behind Trevor. I'd work on my crosswords for a few hours in the morning, then walk down to Beth's house and give Janey a bottle and play sword fighting with Will in the kitchen while Beth seized the opportunity to do exercise videos, thrashing around in her lounge to the thump of disco music.

It was Beth I asked for advice about the cheque from Robert.

"My initial reaction was to tear it into little pieces and post them back to him. What do you think?"

"Are you mad Ellie? From what you say that money is a drop in his champagne bucket but it's a fortune to you and me. Cash it. Take his money. You've earned it."

"Doesn't that make me a prostitute?"

"Only if you let yourself feel that way."

"I don't know — I'll think about it. I could use it to go travelling again I suppose."

"Use it however you like so long as you use it. In fact, ring him up and tell him that it's not enough and unless he sends you more you'll tell his wife."

"First you want me to be a prostitute, now you want me to be a blackmailer. I'll think about it a bit longer, maybe if I live with it for a while I'll know the best thing to do."

"Whatever. It's your money."

"You know Beth, I've been thinking. Gina said something when I told her about me and Robert, something about married men and affairs, and I think it applies to Tony."

Beth looked worried.

"No, in a good way. Gina said that married men always tell their mistresses that they are not sleeping with their wives but they always are. But Tony really isn't sleeping with you. So if Gina is right he can't be having an affair because if he was he *would* be sleeping with you."

"So there's another reason why he's not sleeping with me but it's not an affair?"

"Something like that. Why don't you just ask him what the problem is?"

"Because I'm scared of what his answer might be."

"More scared than you are now?"

"Probably not, no."

"What about seducing him?"

"You mean club him over the head as he gets home from work and drag him upstairs to bed by his hair?"

"Well, I was thinking more of a bottle of wine and a massage but if that's what works for Tony, that's fine. Will and Janey can stay with me. Mum would love to help out."

"I don't know Ellie. It makes me nervous just thinking about it. Anyway hush now — Tony'll be home any moment."

When Tony got home he looked genuinely pleased to see me.

"Ellie — really good to see you. You look well. Thanks for helping Beth out. You've been fantastic."

He gave me a hug. His T shirt was soft against my face, worn out by washing, and he smelled of clean laundry. He looked tired and his hair was thinning at the temples but Tony was still a good-looking man, with a lovely smile and a fantastic bum. He has always filled his jeans well. As he turned away and bent down to pick up Janey I looked down at his bum and then up at Beth. I winked. She looked at his bum too, blushed slightly and stifled a giggle.

I pestered Beth relentlessly and in the end she let me babysit Janey and Will that weekend. I insisted on collecting the kids early, straight after lunch so that their parents could have lots of time on their own. Mum was delighted to see Janey and Will, using her special soft voice that she keeps for small children which, when I hear it, touches some warm memory deep inside me, makes me feel safe and loved.

I sat Janey on my lap while Mum and Will made jam tarts. I loved the solid feel of her chunky baby thighs, her soft little feet, the sweet smell of her skin. I wanted to squeeze her tight, gobble her up, keep her safe.

Mum got out her impressive range of biscuit cutters.

"Which ones do you want to use Will? You pick."

He selected different ones from the ones I chose as a child. He avoided the flowers and hearts and stars, picked a duck, a pig, a teddy bear. Mum helped him cut out shapes from the pastry and then Will dolloped strawberry jam into the centre of them all by himself. The kitchen smelt of hot jam and baking and I felt relaxed and, to my surprise, happy.

"I love cooking," said Will.

"Perhaps you could be a chef when you grow up," suggested Mum.

"I don't want to be a chef! I want to be a cooker. Or a wrestler because I've got muscles on my belly. Look." And Will lifted his T shirt, showing us his flat stomach; his rib cage sticking out, fragile as a bird's.

While the jam tarts were in the oven, Trevor took Will into the garden to show him the sunflowers he had planted. The flowers were as tall as Trevor and their big seedy faces, fringed with yellow, smiled sunshine down at Will.

"Cool flowers Mister," Will congratulated Trevor.

Then Trevor took him to his small vegetable patch, pointing out the pale green lettuce lined up in rows and strawberry plants clutching their bright red jewels. I watched as Trevor picked a few strawberries, wiped them gently against his trousers to get rid of the worst of the dirt and handed them over to Will who said nothing but slowly and juicily ate the sweet fruit.

Afterwards, we all sat round the kitchen table and ate jam tarts with beakers of milk. I had forgotten how good both tasted.

174

The next morning I could hardly wait to return the children to their mother to find out what had happened, but I did the decent thing and held off until 11 a.m. Gina came with me.

"You're looking good Beth," she said, as Beth opened the front door, her hair tousled and her skin glowing.

"I should hope so," Beth said. "I've been hungry since last Tuesday and I've been swinging from the chandeliers all night."

"What's a chandelier Mum?" asked Will.

"It's one of those strap things that you hold on to on the Tube to keep your balance. Now let's get you settled in front of the telly so that I can have a chat with the girls."

"Well?" We said in unison as soon as Will and Janey were safely watching a *Tweenies* video.

"Ellie — it was fanfuckingtastic. Thank you so much. We had the most wonderful night — we drank loads, played our favourite cds in the lounge, had sex on the sofa while we looked deep into each other's eyes. Honestly, it was like we were seventeen again. We did it quickly, we did it slowly, we did it again this morning —"

"Crikey," Gina said, "you two had better not be having more sex than me. That's not allowed."

"And did you find out what the problem was?" I asked.

"The stupid thing is that there wasn't one really. He was tired, I was tired, he thought I'd rebuffed him so he didn't feel sexy, I thought he'd rebuffed me so I didn't feel sexy. It was just really bad communication but it's sorted now. Thank you. Thank you so much."

Beth glowed with love and with good sex. I was so glad for her that things were ok, glad for me too that my icon for a good marriage was still holding true. I was also jealous.

"What about the domestic stuff, all the household jobs you've got to do?"

"We talked about that. He said he feels that I don't appreciate how hard it is to go out to work every day and earn the money and be responsible for all the bills, which is true — I don't — so we've agreed to be more supportive of each other. And we've agreed that I should have some time to do something for myself, so we're going to find the money somehow to put the kids in nursery a couple of days a week and I'm going to enrol on an aromatherapy massage course. I've always wanted to do that and perhaps one day when the kids are older I can get a job in one of those swanky spas in the West End."

"Really?" Gina's voice came from outside where she was crouched down beneath the kitchen window, having a fag where the children wouldn't see her. "I couldn't be doing with that. Halfway through the massage I'd be tapping the client on the shoulder and swinging her legs off the table, telling her to get off because it's my turn now. Why don't you just come down the pub with Ellie and me instead?"

"Where is Tony anyway?" I asked "Have you still got him tied to the bed?"

"Don't be daft. Even I've had enough relationship-reaffirming hanky-panky for a while. Any more and I'd be walking like John Wayne. He's gone to get some lunch. We thought you two might like to stay. But you're not to tease Tony about the sex — you know how scared he is of the two of you."

When Tony got back, he and Beth set to making lunch. Gina and I sat at the table and watched them as they worked. They operated as a team, putting together ploughman's lunches for us all, criss-crossing each other in their kitchen without getting in each other's way, dancing to the steps of a familiar tune. Every now and then they caught each other's eye and grinned. It was good to watch them together. They put heaped plates in front of us — chunks of mature cheddar, fresh French bread, pickled onions. There were bowls of plums and grapes on the table too.

"Great, pickled onions," I said. "Haven't had pickled onions for ages. These are lovely."

Beth looked at me, surprised.

"Trevor made those. He brings us a big jar every six months or so."

"Ah yes, my grandfather's pickling empire. How could I forget about that?"

"That's because you've been hanging out with someone too posh to eat pickled onions," laughed Gina. "I bet Robert only ate caramelised red onions with a balsamic vinegar *jus*."

This was painfully true. I could not for one second imagine Robert sitting with my friends round this battered pine table, marked with felt pen and coffee cup rings; Will taking advantage of the fact that his parents were preoccupied with entertaining their guests to scoop butter straight from the dish with his spoon and shovel it surreptitiously into his mouth. Robert would have been totally out of place in this place — a place where I belonged.

"You're right Gina," I said, "from now on I intend to bring all potential boyfriends round here to take the pickled onion test before I go out with them. And make sure they are not married."

Beth and Tony were not quite certain how to take this comment but Gina and I fell about laughing so they smiled too.

"Anyway," Gina said. "Enough about *you*, let me tell you all about *me*. I have good news. As from this weekend I am the proud tenant of one very overgrown and under-loved allotment. Finally I am a woman of property."

"At long bloody last," said Tony. "What did you have to do — sleep with the bloke who gives them out?"

"Not quite. I just had to give him the impression that I *might* sleep with him at some stage."

"That should've been easy enough," said Tony, "you give everybody that impression."

"Hey you," Gina swatted at Tony with a baguette, "I have never once flirted with you."

Beth looked up from giving Janey a bottle.

"Are you saying my bloke is not fanciable," she teased. "Because let me tell you I fancy the arse off him." She grinned at Tony as she said this and I couldn't work out which emotion was stronger in her face — the love or the lust.

CHAPTER
EIGHTEEN

Given my mother's strongly developed work ethic, it was hardly surprising that she only allowed me a few weeks' grace before I started to get on her nerves and she began to nag me about my jobless state.

"It's not good for you Ellie. Hanging around the house is not going to help you get on with life. You need a job. Something to aim for."

"I've got my crossword puzzles," I said, offering this up weakly, already knowing what her response was going to be.

"Writing crossword puzzles about dogs is hardly a career my girl and you know it. You've spent long enough romping round the world like some harum-scarum. Really Ellie, you need to get a proper job."

I groaned and rolled my eyes like some hormonal teenager, hanging my shoulders in despair.

"Oh good Lord," my mother snorted in desperation.

I left the house at this point. I didn't quite slam the door behind me or tell her that I hated her and that she didn't understand me but I felt like it. I made my way to the allotments, figuring Gina would be there. It was still light after all. I found her working on her tatty shed, sanding down the exterior. She handed me a piece of sandpaper before she even said hello to me.

"Do I have to?" I moaned.

"It's the price of spending time with me nowadays my friend."

I rubbed at a piece of shed half heartedly.

"This bit of sandpaper is blunt."

"Put your back into it then."

I sighed and applied a bit more pressure.

"What do you think Gina? Is it time I grew up and got a real job?"

"Didn't take her long then." Gina knows my mother almost as well as I do. "What counts as a real job anyway?" She was sandpapering so hard I could barely hear her. "Is singing a real job? I doubt your mother thinks so but it pays my bills and makes me happy. It doesn't matter what I think or your mother thinks. What do you want?"

"I dunno. Win the lottery I guess, never have to work another day in my life."

Gina stopped momentarily to blow sawdust off her fingers.

"You'd better start buying a ticket then. Increases your chances of winning no end."

"Actually it's not working I mind so much. It's careers. I don't want a career. What I want is to take off again, do some more travelling. I haven't been away anywhere for ages, not since before Robert. I think it's time I started planning my next trip."

"Don't you need money for that?" Gina looked at me slyly. Ever since I'd told her about Robert's guilty attempt to pay me off she had been on at me to cash his cheque.

"I've told you already! I don't want his money."

"Well in that case you'd better do as your mum says and get a job, start saving up."

"I'm not temping in the City again. I just can't. Too many reminders of Robert. Shit, I might even bump into him." I was disappointed in myself that, after the first shudder of horror, my heart leapt a little with joy at the thought of seeing him again.

"You don't always have to do fancy temping Ellie. You could always get something more local. There are jobs right here in Clapham too you know. You could apply for something permanent and then just leave when you're ready. I could ask Paul if there's anything going at the bank next time I see him if you like."

This immediately got my attention.

"What do you mean, next time you see him? How much are you two seeing of each other?"

Gina blushed.

"Quite a bit actually. Since the last time we had sex for old time's sake we've been having quite a lot of sex for new time's sake."

"And how's it going?"

"Really rather well," she said "so well that I don't want to risk ruining it by talking about it."

I mimed turning a key at the corner of my mouth, throwing the key theatrically over my shoulder.

"Is all this sandpapering really worth it?" I asked, changing the subject. "It's ruining my nails. Wouldn't you be better off just tearing the blasted thing down and starting again?"

Gina was affronted.

"Absolutely not. This shed is going to be fabulous, I promise you; and the allotment is going to be even better. Now, I've got about an hour before I've got to go get ready for work so let's see if we can get the whole of the back done in that time."

I picked up my piece of sandpaper and rubbed until my arms ached.

In the end my job prospects sorted themselves out, without me even having to try that hard.

The very next morning I walked to Clapham High Street, full of purpose. Gina was right. I didn't need to work in the City. I could try my hand at something else for a change. I planned to buy the paper and see if there was anything in the job adverts that I could do, possibly even swing past the Job Centre for the first time in my life. But, as it turned out, when I got to the newsagents I noticed there was a firm of solicitors right next door. Not a big serious corporate firm of solicitors like the ones I temped for in the City, not like Robert's firm, but one that did family law, wills, conveyancing and debt advice: the kind of work that City law firms refuse to do because there's not enough money in it. And stuck in the window was a piece of paper advertising a vacancy for a secretary/receptionist — experience preferred but not essential — please apply with CV to Mr Collins, managing partner.

I rushed home to my computer to tart up my CV. I described in detail my secretarial work in solicitors' offices, stretching my experience out so that it filled the gaps left by travelling. I phoned the number from the advert and spoke with Mr Collins, dropping in my CV to him as requested. That same afternoon Mr Collins rang me back and offered me the job without even interviewing me.

"Your CV looks excellent," he said "I'm sure you'll be just great. And anyway we've got a bit of a typing backload and we need someone who can start immediately. Could you start tomorrow? Say 8a.m.?"

The pay was a lot less than I could get temping in the City but it was right on my doorstep. I could walk to work in less than ten minutes. The prospect of bypassing the miserable crowds queuing up to plunge down the black hole of Clapham North station, and of avoiding sweaty, uncomfortable journeys pressed up against total strangers, swung it for me. I accepted the job.

It was very different from what I was used to. The office was out-and-out shabby, with a couple of ancient tweed-covered armchairs in reception that smelled faintly of damp dog, and a chrome and glass coffee table left over from the eighties. There were no water coolers here, no wall-to-wall air conditioning or gym in the basement, just a battered kettle on top of a fridge and all the tea and coffee you could drink. There was just one other secretary, called Corinna, who had been at the firm for years and years or, as she put it, *since God was a boy*. She and I were expected to look after

184

reception and answer the phones while doing all the typing and photocopying for the five solicitors who worked there.

Corinna was usually the one who opened up every morning and she liked to make a big song and dance about all the hours she put in and the amount of work she got through. It didn't take me long to rumble that Corinna spent the first forty minutes of her working day, before the solicitors arrived, eating toast, smoking and reading celebrity magazines. I didn't say anything to her — it was none of my business — but my silence was not enough. Corinna obviously felt that my very presence in the office was in some way a criticism of her. Perhaps she thought I would tell on her to Mr Collins. Whatever it was, from the moment I started work, Corinna made it her mission to show me that what was actually expected of a secretary first thing in the morning was toast eating and magazine reading, and that I was committing some serious breach of trade union ethics or secretarial honour by actually working. Every time I reached for a tape or went to the photocopier she sighed and tutted, ostentatiously flipping the pages of her magazine. If I got too industrious she would finally say tersely,

"They don't pay you enough to work that hard you know."

I liked the way she always said "you" the implication being that they paid her more than me. They probably did. I didn't care. I could cope with Corinna. I could cope with the lack of a water cooler and the never-ending work load. What I was finding it difficult to cope with was the type of work we did. Collins and Co did almost exclusively legal-aid work and in particular child-care work and it was heart breaking stuff, worlds apart from the business transactions I had worked on in the past. This firm didn't deal with buying and selling companies for millions of pounds, or the contracts of employment of fat cat board directors. What the lawyers of Collins & Co did for long hours every day was help decide the fate of children who had been taken into care for their own protection.

I had a constant lump in my throat as I typed up statements about children tied to their cots, left lying in their own filth for hours with nothing to drink or eat while their parents lay downstairs passed out on drugs, or sitting in the corner of a bedroom watching their mother turn tricks to make enough for her next fix. These were some of the worst, most extreme examples but there were hundreds of cases of more routine, systematic neglect — children not fed or watered or loved. The saddest cases of all were the ones where the mothers had simply fallen off the rails — had not been able to keep things together, had been hard up, desperate and losing their way — and whose children had been taken into care against their wishes. Some of these mothers gave up at this stage, sinking even further into the depression or substance abuse that had caused their problems in the first place, resigning themselves to the loss of their children. Other mothers fought back with every ounce of whatever strength they had left, to get their children back.

I knew I needed to adopt the same sort of approach that the solicitors did — a cool detachment from their daily working life which meant they could dictate reports of children whose parents had stubbed cigarettes out on their naked bodies or who had fed their Alsatian dog every day but their children only every other — without so much as a wobble in their voices. I knew I needed to keep myself aloof and distant and that not getting personally involved was the only way to cope, but I failed miserably at that from the very beginning thanks to Carol Matthews. Because Carol was one of those mothers who had fallen off the rails but was now fighting back and Collins & Co was helping her do that.

It was Emma who got me involved. She was the youngest solicitor at Collins & Co and not the most organised, often forgetting she was due somewhere until ten minutes beforehand when she would fly out of the door, effing and blinding, her bag undone, dropping her car keys and her purse and getting herself into a right state. She had collected fistfuls of parking and speeding tickets in this way and lived in dread of losing her driving licence. It only took me a few days to work out that Emma was also a party girl, working till 8p.m. every night and then going straight out from the office to join her mates. She would arrive at the office the morning after the night before clutching a tall latte from Starbucks (with two extra shots of espresso) and a big bag of giant, chocolate-chip cookies.

"Ok everyone," she'd announce. "Be gentle with me today. I've got low self esteem."

Just two weeks into working at Collins & Co, I got a frantic phone call from Emma. She was stuck in court at a hearing that had overrun.

"Ellie, is there a lady called Carol Matthews waiting for me?"

"Nope, not yet. Want me to make her a cup of tea when she gets here?"

There was a rule at Collins & Co, which I suspected originated from Corinna, that clients in reception did not as a matter of course get a cup of tea. A cup of tea for a client necessitated a direct request from the lawyer to Corinna, preferably at least 24 hours in advance. As a result very few such requests were ever made.

"No it's not tea I'm after. You've worked in lots of law firms haven't you Ellie?"

"Quite a few, yes."

"Listen, everyone else is out at meetings and I'm desperate. I need you to kick off the meeting with Carol Matthews for me. Tell her you're my assistant or something and that I've been unavoidably detained and just keep her talking till I get there. I've got a bunch of psych' reports I need to discuss with her but the thing that niggles me about Carol is her drinking — I've got a gut feeling that she drinks more than she'll admit — and I'd really like to know what you think when you meet her, how she comes over to someone who's new to her story. It'll give me an idea of what sort of witness she'll be in court. Take a look at her file to get a bit of background first. Do you think you can do that?"

"I think so," I said, not thinking anything of the sort.

By the time Carol Matthews arrived in the office, I had managed to speed read the first few pages of her file. She was a single mother whose children had been taken into care after the school had drawn the local authority's attention to the fact that their hair moved. Head lice is a common problem in schools and most parents attack the problem with commercial nit shampoo or the more hippy and environmentally sound option of tea tree oil, lots of conditioner and a fine-toothed metal comb. It was clear to the school after a few weeks of watching her boys' hair stir gently, due to the number and sheer size of the lice crawling through it, that Carol was not planning on following either method and so the head master called social services. Social services organised a home visit and found Carol sitting on the sofa off her head drunk and staring at a blank television screen; her youngest child wearing a nappy that had not been changed for such a long time that excrement was pouring down her legs. When social services changed the baby they found a nappy rash so extensive that the child was chapped and bleeding. The house was dirty; there were no nappies or wipes in the house and no food other than a third of a packet of cornflakes and a carton of milk. This was more than enough for the local authority to seek and obtain from the court an interim care order for all three children, who had been placed in short-term foster care and had stayed there ever since.

A brief read of this history meant that I was not pre-disposed to take to Carol Matthews when she finally arrived. The way she looked didn't help much

189

either. She was about 5′9″ but extremely skinny; Victoria Beckham-style skinny, and she wore stone washed denim jeans so tight that her hip bones jutted out through the denim like a wire coat hanger. Her hair was bleached blonde, shoulder length and scraggy, and she was wearing flip-flops. Her feet were dirty and she was wearing a toe ring. She was not at all pleased to find out it was me ushering her into the meeting room and not Emma.

"What do you mean Emma's going to be a bit late?" she said aggressively. "I've had this appointment arranged for days now and I expected her to be here. And who are you anyway?"

"I'm her assistant."

"Bollocks you're her assistant. She's never mentioned an assistant to me all the other times I've been here. You're just the apprentice you are, aren't you?"

Carol had promoted me quite considerably. I thought it best to confess while I still could.

"You're right, I'm just training, long way to go yet before I qualify. But Emma wanted me to kick this meeting off before she got here to save you some time. I'm sure you're a busy woman."

"Lady," Carol said through gritted teeth, "I'm not busy at all at the moment. My kids have been taken off me remember?"

"Hmm, yes well. Shall we get on? How've you been coping?"

"Have you got kids Miss . . .?"

"Taylor. But please, call me Ellie."

"Ok then. Ellie. Do you have kids?"

"No I don't."

"I figured. If you did, you would already know the answer to that question. I've got three kids Ellie. Does it say that on my file? Three beautiful kids. Jimmy who's ten and Franklin who's nine — two boys — and then my baby girl, Cristina, who was nine months old when they took her off me and who is now 20 months and being looked after by other people. She's been away from me for more than half her life. You can't even begin to imagine how terrible that is. Some other woman has helped her learn to walk, say her first words — not me — her mother. And my boys aren't little any more. They're old enough to know how it feels to be abandoned by their mother and two visits a week at a contact centre, playing with skanky local authority toys, doesn't help them believe me any when I tell them I'm doing everything I can to get them back. So Ellie, to answer your question, I'm barely coping at all."

I blushed, fiddling with the papers on file, trying to hide how sorry I felt for this family and failing, trying to think of some polite, subtle way of getting to the question Emma wanted answered and failing at that too.

"Does the drinking help you cope?"

Carol's teeth were still gritted. "What do you mean 'the drinking'? You make me sound like I got a drink problem or something. I haven't got enough money to have a drink problem sweetie. Maybe I can stretch to a half bottle of vodka of a weekend if I'm a bit flush, more often a can of cider of a night time. My kids weren't taken off me because I had a drink problem.

Do you want to know why my kids were taken off me Ellie?"

I said nothing, just kept looking straight at her, adopting what I hoped would look like an expression of professional objectivity.

"I'll tell you why. Because I'm poor, that's why. So my kids had nits? All kids get nits. So I only had cereal and milk in the house? So what? I was due a benefit cheque the next day. Until then the kids had to make do with cornflakes. Is that so awful? Just for one poxy night? They get free school dinners and now that Jamie Oliver's got his way my boys eat a cooked dinner at lunchtime. One night of cornflakes wasn't going to kill them."

"I don't suppose it would, no. But the thing is social services say that you seemed drunk when they visited and smelled strongly of alcohol. I'm just trying to establish why that might be."

"Why that might be?" She was staring at me now, clenching her fists so that the tendons in her skinny little arms and her neck were flexed and prominent, and her head wobbled aggressively as she repeated my words, mimicking me. "Well it could just be because there wasn't enough of them cornflakes to go round. So I was going to go hungry that night. Again. So I drank a couple of cans of Tennants' Extra that my old man had left knocking around and they hit me for six because I hadn't had anything to eat all day. Do you really think I would buy booze over food or nappies? Do you?"

I had known Carol Matthews for all of about fifteen minutes and I had absolutely no basis for what I thought but sitting there, staring her straight in the eye, I believed without the slightest doubt that she would do no such thing.

It was Carol who looked away first, glancing down at her hands. I noticed that her nails were bitten right down and that she had picked the skin around them so badly that it was cracked and bleeding.

"Listen darling," she said more quietly now, "I promise you I haven't got a drink problem. What I've got is a money problem and they can't take my kids away just for being poor. It's not fair."

She's right, I thought, that isn't fair.

I flicked through the file some more, trying to think of something legal-sounding to say. I could think of nothing other than what was on my mind.

"You must miss them something awful?"

"Every second of every day, and all through the night too, because I can't sleep without my kids under the same roof as me." This was the point at which Carol Matthews started to cry and also thankfully the point at which Emma turned up. She didn't say much — handed Carol a box of tissues and motioned at me to pass the file over to her.

"Ok Carol. We haven't got much time left. Let's go through the paediatrician's report and the psychiatrist's report as quickly as we can."

I got up to leave, but Emma shook her head, waving at me to sit back down.

"You may as well stay now you're here Ellie. We've got a trial date in less than two months and I could really do with the help."

CHAPTER
NINETEEN

That was the sum total of my induction into care proceedings. I felt like a dog that had been thrown in the lake to see if it could swim. I did but not particularly well. I reported back to Emma the conversation I had had with Carol about her drinking.

"For what it's worth I don't think Carol has any more of a drink problem than you or me. I mean I'm sure she likes a drink — most people do — but I don't think she abuses alcohol and I don't think she spends all her money on it."

"Good. Thanks for that Ellie. That's really helpful. It makes me feel a lot more confident that working my arse off to keep this family together is not going to be a monumental waste of all our times."

I did a lot of work on Carol's case after that. Not real legal work but a lot of photocopying, preparing bundles of papers for the court, ringing round psychiatrists and doctors to book them to attend the trial — stuff that was hardly taxing but time-consuming and that needed to be done to prepare for the case. This was the sort of stuff that Emma would otherwise have to do herself and the more I showed myself capable of following the instructions she gave me each morning, the more she gave me.

I also did a lot of talking with Carol. After that first meeting, she was no longer as prickly with me. I seemed to have gained her trust by asking her whether she missed her kids.

"You know how I feel don't you Ellie," she would say when she called in at the office which was almost daily because Carol didn't have a telephone, or at least not one that hadn't been cut off, and all communication with her was by letter or face to face.

I didn't really understand how she felt. As she'd pointed out when we first met I didn't have kids. But I thought about how distraught Tony and Beth would be if their kids were taken away from them and that gave me some inkling at least of what Carol was going through.

Childcare proceedings are nothing like the court stuff you see on telly. There isn't a jury for a start or kooky little attorneys who prepare by singing along to Barry White in the toilet beforehand. Childcare proceedings are all about reports — acres and acres of paper from social workers, guardians, doctors. That amount of paper is not generated overnight. Carol's children had already been in care for almost a year but Emma told me that a separation of that length was not at all unusual as it takes months to complete all the assessments and for a court to then decide whether a child should stay in care long-term or be returned to their family. During that time Carol had only been allowed to see her children for two afternoons a week at

196

a custody centre at which her interaction with her children and their response to her was also monitored.

There was a reason for that. Despite what she had told me about not having a drink problem, this was not the first time that social services had got involved with Carol's family. They had paid her a visit on two previous occasions, both as a result of reports of domestic violence. Carol's husband was a parttime bar man but a full-time drugs dealer and violent with it. Her neighbours had called the police one night when they saw Carol outside in the street, heavily pregnant and dressed only in her nightie, weeping loudly and bleeding from her nose. They called again one afternoon a few months later when Carol had locked herself, the boys and her newborn baby in her husband's car and he was banging on the roof, shouting at her to get out or he would kill her.

Carol dismissed any concerns we raised with her about this.

"He's not a problem for us anymore. He's back inside again and he'll serve a three year stretch minimum. He only stayed out of prison long enough this time to give me Cristina and a couple of black eyes along the way. He's out of our lives for good and I won't be taking him back when he gets out. I learned my lesson last time. The hard way. Honest."

Her husband might not have been a problem for Carol any more but he was still a significant problem for her sons. The psychiatrist reported that both boys were still traumatised by what they had witnessed in the periods of time their father was out of jail and this manifested itself in a number of ways, including bullying at school, bed-wetting and, in the case of the younger boy, starting to suck his thumb again. The social workers were not as certain as Carol that she would not allow her husband to move back in when he was released because in the past she had always taken him back, despite the violence. Also the boys had not bonded with their younger sister and the psychiatrists attributed this to the fact that they were angry with their mother for taking their father back and even angrier with Cristina as the product of that reunion. The fact that the boys were with one foster family and Cristina with another had not helped matters, although all three children were reported to be doing well in care.

Emma was not optimistic about Carol's chances. Not optimistic at all.

"I think there's a real risk she might lose," she explained. "It's the needs of the children that are most important in these cases, not what the parent needs. Although it's pretty obvious that the best option for Carol is to get her kids back, it's nowhere near as clear that it's the best option for them."

"Which way do you think it will go El?" Carol asked me almost every day. "In your experience like?"

I had very little experience but knew enough to say: "We'll just have to wait and see Carol."

When I worked for law firms in the City there was always some social event or other going on after work. A lot of the time it was organised and paid for by the firm. Part of the price of keeping your staff happy and motivated to continue working incredibly long hours appeared to be taking them out on a regular basis, putting one of the partners' credit cards behind the bar and getting them all drunk. It didn't come as a surprise that there was nothing like that at Collins & Co.

"We have a staff meeting once every quarter," Corinna informed me, "and there's one coming up in a couple of weeks so put it in your diary as you will be expected to attend. Afterwards we usually go down the pub for one drink. Just one mind and we all pay for our own because there's no point getting into rounds. It's not that we're not a sociable crowd but all of us here have got lives to get home to."

I couldn't help noticing Corinna's extra emphasis on the word "us". Perhaps I was paranoid but I had a very strong feeling that as far as Corinna was concerned I was never going to be included within the definition of "us".

It was in the pub after my inaugural staff meeting that Emma suggested I should consider taking my career in the law a step further.

"You'd be a fab solicitor Ellie. You're loads more organised than me and your help on the Matthews' case has been invaluable. I don't know how I would have managed to do it all myself. You really should think about it."

I didn't tell her that she was the second person to suggest I qualify as a lawyer but that I had no intention of staying at Collins & Co long term.

"Thanks Emma. That's really kind of you and I'm flattered but I couldn't afford to go back to studying."

"You don't have to. Not full-time at least. You could do the exams part-time or on day release and carry on working. Mr Collins would go for that — he thinks you walk on water."

She was being so kind and encouraging. Guilt swept through me for having taken this job, knowing that I planned to go off travelling again just as soon as I could afford to.

"I'm not certain I'm cut out to do more exams but it's something to think about. Thanks for the suggestion."

After my first reluctant stint at helping Gina with her allotment, I grew to quite enjoy the work, which was just as well as otherwise I would not have seen much of her that summer. She meant it when she said she was going to transform her precious allotment but it was a long, slow process.

The first job was to get gorgeous Gabriel round with his rotovator to get rid of the brambles. This took an entire weekend and while Gabriel worked, Gina had long discussions with him about what she should plant.

"I've heard potatoes are the best because they break up the soil. What do you think Gabriel?"

"Actually, that's a bit of a myth. It's not the potatoes that break up the soil but turning it over to get it ready for planting them in the first place, but anyway it's way too late in the season to plant potatoes," Gabriel advised. "If you get cracking you've got just enough time to sow carrots and runner beans although you'll need to get some manure in if you want a decent crop. Then you could try beetroot, turnips and salad onions in the next few weeks. Even a bit of spinach and some salad leaves for the winter."

Gina took his advice. When the briars had all been removed she dug in bags and bags of manure she got from Trevor's old friend the rag and bone man, got herself her very own set of bamboo canes and set about planting her beans and carrots.

Once we had finished sanding down the shed, she painted the outside midnight blue and the inside bright white. She replaced the broken glass windows with new reinforced glass. There was enough room for a couple of old Lloyd Loom chairs which she also painted white and kitted out with cheap but cheerful cushions from Ikea. She fitted out her shed with all her garden implements, stacked the shelves with seeds and fertiliser and put in an old radio and kettle. She even had a supply of booze in there and some glasses.

"I'm going to work on my allotment every morning and then listen to Radio 4 and finish off my education while I get gently pissed on sherry," she said. In fact, she mostly drank tea but she did at least know the sherry was there if she fancied some.

Paul helped out with the allotment a lot. He seemed to enjoy it even more than Gina, enthusiastically double-digging in manure. He even bought Gina a special box for her compost and printed off pages and pages from the internet about how to achieve a fast hot-rot. He spent most of his weekends there, even

201

working on the allotment in the evenings after Gina had left to get ready for work.

One Friday evening after a long digging session the two of us were sat outside the shed drinking lager and watching Paul, who had insisted on working on a bit longer. I liked digging, driving my sharp, shiny, spade deep into the soil, slicing cleanly through the earth like teeth through chocolate cheesecake. I liked too the way my body felt after digging. It was tiring and my muscles ached but when I looked out at the allotment I could see the rich, dark soil we had turned over, free of weeds and ready for planting. It was a good feeling, full of achievement, and beer tasted wonderful afterwards, cold and strong.

Gina was picking dirt from under her finger nails and smiling to herself as she watched Paul dig.

"I know I said I wouldn't ask, but you two seem to be getting closer and closer."

"Do you know what Ellie?" Gina said "I'm really enjoying spending time with Paul. I haven't looked at another man all summer."

My mouth dropped. Paul was a handsome man but a quiet one and he didn't have the jaw-dropping good looks of some of Gina's other conquests.

"Don't pretend to be all surprised," she said. "You must have known something was going on when I stopped flirting with Gabriel. I know Paul's not, well, dazzling — but he makes me feel comfortable with myself, like I don't need to prove anything. He knows me, all the different sorts of woman I am: the singer, the gardener, the wanton woman — he even knows about the long list of men I've slept with — and he still likes me and wants to hang out with me and have lots of sex with me. And I'm really enjoying it. I can thoroughly recommend having sex with men who are already your friends."

I looked over again at Paul with renewed interest. He was still working hard as the sunlight faded and lengthened around him, wiping his hands on the seat of his trousers to get a better grip on his spade.

"Crikey. That's not the way I saw things panning out all those years ago when you dumped him and went off with the bloke from the 24-hour garage."

"Me neither. I thought we were just having a bit of rebound sex to take the sharp edges of both our lives. We've done that plenty of times in the past and then after a while one or other of us has drifted on to someone else and we've gone back to being just mates again until the next time. But this time I don't want to move on to someone else just yet — I'd like me and Paul to hang out together for longer."

"Wow." I was stunned. "Have you told him?"

"Nah — I'll let him work it out for himself." She took another swig of her lager, smiling to herself as she watched Paul work from the window of the shed. "Talking of flirting with Gabriel, I think you should have a pop at him. It would do you good — you're in need of some fresh lips."

"You think?"

"Definitely! He's gorgeous. And he asks after you every time I see him."

"Won't you mind?"

"Nope, not a bit." She nodded her head in Paul's direction. "I'm good right now thanks." She motioned to him to come over and join us, miming beer-drinking gestures at him.

"Give me a beer and give it to me now," he said as he approached us. "I've done real manual labour and I've earned it."

Gina handed him a bottle. He popped the top and drank it down in one, wiping the back of his hand across his mouth.

"Didn't even touch the sides. Just look at my hands," he said, showing us his muddy blisters. "Before I became a real man and learned how to dig dirt I used to have the soft hands of a banker."

"A what?" Gina asked.

"A banker, Gina. Starts with a B. Although come to think of it —"

He caught Gina's eye, grinned at her, reached for another beer. The three of us sat for a while longer, drinking lager and watching the sun set, until I realised that there was a degree of sexual tension around the shed which did not include me and left them to it.

CHAPTER
TWENTY

The next morning Gina rang me

"You didn't have to slope off you know. We weren't going to have sex in the shed or anything!"

"Really?"

"Well not while you were there anyway."

"And after I'd gone?"

"You know me. A girl's got to get it while she's got the chance."

"Which is precisely the reason I left."

"In that case, thanks. Listen — it's time you, me and Beth had a girls' night out. It's been ages since we've done that. I'm not working this Friday so how about it?"

"Ok, sounds fun."

As the three of us walked into one of Clapham High Street's trendy wine bars that Friday and into the babble and flutter of an excited crowd out on the pull, I was delighted to feel again a tight little bubble of excitement just under my breastbone,

We found ourselves a table and ordered a bottle of white wine. Just half a glass in, Beth lifted her leg and showed us her calves.

"I had my legs waxed for the first time today," she said proudly. "Have a look at that. Smooth as a baby's bottom and no shaving for at least three weeks."

Gina peered closely at Beth's legs.

"Not quite a baby's bottom. I can see some in-growing hairs right there."

"Don't look that closely. The girls on the beauty course have only just started doing waxing. They need a bit more practice yet. It's still a darn sight better than attacking them with one of Tony's old razors every few months."

"So now you've got legs like a baby's bottom are you going to be getting yourself a ra-ra skirt and showing them off more?" I asked.

"You must be joking. Someone would have to invent a way of waxing the cellulite off my thighs before that day comes. Nah — it'll just be nice for Tony to get into bed with someone whose legs aren't hairier than his for a change."

"How are you getting on with the course? You enjoying it still?"

"I love it. Absolutely love it. It's great to do something that's just for me. Where no-one sees me as Tony's wife or the mother of two kids. Just another woman training to be an aromatherapist. I love everything about it — having a laugh with the other girls, learning all about essential oils and how to blend them. Got to say the best bit of all is dropping the kids off at the nursery. That bit is particularly good."

"Doesn't having to rub the skin of strangers get on your nerves?" Gina wrinkled her nose.

"Not at all. I really enjoy it."

"What — even all that dolphin plinkety-plonk music?"

"Even that. I find it restful. And I like the way everyone getting a treatment relaxes so much and feels better afterwards. People are always glad to see me. It's really rewarding."

"God!" said Gina, topping up our glasses and ordering another bottle simultaneously. "I wouldn't have the patience. I would be looking at the clock all the time, waiting for it to be over."

"The time goes really quickly, honestly. You go into a bit of a trance and before you know it it's over. And it must use up loads of calories because I'm losing a bit of weight. Mind you, people do make funny faces when they're getting a massage."

"What do you mean?" I asked.

"Well you know the face that people do when they're sunbathing? The one where people turn their faces up towards the sun and stick their chins out and do a little tiny smile?"

Gina and I looked at each other.

"Sort of."

"Well they do that face when they're getting a massage too. It's kind of weird at first and of course you don't see it all the time because a lot of the time they're lying on their fronts but when you ask them to turn over, they're doing that sunbathing face."

Gina laughed.

"Rather you than me babe. I'm just glad you're getting so much out of it. You like aromatherapy and

207

Ellie likes typing depressing reports all day. Weird but whatever floats your boats is just fine by me."

Beth turned to me. "You still sticking it out at that law firm then Ellie? Not got enough in your war chest yet to pack it all in and buy yourself another round-the-world ticket?"

"Not quite enough yet, no. So I'll be staying around. For the time being at least. Anyway, it's nice being able to see you guys a lot, hang out again with Mum and Trevor. It feels like, well it feels like —"

Beth finished my sentence for me. "It feels like home Ellie because that's what it is."

"Why didn't I think about living at home and getting a job round here before? I used to earn better money but spent most of it on rent and travel."

"You never thought about it before because you didn't want your mother and grandfather cramping your style past the age of 21 before." Gina said. "You must be slowing down in your old age. Anyway, isn't that other secretary driving you mad, the older one, Corinne or whatever her name is?"

"Corinna. A. It's got an A on the end. Very important that A. And yes she is getting on my nerves. I mean she's nice enough and she's been working at the firm for donkey's years which deserves some respect, but she just does not stop talking."

"What does she talk about?"

"Everything really, but mostly celebrities. You know she buys one of those chat magazines almost every day. *Hello, OK, Goodbye* — whatever they're called. I didn't even know there were enough of them around to

208

be able to get a new one that often. And then she talks at me all day, pointing out which celebrity had sweaty arm pits at the Oscars and which ones have had boob jobs. She could do a PhD in celebrity-watching if she didn't have to go for a fag break every ten minutes."

"You're exaggerating obviously," Gina sat back in her seat, took a long swig of her wine.

"Just a little bit. But she does go out for a fag a lot which means that while she's out the front smoking, I'm the one doing all the typing. She's even got her own special ashtray — a little golden thing with a lid she keeps on her desk — and she takes that outside with her when she goes for a cigarette and taps her ash in there so as not to make a mess on the pavement."

"Very responsible woman," Beth said. "Taps her ash into her ashtray, blows her smoke into the street and into the lungs of all the kids walking by. I love her already."

"That's not the half of it. She's got a gold toothpick round her neck on a chain although I've never actually seen her use it. And today she had on a black PVC skirt, very shiny, and an acrylic jumper with a butterfly motif, finished off by a huge black belt with a butterfly clasp. I had a headache at the end of the day just from looking at her."

Gina shook her head in mock horror.

"So wouldn't you prefer to go back to work in the City with all the high-powered, better dressed PAs reading the *Wall Street Journal?*"

"Nah. I enjoy this job actually, though it's a strange thing to say because it's one of the saddest jobs I've

209

ever done, not to mention a lot of hard work. But it feels good to be working for ordinary people with real life problems, not some big faceless company buying another big faceless company for zillions of pounds. I don't think I could do it long-term — it's way too stressful — but it's good for now."

"And Robert? How do you feel about Robert these days?" Gina asked.

"Um, trying not to feel anything at all, getting there bit by bit, day by day. Do you think we could change the subject now please?"

Gina swiftly turned her cross examination on to Beth. "And you and Tony? Everything ok with you two now?"

"Brilliant," Beth said. "Tony's very frisky nowadays. We've no problems there any more."

Gina made a face. "Frisky? Don't call him that. You make him sound like a West Highland white that needs a walk."

Beth grinned. "Well he's like a West Highland white with two dicks when I practise my massage on him."

"Enough!" Gina announced. "You're painting a picture with words that I really would prefer not to see. Come on then. Let's drink a toast to us lot being out together again on a Friday night."

We raised our glasses high, chinked them together enthusiastically.

"Right then!" Gina announced, "Now I've got you all here I can tell you that I'm thinking of asking Paul to move in with me."

Beth looked horrified. "What do you mean? Paul's got a lovely big house — massive — and you've just got a little flat. Why should he move in with you? Why don't *you* think about moving in with him instead?"

"Precisely because he's got a lovely big house which will rent out easily whereas my flat would not."

"Oh really, is that it?" Beth sounded cynical.

"That and the fact that I like my flat better. It's cleaner and better decorated and I know where I keep the sugar and the Super Glue. And if it doesn't work out I want him to be the one who has to move out not me."

I could see the wisdom in that statement. What I was worried about was Gina deciding after all those years of living alone to live with a man. Not just Paul. Any man. I could not imagine ...er accepting the sort of compromises she would need to accept if she and Paul were going to live with each other successfully.

"I can see from the look on your face that you don't think that's a good idea Ellie." Gina said haughtily.

"I'm not certain it is," I replied bravely. "I think you're going to find it difficult living with a man."

"What are you trying to say?" Gina was annoyed with me, her comment frosty.

"Just that you like things your way and being free to do them your way whenever you want to. When you live with a bloke you have to do things their way sometimes so that it's fair."

"How would you know? When did you ever live with a man?"

"I haven't Gina, as you know. But you've got annoyed in the past when boyfriends came to stay just for the weekend. If Paul moves in with you he'll be there all the time. You won't be able to kick him out whenever you feel like it."

Beth nodded in agreement. "It's true Gina. You do have to make all sorts of compromises when you live with a man. They're programmed differently from women."

"How hard can it be?! Millions of women do it every day."

"I'm just saying, that's all. When Tony and I first moved in together he would get out of the shower and drop his towel on the floor of the bathroom and leave it there in a smelly heap until the next time he took a shower. He never willingly changed the sheets, wanted to watch sport on the telly all the time and thought pizza was a balanced diet. You know, the first time I asked him to sort the dirty washing into loads for the machine — you know a dark load and a light load and so on — he sorted it into one load of his clothes and one load of mine."

"He's not like that any more though is he?"

"No, thank God. But it's taken years of nagging to get him to change even a little bit. Even now he still can't see dirt and he thinks toilets are self-cleaning. And from what I remember of living with Paul, I don't think he'll be any better than Tony."

"I can nag. I think I'd be pretty good at it."

"I'm sure you would be. The thing is; it's not much fun having to nag. It makes you feel like your bloke's mother and that's a killer blow for romance."

"You managed it. Why do you think I won't be able to?"

Beth hesitated before answering that question and then said calmly, "Because you and I are different people Gina. Very different. And Tony and I got married when we were really quite young and we hadn't lived alone for years before we tried living together and we weren't so set in our ways. It'll just be more difficult for you and Paul that's all."

"I disagree. I think we'll be just fine. I think you're just having a go at me because you don't want me and Paul to be together. Aren't I good enough for your brother or something?"

This was grossly unfair and Beth looked stunned at Gina's comment but she held it together. It was testament to her newfound confidence that she did, because the Beth of just a few months ago would have burst into tears at a hurtful comment like that.

"That's not it at all Gina and you know it. However, at the risk of pissing you off even further, and speaking as Paul's sister for once rather than your friend, I am worried that he'll rent out his house and come and live with you and then a few weeks later you'll get fed up with him like you usually do and chuck him out and he'll have nowhere to live."

"You just don't get it do you? I'm tired of my old life. I'm fed up of being the single girl about town living a mad, wild, dangerous life and providing entertaining stories for you lot. I *want* to grow up. I want to be in a proper relationship with a decent man and sit down for Sunday dinner with him and buy Tupperware and beach towels and all the other boring household items that couples own. Paul is the first bloke I have ever even contemplated living with. I want to live with him, be with him every day and every night. I love him, ok?"

Gina got up and flounced off to the toilet. Beth and I looked at each other in astonishment. Gina had never once admitted to being in love with any man.

"I knew she was keen on him but I didn't expect that," I said in wonder.

Beth shook her head. "Me neither. I wonder if she's told Paul?"

"Which bit? The bit about moving in or the bit about being in love with him? I doubt she's told him either. She'll expect him to work it out for himself again."

"Ellie, the last thing I want to do is piss Gina off. I'm a bit scared of her you know?"

"Me too, sometimes."

"But she and Paul mean so much to me and them being together again means a lot too and I would hate it if they went into this living-together thing without thinking it through. Paul's loved Gina forever. I think that's why he's never settled down. Gina was always there — popping back into his bed every now and again and making every other woman seem boring and less shiny when she did. If she loves him like she says she does that's a very precious thing and I would hate them to spoil it by moving in with each other too early."

We were both a bit surprised when Gina came back from the toilet just a few minutes later. When she flounced off like that, as she did quite often, she usually didn't come back at all.

"Right then you two. I had a think about this in the ladies. I know you're only warning me about stuff I need to know and I'm grateful for that — you both want the best for me and Paul and a lot of what you say makes sense, so I'm going to take your advice and leave things as they are for now just to show you two that this isn't just some silly whim. I'm sorry for what I said to you Beth — you're Paul's sister and it's only natural you should be worried about him."

Beth and I stared at her. For once we were both at a loss for words.

"So," Gina continued, "enough about men for now. Let's go to La Rueda shall we and eat tapas and flirt with the Spanish waiters?"

I looked over at Beth. "She's matured," I said, "but thankfully not too much. My turn to pay the bill — you two can pay in La Rueda — I'll settle up if you like and see you up there."

Beth and Gina gathered up their bags and clattered out of the door to walk the few hundred yards to La Rueda. It was while I was stood patiently at the bar, credit card in hand, that I spotted Carol sitting in the far corner of the bar with a man. She was wearing a little, low-cut top which clung tightly over her small breasts, a lot of make up, big hoop earrings. Her straggly blonde hair had been back-combed furiously and lacquered so that it stuck out over her head in big spikes like Kim Wilde's in the late eighties. I couldn't see her legs but I would have bet a week's wages that she was wearing a very short skirt. The man she was with must have been in his late forties, he was wearing a pinstriped suit, with a big, round, florid face. They were both absolutely wasted. It took a full five minutes of staring straight at her for her to spot me, another three before she staggered up from her seat to sway towards me.

"Don't you dare judge me Ellie," she slurred. "Don't you dare. It's five more days before I get to see my kids again and I'll be stone cold sober long before then."

"I thought you said you didn't drink," I said.

"No I never, lawyer lady. I said I didn't have a drink problem and I don't. Just cause I'm arseholed tonight doesn't mean I've got a drink problem, it just means that tonight I've managed to get that nice kind rich gent over there to buy me double vodkas and lime all night."

"You want to watch yourself Carol. He might be expecting something in return."

Carol laughed loudly at this, smacking her hand down on the side of the counter gleefully.

"Of course he's expecting something for it love. Do I look like I was born yesterday? Man like that doesn't buy drinks all night for someone like me for nothing. So I'll have to take a walk up a back alley with him after closing, let him feel me up, give him a hand job. I'm not going to care about that by the end of the night. I'm shit-faced already and so's he. I doubt he'll even be able to get it up so with any luck I may even get out of the hand job."

I looked up again at the man Carol was with. He looked ordinary enough. Bit fat. Bit sweaty. Very drunk. Not like an axe murderer or anything.

"Still, be careful Carol, you don't know what sort of a person he is. You've got a lot riding on the next couple of weeks. You don't want to ruin everything you've been working for."

Carol wasn't laughing now.

"That some kind of threat El? You going to rat on me, file a big report in triplicate about me getting drunk on someone else's money of a Friday night? Are you eh? I'll tell you something for nothing. If I had my kids at home I wouldn't need to be here right now getting off my face. I would be at home with them, watching telly, having chips from the chip shop and a can of pop. But if I'm shit-faced it doesn't hurt as much not being with them and tomorrow my head'll hurt so much I won't be able to think and then the next day it'll be just three days till I see them. Seventy-two hours. I'm not much of a one for maths me but I can do my 24-times table by now because I count the hours down till I'm with them again. So if you're going to tell tales Miss Taylor, you make sure you tell them at the same time just how much I miss my babies. Now, if you'll excuse me. I've got someone waiting for me."

And with this Carol made her way unsteadily back to her benefactor. I watched her as she dropped back into her seat and heard her greeting him in her best Peggy Mitchell voice, "Hello darling, did you miss me?"

She made a great show of embracing him enthusiastically before lifting her drink to her mouth, finishing it in one long swallow and banging the empty glass down on the table. She looked straight at me as she did this and made a tiny but very definite motion towards the door with her head. I knew what that meant. It meant get out of here right now.

CHAPTER
TWENTY-ONE

I asked Gabriel out. It was the first time I had ever done anything like that. In the past I had always waited for the man to make the first move but this was a strange time in my life. My heart had already been broken and I didn't fear rejection any more. I could not possibly be more hurt than I had been already and, in any event, I would be going off travelling again fairly soon. I had nothing to lose.

He said yes.

"That's great," I said. "Just one thing — do you like pickled onions?"

"I love them. Is that a problem?"

"No, not at all."

I took him to the pub for our first date. It was not the sort of place I would normally have chosen for a first date but it was a Friday and I like going to the pub on a Friday night. There were no staff in starched aprons here, no flowers or tea lights or olives in glass jars. Our pub is a big, run-down old place with grubby maroon upholstery and fag burns on the top of the toilet cisterns; and the only food items for sale are packets of crisps and pork scratchings.

Gabriel was standing at the bar when I arrived, sipping a pint of Guinness. He was wearing brown moleskin trousers which made his long legs look even longer and a plain black T shirt. His dark hair was cropped very short and I noticed he was greying slightly at the temples but that it suited him. It is an annoying fact of life that a bit of grey hair looks good on most men but that the same is not true for women. He turned and smiled at me as I approached the bar and I saw that one of his front teeth was chipped, and that his eyes were very brown and full of humour.

"What do you want to drink?"

"I'll have a white wine and soda," I said. "Actually soda that. I'll have a pint of Stella."

"Pint of Stella please," Gabriel said to the bar man. "Looks like the lady means business tonight. And can I have some change for the pool table please?"

It was early and the pub was still fairly quiet so we had the pool table to ourselves for a while. I beat him twice. He beat me three times. It was easy to chat as we played.

"So how did you get into gardening?" I asked him.

"I used to have a serious job in the City," he explained, "but I wanted a change and gardening was about as far away from broking as you could possibly get. Didn't know anything about it to begin with, so in the early days I did a lot of garden clearance, weeding, clearing garden waste; that sort of thing. That's how I got the rotovator. But now I'm pretty good at real gardening too. What about you? Gina said you used to work in the City too."

"I'd hardly call it working in the City. I only ever temped in big law firms. Now I'm working for a little law firm here in Clapham but only until I've got enough money together to go off and do some travelling."

"That's exciting. I never managed to do any travelling. I was working too hard for years and now I'm a sad old git who wouldn't want to leave his allotment. Where are you planning on going?"

"Not certain. South America maybe. I've been there before and it's amazing. Or maybe Asia. I've got some time to think about it anyway. It'll take me a few months to get enough money together."

"So you'll be staying in Clapham for a little while then?"

"For a little while, yes. Until the end of the summer at least."

I enjoyed talking to him. He was good company, relaxed and assured but not over confident and he asked questions, didn't talk too much about himself. As the pub began to fill up and we switched to playing winner stays on at pool Gabriel took a few games from the regulars, even one from Clive.

"Been giving you private tuition has she?" Clive asked, grinning at me as he set up the table for the next game.

"Not yet," Gabriel said, "but maybe we'll get to that eventually."

Clive regained his form in the second game and Gabriel handed over his pool cue good naturedly to the next player who had his money lined up on the table.

"I really enjoyed that. This is a great pub. A real local. And the Guinness is good."

"You must tell the landlord that," I said. "He's Irish and very proud of the state of his pipes."

"Much better to look after your Guinness than your carpets," agreed Gabriel, lifting up on the balls of his feet so that the carpet made a sticky squelching noise.

There was no doubt about it. Gabriel was attractive. He was fit from all the gardening and had lovely strong arms with just the right amount of biceps — not so much that he looked over-muscled like a body builder but still with plenty of definition — and his bum out-bummed even Tony's. Robert was attractive too of course — too attractive for my own good — but Robert's job was sedentary and he ate a lot of client lunches and whilst not fat exactly he was, well, a bit flabby. And pasty. Whereas Gabriel was tanned from working outdoors. And he had little wrinkles around his eyes that crinkled when he smiled. And I was pissed and it was time for me to go home.

"Would I be pushing my luck if I asked to come home with you?" Gabriel asked when I explained that I needed my bed.

"You've no chance mate," I said. "I'm living at home with my mother and grandfather. Teenage rules apply."

So we snogged for a short while outside the pub before he walked me home. It was a proper snog too — exciting and fumbling and he grabbed my arse as he kissed me hard. It was a long way off Robert's gentlemanly kisses. Not just fresh lips but hot too. I half expected him to try to cop a feel of my boobs. But he didn't.

When you really miss someone, their absence is a physical presence, an imprint on your mind and on your body. You carry that absence around with you at all times. That night with Gabriel, the burden of my loss began to lighten. I started to shake Robert off my back.

Gabriel called me early the next morning.

"Thanks for last night. I enjoyed it."

"Me too."

"I was wondering if you wanted to come over to my house for dinner tonight?"

I hesitated. I was pleased he wanted to see me again so soon. I wanted to see him again too but I wasn't certain if I was up to spending an evening alone with him in his house just yet.

Gabriel heard the hesitation in my voice. "It wouldn't be just the two of us. I've invited Gina and Paul too and there'll be another couple there, friends of mine."

I was relieved that it wouldn't be just the two of us but also sort of annoyed that he didn't want to be alone with me.

"That would be fun," I said, "especially if Gina and Paul are coming too. What time?"

"Seven thirty." He gave me his address. He lived just a few streets away from Tony and Beth. "See you then. And Ellie —"

"Yes?"

"I'm really looking forward to seeing you again."

I was grinning to myself as I put down the phone.

Before we went over to Gabriel's, Gina suggested that we stop off at Tony and Beth's and have a drink with them first. She was wearing a fifties-style, orange-flowered dress, sleeveless with a sweetheart neckline and wide shoulder straps. It fitted tightly at her narrow waist, flared out over her hips. She'd teamed her frock with high heeled white shoes and a matching white handbag. All she needed was a head scarf and she would have looked like a darker-skinned version of Doris Day but as always Gina could pull it off. I felt under-dressed next to her in my jeans and flip-flops and a little turquoise beaded top.

Will threw himself at Paul the moment we walked through the door and there followed an extended bout of wrestling on the living room carpet while Beth opened bottles of cava and dumped fancy crisps in glass bowls.

"Honestly," she said. "I swear that Will can smell testosterone before it even comes through the door. He gets all feisty the minute any man is in the vicinity. Cava everyone? Will! Paul! Enough of the wrestling."

Will reluctantly disentangled himself from Paul and plopped himself down on the settee. He was quiet for a few minutes while he caught his breath and then, having helped himself to crisps, he crossed one leg over the other and looked questioningly at Paul.

"Uncle Paul? Do you want to know something?" he asked through a mouthful of crisps.

"What's that then Will?"

"Mum and Janey haven't got a willy. Just a bum."

Gina laughed so hard that Cava came out through her nose.

I was quite tipsy by the time we left half an hour later. All four of them came out to wave us on to our next destination, Will leaning against Tony's legs, Beth holding Janey in her arms, the picture of domestic bliss. It gave me a good feeling to watch them; my friends, happy again, and I had helped make that so. I didn't even mind that Gina and Paul couldn't keep their hands off each other as we walked to Gabriel's — I even felt I'd had a part to play in that, like I was south London's very own cupid.

Gabriel lived in a small terraced house very similar to Tony and Beth's. There were dozens of terracotta pots in his paved front garden, brimming with flowers and shrubs, and his front door was painted fern green, a Farrow & Ball colour if ever I saw one.

"Welcome," Gabriel said as he opened the door. "Come in, great you could come."

We all squeezed in. The house smelled deliciously of warm bread and garlic. Gabriel dealt with the formalities of hanging our coats on the banisters at the bottom of his stairs, accepted our offerings of more Cava and red wine.

"Come through, come through. These are my friends, Dave and Charles. Dave and Charles, this is Paul and Gina and this is Ellie."

He didn't say it but there was a faint undertone of "ta-da" as he introduced me. Dave and Charles checked us all out. Gabriel went up in my estimation a little further for not having felt it necessary to explain to us that his friends were a gay couple before we arrived.

"Help yourselves to wine," Gabriel said. "I've just got to go check some stuff in the kitchen."

I followed Gabriel into the kitchen, watched him as he slid a dish into the oven. When he was done I sidled up behind him, put my arms around his waist and as he turned towards me gave him a hot heavy kiss.

"Crikey Moses," he said. "It's only a bolognaise."

"I didn't know anybody other than my grandfather actually said crikey Moses," I giggled. "Is there anything I can help you with?"

"Nope, it's all under control. Just get back into the living room and referee Dave and Charles — they had a massive row before getting here and the atmosphere in there is decidedly frosty. Here — dish these out while you're at it."

Gabriel handed me a ceramic platter of crostini — tiny bits of baguette topped variously with pesto or goat's cheese with cranberry sauce.

"You can cook," I teased, "and you garden too. Are you sure you're not of Dave and Charles' persuasion?"

Gabriel flicked me on the bum with a tea towel as I walked back to the living room, holding the platter high above my head in what I hoped was an approximation of waitress silver service.

Dave and Charles appeared to have more or less made up by the time I got into the living room and were telling Gina and Paul about their home in

Wandsworth and their DIY skills. They were big fans of all the home improvement programs on telly.

"I love that Kirsty Allsopp," Dave swooned. "She has the most divine taste in clothes and her shoes are just fab."

"It's Kevin McCloud for me every time," said Charles, "he's just so sensitive. So understanding."

I picked up my glass of wine and cheekily wandered off to have a little nose around Gabriel's home. In Tony and Beth's house the two downstairs living rooms had been knocked into one to give more family living space but Gabriel's house still had two small living rooms. The front room where we had been sitting had stripped floorboards, a marble fireplace and two ancient, caramel-brown leather sofas, battered and scuffed. The back room looked like it must be his office, equipped with a big desk and a computer and lots of bookcases. Gabriel seemed to have eclectic reading habits. I spotted books by Ian McEwan, Hanif Kureishi, Joseph Conrad, and Graham Greene but also Tony Parsons and Nick Hornby. No Dan Brown. Good. Even if he had read any he had the good sense not to advertise the fact. There were whole shelves of gardening books but also poetry books and cook books including ones by Jamie Oliver, Nigel Slater and the Moro cookbook.

Pinned above Gabriel's computer was a small scrap of paper, a transcript of a poem by John Betjeman.

I made hay while the sun shone
  My work sold
  Now if the harvest is over

226

And the world cold
Give me the bonus of laughter
As I lose hold

Gabriel came in behind me as I was reading it.

"I like that," I said, "that seems to me to be a good way of looking at life. Oh hang on. Maybe not. I thought it said the bonus of *lager* as I lose hold."

This time it was him who kissed me, grabbing my face in both his hands and pulling me towards him.

We had a wonderful evening. Dave and Charles were a great laugh, bitchy and acerbic and commentators on life, love and television. They had been among Gabriel's first customers when he started out.

"We knew he was straight," said Dave.

"But he was so cute we just couldn't resist him," chuckled Charles.

Gabriel served the spaghetti bolognaise in big, cream-coloured pasta bowls with a crisp, green salad and French bread and butter. For pudding there was Greek yoghurt, with a sprinkling of brown sugar, served with blueberries and chopped-up peaches. The food was good, the company was better and there was tons of wine. It was good to spend time with people who were not looking at their watches so that they could rush off somewhere else. Paul got rather sloshed and it was entertaining hearing him trying to explain to Dave and Charles how he and Gina had been together a very short while or a very long while, depending on how you calculated it.

"This is the thing Charles. Gina and I. We've got history."

Charles looked deep into Paul's eyes.

"Do tell," he said, taking a deep swig from an enormous glass of red wine.

"Well," said Paul, taking a full swig of his own drink in return. "I've loved Gina since I was seventeen years old. Well most of the time. I hated her for a bit after she dumped me the first time. Now I'm just waiting for her to realise that I'm the man she's supposed to be with but I think it's going to be a long, cold, lonely wait. I swear I wouldn't be in with a shout now if she didn't want me to help her with her bleeding allotment."

Dave and Charles looked at Gina in her fifties get up.

"You have an allotment?" Dave looked incredulous.

Charles was equally disbelieving. "You don't look like the kind of girl who doesn't shave and knits her own yoghurt."

"And you two don't look like the kind of guys to display stereotypical discriminatory assumptions towards allotment owners," Gina retorted, holding out her work-worn hands, and showing them the digging calluses on her palms as proof.

"And," she said demurely, "I assure you I most certainly do shave — I can show you if you like."

"Oh no thanks dear," Charles made a face like he'd just sucked a lemon. "Dave and I don't have much interest in female flesh."

"You don't say," Gabriel was smiling to himself as he opened another bottle of red. "We would never have guessed."

228

I sat at the table, listening to Paul regale Dave and Charles with his love for Gina, watching her cringe but enjoy it at the same time. I also watched Gabriel serving people food, keeping their glasses topped up. He hit just the right balance between looking after people in a laid-back fashion and enjoying himself at the same time. I liked his house — it was friendly and warm, stuffed with books and pictures. It was clean without being too tidy and there was a small tabby cat sleeping in the open airing cupboard outside his bathroom.

"What's your cat called?" I asked as I sat down after one of my excursions to the toilet.

"She's called Maud Gonne," Gabriel said.

"Wasn't she the woman Yeats fell in love with, the poet?" I asked.

"Bravo!" Charles clapped at me. "Go to the top of the class. You'll definitely have old Gabriel here eating out of your hand if you also know something about poetry."

I stayed with Gabriel that night after everyone else had gone, Dave and Charles blowing everyone theatrical kisses as they left, Gina and Paul sliding off shortly after, evidently keen to have some more old time/new time sex. I didn't really plan to stay but before I knew it I was clearing the kitchen with Gabriel and he was opening yet another bottle of red wine and putting Paul Weller on the CD player. I watched him as he tidied his kitchen, piling up dishes and throwing away leftover spaghetti. I was fearful of breaking the skin of the moment by hasty action but in the end I wrapped my arms around his waist, and waited as he put down the dishcloth.

"Want to make some hay?" I asked.

Having sex with someone for the first time is both wonderful and awful. There is the excitement of new intimacy but also the awkwardness of knees and elbows that don't yet know how to fit together, what goes where. You don't know what noises are acceptable to make, whether you will be able to fall asleep, how you will feel in the morning. With Gabriel, there was all the usual awkward bumping and grinding and nervous giggling but there was also moonlight slanting into his bedroom and the feel of limb against limb and lip against lip and most of all, and this was strange so early into a relationship, there was a feeling of ease and familiarity.

In the morning when I woke up, Gabriel was already up and about, banging around in his kitchen. Even though he was only downstairs I texted him.

I wrote, *Come make love with me but bring me tea first.*

He texted me straight back. *Want a bacon sandwich to go with that?*

I plumped up the pillows and settled back to wait for Gabriel. I had a feeling this was going to be another good day.

CHAPTER
TWENTY-TWO

Gina had invited all the guests from Gabriel's dinner party to come to hear her sing at a small blues club in Brixton the following Thursday by way of a thank you for dinner. Gabriel had said yes straight away which was, in itself, a pleasant change. Robert always had to spend at least half an hour consulting his Blackberry and his secretary before committing to any social arrangement and even then would make it clear that his acceptance was provisional only and subject to work requirements. I don't think he would have turned up to a blues club in Brixton anyway. He would have found some urgent completion meeting to go to instead.

I can walk to Brixton in about fifteen minutes from Trevor's house, taking a few short cuts through some backstreets. It's not perhaps the most picturesque of routes but it gets you there quickly. Brixton may not be that far away but it has a totally different feel from Clapham, a sort of raw energy with an edgy undercurrent. As soon as you get on the high street there is altogether a different mix of people — women in traditional dress talking patois and market stores selling plantain and yams. That's one of the things that is so special about London — just a few stops on the

Tube and you can be in a totally different place. It's a city where cultures rub along together, all leaving their own kind of mark, their own look and feel and flavour.

Gina doesn't play the club in Brixton very often, just sometimes when she feels like it because the owner plays mean harmonica and she likes to go listen to him every now and then. It's my kind of place — small and intimate with the lights always turned down low — and that night it was packed full of people drinking and talking as they waited for the music to start. Gabriel was the last of our crowd to turn up and as he walked across the room to join us at our table, wearing a faded pair of jeans and a white linen shirt, open at the neck which showed off his tan, I caught quite a few women checking him out. Seeing him stride along, unaware of how handsome he was and the admiring looks he was getting, I felt a small curl of pleasure in my stomach stretch and twist.

"Ooh, get you," Dave greeted him. "Don't you look all Julio Iglesias tonight. Fabulous tan dear."

"Strictly a gardener's tan," Gabriel grinned, opening the neck of his shirt wider to show that only the V of his neck was brown and that beneath his shirt the rest of his skin was pale.

Charles craned forward for a better look.

"Down boy," Dave said, pulling Charles back into his seat. "Do put it away Gabriel. You'll have him all hot under the collar."

I didn't know about Charles but when Gabriel put his hand on my shoulder and squeezed it ever so slowly

232

and gently I was certainly feeling hot but not just under my collar.

"I'm going to the bar," Gabriel announced. "Tequila slammers all round?"

"Yippee!" Dave clapped his hands in glee. "Gabriel's on a bad boys' night tonight. I love it when he gives me reason to be badly behaved."

Gabriel returned with an entire bottle of Tequila — cheaper than buying shots for everyone he claimed — some glasses, salt and lemons. He showed us with an ease that could only have come from long practice how to do Tequila slammers and we were all fairly well oiled by the time Gina came on to sing.

She was wearing the Farrah Fawcett wig that night and a long slinky sequinned silver dress and I looked over slyly to watch Gabriel realise that the glamorous blonde on stage was the same girl who had been sitting round his table the weekend before. He leaned over to me, not taking his eyes off the stage.

"Is that really Gina?" he whispered.

I nodded. "Sure is. Take a look at Paul if you don't believe me."

One look at Paul, his tongue practically hanging out, assured Gabriel that the wavy haired blonde was indeed Gina.

Gina opened with "The First Cut is the Deepest". I had heard her sing this song countless times but she seemed to sing it better than ever that night. It might have had something to do with the balmy night air or the number of slammers I had had or the press of Gabriel's thigh against mine, but hearing Gina sing made me feel like all my emotions were on the outside of my skin — the frustration of my time with Robert, the sadness at how it had ended and the exciting tingling of this new relationship. Gina sang the blues and I felt them rolling and swelling in my chest and tears pricking in the back of my eyes. I didn't want her set to end but when I heard the first few bars of "Knocking on Heaven's Door" I knew Gina was drawing to a close. She likes to finish off with her rendition of this song which is somewhere between the Bob Dylan version and the Guns and Roses one — not quite the blues but a song loaded with sentiment and emotion all the same. I watched her as she sang it, hardly ever taking her eyes from Paul who didn't take his eyes off her once.

Gina never does encores — she likes to leave her crowd wanting more — but it was fun for me to listen to the clapping and cheering and the demands for more and I was tremendously proud of my talented friend. As the clapping finally died out Gabriel grabbed me by the wrist, pulling me slightly to one side of the table.

"Have you ever done a slammer from someone else's body?" he asked.

I looked at him confused.

"I'll show you," and he proceeded to lick the inside of my forearm softly and gently for what seemed a very long time before sprinkling me with salt. Then he licked off the salt. The warm wetness of his tongue on the inside of my arm was so sexy that I could not speak, just watch him as he sucked his slice of lemon, threw back another slammer.

"Your turn now," he said, handing me the salt. I did as he had done, knowing how my tongue would feel against his forearm. The tequila made my head buzz and I could still taste the strength of the alcohol on both our tongues when Gabriel pulled me towards him and kissed me very long and very hard, one hand pressed into the small of my back as he held me close.

"Oh puhleeze," I heard Dave say from some far away planet a million miles away. "Get a room you two".

I spent a lot of that summer with Gabriel. He was a good cook, great in bed and not half bad at pool either. Being with him was a very different experience from being with Robert. He didn't talk nearly as much for a start and it was odd at first being with someone who answered his mobile phone when I rang, who wasn't permanently in a meeting or trying to meet an important deadline, who asked me if I fancied a drink after work and then actually turned up on time.

He was easy company, happy to fit in around whatever else was going on. Although neither of us said it out loud, we both seemed keen to keep our relationship light-hearted and fun. We didn't talk much about feelings or other deep stuff and we avoided the discussion that most couples have at some point or another about where our relationship was headed. This suited me — I didn't want to give too much of myself to somebody else while so much of me, despite my best efforts, still belonged to Robert, and as soon as I had enough money saved I planned to go travelling again anyway. Our arrangement seemed to suit Gabriel too. I thought of our relationship as my compensation for what I had gone though with Robert, a summer of love before I made my way off somewhere more exotic than Clapham. I knew it would come to a natural end when the time came to pack my bags but I intended to enjoy it until we got to that point.

Gabriel was very much his own person. He was used to living on his own and was competent at it. There was milk in his fridge and toilet paper in his bathroom and he put his own Hoover over from time to time and knew when bin day was. He could be a little remote sometimes — he was very comfortable in his own company, enjoyed time alone reading or listening to music and seemed to zone me out when he was doing other things. I knew he liked being with me but he didn't *need* to be with me and he certainly didn't feel the need Robert did to explain in minute detail his working day. He hardly ever told me what he had been up to and it became something of a standing joke between us when I asked him how his day had been for him to reply only,

"Good. I did gardening."

Our relationship was casual in the sense that neither of us tried to own the other. We didn't actually sit down and agree that we wouldn't see other people. Having that sort of conversation is the precursor to the discussion entitled "Our relationship — where is it going?" that we were both studiously avoiding. In any event we saw each other a lot. It wasn't so much that we had agreed our relationship was exclusive; it was more that we had insufficient time left over to see other people.

Gabriel was always happy to see me but equally happy to be on his own. I was glad about all of that but I did wonder sometimes if he would even notice if I wasn't around or whether he would just be glad of the opportunity to spend some time by himself at home and catch up on his reading.

One Sunday night when he was lying on the sofa wading through the business sections of the newspapers and I was sitting on the floor flicking through the magazine supplements I asked him straight out.

"Tell me. If I wasn't here right now would you be bothered or would you be equally happy just reading the paper all night?"

He didn't even bother to look up from his paper.

"Are you kidding? When I've finished the paper I'm going to take you upstairs and shag you stupid. And then I'm going to hold you till you do that funny little jerk thing you do when you fall asleep. You're damn right I'd be bothered if you weren't here."

And he carried on reading his paper.

A major difference between Gabriel and Robert was how low maintenance Gabriel was. He could shower, pull on a pair of jeans and a T shirt and look knee-tremblingly handsome in 20 minutes flat. He smelled of soap and sometimes at the end of a long working day a little of B.O. but in a good way, like the first yeasty sniff when you pop open the top on a bottle of French lager. Robert was, well, if I'm truthful, a bit anal about his personal hygiene and clothes. His shirts had to be starched, his shoes had to be polished, he had his haircut every three weeks and he was forever fussing with his nails. And shopping! Robert liked shopping more than most women I know put together. The fact that he looked so good in his City suits was no accident — he spent a lot of time putting that look together — and all his clothes had the name tags of other men on them — Paul Smith, Oswald Boateng, Hugo Boss and Ralph Lauren.

I did not share my observations about these differences with Gabriel. I don't think I would have wanted to anyway but one of the few, semi-serious things that Gabriel did tell me when we started dating was that he didn't kiss and tell.

"I don't mean to be rude but other women I may have slept with are really none of your business Ellie. There have been other women — I'm 35 and it's not like I've never been kissed — but all you need to know is that I'm not gay, I'm not married and I've no kids."

"That you're aware of."

"Believe me Ellie. I've no children anywhere. I can assure you of that."

I was relieved that Gabriel didn't want to talk about our pasts. I certainly didn't want to have to tell him about Robert. I preferred being the person he thought I was — a happy-go-lucky type, a traveller home for a short while, a girl whose heart was whole and healthy and who would soon be on her way again to another far-flung corner of the world. I didn't want Gabriel to know about the monumental fuck up I'd made with

Robert and I didn't want him to judge me for having got involved with a married man.

This didn't stop me wondering sometimes about Gabriel's past and his former girlfriends — had there perhaps been some Mexican beauty, hot blooded and fiery who had taught him to be an expert at Tequila slammers and Tequila kisses or a French fancy who had taught him how to cook and bought him those lovely pasta bowls? Or perhaps there had just been other south London girls like me. Maybe a lot of south London girls like me.

There were certainly no clues to the identity of former female visitors in Gabriel's house, which was all very masculine. The long, narrow kitchen was fitted with ultra modern units, with a stainless steel work surface and a black slate floor, and he had a shower so powerful it could wobble cellulite but there was nothing girly — no cushions, no vases, no framed photographs. Not even a tampon or a lipstick hidden away in the bathroom cabinet. I knew because I'd checked.

One of the downsides of living at home was that Gabriel ended up meeting my family much sooner than I would have liked. My mother and Trevor are not the type to allow callers to wait around on the doorstep. Just about anyone who appears at our front door gets invited in and Gabriel was no exception.

I was anxious the first time this happened, worried perhaps one of them would mention Robert, say how glad they were I had met someone new, someone who bothered to come in and say hello. I should not have worried. They were the soul of discretion.

"You must be Gabriel," Trevor said the first time he opened the door to him. "Come on in. Have you got time for a cup of tea before you and Ellie go out? She tells me you're a landscape gardener. I'm a gardener myself. Only amateur of course."

After that, Trevor took Gabriel for a tour round his garden every time he came round.

I would watch them as they walked about, inspecting Trevor's sweet peas or his beloved strawberry plants, sticking their fingers into the soil or bending down to crumble it between their fingers.

"Come and have a look at this," Gabriel would say, "I've always been one for nuking slugs with pellets but your grandfather sets traps for them with beer and gets them right royally drunk before drowning them. A much nicer way to go and organic too. It's like a little pub just for slugs, Sluggy O'Murphy's."

All I did was roll my eyes at them both from the safety of my bench. I heard more than enough of this sort of talk whenever Gabriel and I got together for a drink with Gina and Paul.

Teresa was particularly taken with Gabriel, which was surprising because Teresa took a long time to warm to people and her natural inclination was to distrust people for a minimum of a year.

"It must be because Gabriel is so good looking," my mother explained. "And because he always kisses her when he sees her."

When I told Gabriel this he blushed slightly.

"Ah — there's a bit more to it than that."

"What do you mean?"

240

"Well you know Teresa is quite small?"

"Yes"

"And I'm quite tall?"

"Well yes — where exactly are you going with this Gabriel?"

"Thing is, the first few times I kissed Teresa I put my hand round her waist but I misjudged the height thing."

"Get on with it Gabriel."

"I misjudged the height thing and I put my hand on her boob instead of her waist. I'm sorry — I didn't mean to — it's just that her boobs are a bit, well, low lying."

I laughed my head off at that. All these years of thinking that Teresa was an old sourpuss who fancied my mum when in fact all it took to get on her good side was for a nice-looking bloke to feel her up a bit.

Mum, Teresa, Beth and Tony — they all approved of Gabriel. He didn't have the kind of flashy charisma that Robert had, he didn't command attention, but he did make everybody who spent time with him feel comfortable, most of all me. I wondered sometimes what Gabriel's family was like and if he was as easy going with them as he was with my family. His parents and sisters lived in Suffolk and he went there to visit them from time to time, but he never invited me to come with him and I never suggested he should. People who were only having a summer of love didn't normally get introduced to the parents and one thing's for certain; if I hadn't been living at home I would not have taken Gabriel to meet mum or Trevor either.

CHAPTER
TWENTY-THREE

As the summer wore on I thought of Robert less and less. Even though I had only moved south of the river I felt like I had moved to another city altogether — I didn't go into town, didn't go into the City. I lived and worked in Clapham, near my friends, near Gabriel. My whole life was contained in less than half a square mile and that suited me just fine.

It was surprising therefore that one Saturday my mother managed to persuade me to go on a shopping trip with her to Peter Jones in Sloane Square. She needed to buy an outfit for a wedding she was going to with Teresa and nothing else would do except Peter Jones. I felt like I was on holiday as we strolled down the King's Road, had coffee at Starbucks and looked in all the shop windows as we walked on by. The King's Road is in a different world altogether to Clapham. Pretty people with money spend time on the King's Road — they pop into Heals to buy their furniture, into Bluebird for flowers and fresh bread, into Oriel for a cup of coffee when they have finished shopping. Life there is beautiful and rich and always pleasant. It is the kind of life we would all like to live if only we all had the benefit of a private income.

My mother loves Peter Jones. She always says there is nothing a person needs that can't be bought at Peter Jones. And she is right. You can buy widescreen TVs there and three piece suites but you can also get needles and thread, hooks and eyes and things with which to stuff cushions or clean leather.

It was in Peter Jones that we bumped into Robert and Ann.

Whump. In a split second I took in the family scene. Robert, handsome as ever, jiggling the pram back and forth, a tiny pair of arms flailing around inside, Ann next to him, rummaging for something in an enormous nappy bag, her smooth, straight hair falling around her face. My first, rather shallow, thought was how did I look? I was wearing jeans which Robert hated and I no longer straightened my hair the way Robert liked me to and it was back to being curly and wild again. At about the same time as I was answering my own question in my head and telling myself that it didn't matter a jot what I looked like, I noticed that Robert and my mother were looking at each other and I realised with a sinking feeling that I had never actually got round to telling her about Robert being married and why our relationship had ended.

I looked at her pleadingly, begging her with my eyes not to say anything, to pretend that she had not seen them. She got something of my message but that did not stop her marching over to Robert.

"Robert, how lovely to see you again. Is this your baby? Isn't he beautiful?"

I looked into the pram. It was blatantly not true that the baby was beautiful — it was tiny and wrinkled and had a yellowish tinge.

Even Robert was not a sufficiently smooth operator to get through this little incident without blushing. I was gratified that he looked so uncomfortable.

"Hello Sarah, Ellie," he nodded in my direction. "Ann, this is Ellie and her mother Sarah. Ellie used to temp at the firm."

For a split second I thought of saying something, of telling Ann what I had urged Robert not to tell her before — that yes there had been someone when he'd tried to leave her and that that someone was me. And then I looked at Ann who was victoriously pulling a white muslin square from the nappy bag and she smiled at me. She had a nice smile — open and welcoming — and she was a very pretty woman even though she was tired and pale.

"How nice to meet you both," she said. "This is our son Tobias. He shocked us both by arriving five weeks earlier than expected and he's been making his presence known ever since."

She looked down at her scrap of a baby, and wiped his face gently with the muslin smiling at him proudly. I caught Robert looking at me anxiously. I could tell he was willing me not to make a scene, which I could have done. Could have done so very easily, particularly as, standing next to Ann, I recognised her perfume, the same unmistakeable lime blossom Jo Malone cologne that Robert had liked me to wear.

Instead I put my hand in the pram and Tobias caught hold of my finger, gripped it tightly; trustingly. And at that moment I knew there was nothing I might want to say that was worth causing hurt to this little boy.

"He's lovely," I said. "Really lovely. Congratulations to you both. I'm glad he arrived safely. We'd better be off now — so little time, so much shopping to do, you know how it is. Bye now."

I put a hand under my mother's elbow and steered her firmly away.

"We are going for a coffee right now my girl, and you are going to explain what exactly all that was about," she hissed at me through gritted teeth.

"Fine, but not in here ok? I don't want to see them again if possible."

And so I had to tell the whole story again. I was surprised to find that it no longer hurt to go over old ground. In fact the thing that hurt the most was my pride at being so naïve. When I got to the bit about the cheque, my mother's mouth dropped open.

"That's an awful lot of money. What have you done with it?"

"Nothing. I'm not certain I want to accept his money."

"Cash it!" my mother ordered. "Go on! Cash it. Seems to me like you earned it many times over. I was never comfortable about your relationship with that man — you became someone else the whole time you were with him. Take his money."

"You know what Mum? I've just realised today that I should be grateful to Robert. If it hadn't been for him I wouldn't have come back home to live, would probably never have spent this much time with you and Trevor again. And I'm really glad I've had this opportunity: I'd forgotten how much I like hanging around with the two of you."

My mum smiled gently. "And don't let's forget meeting Gabriel."

"And there's him too of course."

So I dug out the cheque and on Monday, during my lunch hour, for once I did as my mother had told me and went to the bank. I filled in the payment slip and handed it and the cheque to the cashier in the bank and was pleased that all I felt as she stamped them both with a flourish was a little bit better off.

Later that day I sent an email to Robert — I could have phoned him I suppose. I had proved in Peter Jones that I was long past the point of bursting into tears if I heard his voice, but I really didn't want to talk to him again in person. The email I sent said:

Robert,

It was actually quite nice to see you and your family the other day and I really hope that things are working out for the three of you. After a horrible start this summer has turned out to be a really good one and even if I haven't quite forgiven you for what happened I've forgiven myself and that's a good start.

You will have noticed that I did not cash the cheque you gave me for ages. That's because I didn't know if I wanted to take the money or not

— didn't know if accepting it made me feel cheap. Anyway I've now decided to cash it because I've realised I'm far from cheap.

I hope you have the kind of life that you deserve. Mine is much happier now than it was a few months back.

Regards

Ellie

Surprisingly I got an answer back almost straight away.

Ellie

I wish I could say it was nice to see you too. When I realised it was you and your mother, my heart was in my throat, thinking you might say something to Ann. Thank you for not doing that. You are a much better person than I will ever be and you had nothing to forgive yourself for.

You earned that cheque. I had a good billing year last year and a big bonus and a great deal of that was due to you. I hope you do something you enjoy with it. I'd like to think you'll spend it travelling to yet another country I'll never see.

I know you don't believe me but I really did love you. I hope I don't get the kind of life that I deserve but that you do get the life you deserve.

Robert

I showed the letter to Gina.

"Sounds like he's saying you earned that money for services rendered in the bedroom."

"That's not what he's saying at all. He's saying that I helped him to bill a lot."

"How exactly did you help him do that then?" she teased. "By lying on your back and alleviating his stress?"

"Well if that's how I did it Robert owes me much more than £10,000."

And I winked at Gina who just laughed.

I didn't say anything at work after my encounter with Carol in the wine bar. I thought about it. I thought about it for a long time. Part of me felt I should definitely report back what I had witnessed because I had been so very certain that Carol didn't have a drink problem and her behaviour that evening might have had a bearing on that. But another part of me, a bigger part, was still certain that Carol did not have a drink problem — she was just out getting drunk of a Friday night that's all, which was the exact same thing I had done after I'd left the bar and caught up with Gina and Beth at La Rueda and I certainly didn't consider that I had a drink problem. And was the way she was funding her evening that different to me living in a rent-free flat and cashing Robert's cheque? Not really, I reasoned, not really at all. And did she deserve to be judged on the way she acted when she didn't have her kids to look after? I woke up at 4a.m. lots of mornings trying to decide what to do and then at some point, without me realising it, the decision had already been made. I hadn't said anything to Emma at the time and then after a while it became too late to say anything anyway.

Carol and I never talked about that evening or indeed her drinking ever again. She was very nervous at her first few meetings with Emma afterwards but when it became apparent that I hadn't said anything, and wasn't going to either, she relaxed and we all concentrated our efforts on preparing for the final hearing of her case. I wonder sometimes if I had said anything whether it would have made a difference to the court's decision but I comfort myself that it wouldn't have. Really it wouldn't. Because what the court decided was that Jimmy and Franklin should be returned to their mother but that Cristina should remain in foster care for the time being. They said they would keep the situation under review and that Carol should have regular contact with her daughter, but the conclusion of all the reports was that although Carol was capable of taking adequate care of her boys, she had not been giving her youngest child the care and attention that a baby needed and had dumped a lot of the daily responsibility for looking after Cristina on her sons. This had only added to the boys' resentment of their sister and all things considered it was not in the children's best interests for all three of them to be with Carol. What the court decided was that Carol couldn't have her baby girl back.

Two out of three isn't usually that bad an outcome but it doesn't work like that when you're a mother. When the judge explained what he had decided Carol dropped to her knees like she'd been punched really hard in the stomach and all the air had been forced out of her. The lost, empty look on her face when she finally managed to stand up will stay with me for ever. She was bereft. But nothing was going to dent Carol's determination to get her family back together.

"I'll get my baby back, don't you worry. If I have to crawl over broken glass on my hands and knees I'll get us back together as a family again. Best interests, my arse. Cristina's best interests means being with me and the boys. We're her mother, her brothers; not some poxy foster family. I'll fucking show them. This time next year I'll have all my kids back, just you watch. If it fucking kills me we'll be together. Just you watch me."

I was pretty confident she would get there in the end. And I was entirely confident that if getting Cristina back meant never having another drink again for as long as she lived, Carol would do that in a heart beat and it would be no sacrifice at all.

I was exhausted when we got back to the office after the court hearing. My whole body was heavy with sadness and my legs felt like they were made of cement and wouldn't bend properly. Emma on the other hand sat straight back down at her desk and got on with her work.

"Now that's out the way for a while I can catch up on the Northcote case and I've got the Davis case coming up for hearing in three weeks. I could do with your help on that one now."

She looked over at me and must have been able to tell from my face how I was feeling.

"Sorry Ellie, I forget what it feels like the first time, before you get used to it. It gets easier, honestly it does. We did everything we could for Carol and now we've got to put her out of our minds and do everything we can for the next one. Look, it's Friday night. Why don't you push off home a bit early today and we'll talk about the other cases next week?"

I nodded my thanks to her and, without another word, grabbed my bag and left.

CHAPTER
TWENTY-FOUR

Gabriel and I had got into the habit of meeting in the pub for a few drinks straight after work of a Friday night. He was usually there before me, still wearing his grubby gardening clothes, playing the quiz machine while he waited for me. Every time I walked in and saw him standing there, mucky from his day's work with a pint in his hand and deep in concentration, my heart did a little jig of joy because he was handsome and funny and we had the whole weekend in front of us but that day, the day that Carol lost her case, I didn't feel up to the pub. I rang him and suggested we meet at his house instead.

Even though I saw Gabriel at least three or four nights a week, we didn't have the sort of relationship where we turned up on each other's door steps unannounced — that wasn't how our thing worked. We always made arrangements by phone first and that was exactly how I wanted it to be. I had no intention of ever again waiting at the window in the hope that someone might turn up.

"Ok, sure. If that's what you fancy," he said. "See you about eight then? Do you want me to cook something?"

"No," I said, "I don't feel much like eating."

I didn't. What I fancied was getting totally stoned so I arrived at Gabriel's bearing Sandra's previously unopened bag of emergency spliffs. Gabriel readily agreed to sit out in his back garden and share one with me. It was a shame for someone who gardened for a living to have such a tiny garden — just a bit of decking really, big enough for a small round table and the two chairs we were sitting on and a lawn which was beautifully kept but only about as big as two duvet covers. Gabriel had trained five or six clematis on wicker trellises around the garden walls and over the course of the summer these had flowered gloriously at different times, with colours so vibrant they looked almost plastic: from palest pink to imperial purple and with the flowers as big and bright as a dishful of jelly at a child's tea party. Now, with August drawing to a close, the clematis had all but finished and the evenings were getting cooler and darker. I lit a bunch of tea lights in jam jars to cast a cheery, flickering light over our faces and held my hands over them to feel the warmth of their glow.

"Hang on, I'll run upstairs, and get you a fleece," Gabriel said.

I watched him as he jogged gently back through the kitchen. Gabriel moves with a natural grace, long legged and fluid, in control of his own body. He is one of those men who can ride a bike without holding on to the handlebars and make it look easy and natural. He was back within seconds and as he handed the fleece to me I did not thank him but reached up and ran my hand over his head. His short, dark hair parted beneath my fingers and even in the half light I saw the vulnerable white skin of his scalp beneath.

He took a long drag of the joint, threw back his head and exhaled slowly as he passed it to me.

"Jesus. Sandra was right. That stuff is good. Even my toes are relaxed."

"Yep she's a wicked stepmother all right." I said, taking a long drag myself and handing it back to him.

"Eh?" Gabriel looked at me, a foggy look of confusion on his face. "Oh I geddit, wick — ed stepmother," and he made a snapping movement with his fingers.

"That's right. Not a joke that benefits from being repeated really."

"You ok Ellie?"

"I'm fine," I said. I wasn't but Gabriel and I didn't talk about the big stuff. We were all about keeping it light, keeping it fun, keeping it easy going.

"Are you sure you want to keep doing this job? It seems kind of heavy?"

I raised my hand, made the two fingered sign of peace at him. "Apparently, it ain't that heavy man, not if you don't let it be."

"Seems pretty heavy to me. A lot of hassle for bugger-all money. You know, when I bailed from broking I decided I could either have a job that made me rich but stressed me out and soaked up all my life, or a job that paid badly but left me with some life left over at the end of the working day. I figured I could choose having money or time and I chose time but the job you're doing seems to involve long hours, not much money and loads of grief."

"Do you really think life is as simple as that? Time or money?"

"It was for me. When I was a broker I earned tons of money but I was working twelve, fourteen hours a day, weekends too. My bosses made it crystal clear that if I wanted to continue earning at that level I would need to carry on working like that for the rest of my life. I had lots of money but no time to enjoy it. So I worked my guts out until I paid off the mortgage on this place and the day after I handed in my notice. And I've never been happier. You know, I worked all those hours but I could never sleep at night — my brain was so fired up it wouldn't shut down — now I fall asleep pretty much as soon as my head hits the pillow."

"Well bully for you Gabriel. Why don't you just get over yourself! What you've done is not an option for most people. Us ordinary people can't just decide to work our socks off and make enough money to buy a house outright. We get the best job we can get and work every bit as hard as you ever did and we're still lucky to make the rent at the end of the month. Your choice isn't open to me — I'm not trained to do anything that earns a lot of money even if I wanted to earn it. And anyway, life doesn't always come down to your two choices. Emma could choose to work as hard as she does somewhere else and make a fortune but she doesn't. She does a really stressful, difficult job for not much money because there are people out there who need someone like her."

"Ok, ok, I accept the point you're making. You know, I did say that *for me* the choice was money or time. I wasn't trying to make some big social comment. People like Emma who work that hard without getting the big bucks are a rare breed and I admire them for it. Anyway, why we are we having this conversation? I thought you were only planning on staying there for a while and then going off travelling again? Isn't that you making the choice of time over money, just the same as I did?"

"We weren't talking about me. Apparently we were talking about you."

"No we weren't. We were talking about life in general and I just told you my opinion on the choice between having a career and money or having a life, and in my opinion, and it's only my personal opinion so don't get all ratty with me, money doesn't make you happy."

"It's all right for you to say that, sitting out here in your mortgage-free garden."

"Chill Ellie," Gabriel sighed, handing me the joint back. "Have another drag on Sandra's premium organic spliff. I know I've been lucky. I had a job that paid well and I got out of it before I got so sucked in I couldn't get out. I see some of the boys I used to work with from time to time — they're still working as hard as they ever did, keeping up mortgages on massive houses in Surrey and summer homes in Tuscany, a 4×4 for the wife and three kids and a Porsche for themselves, just to broadcast to their neighbours how well they're doing. They never see their kids and hardly ever see their wives. Half of them end up shagging some blonde bimbo from the office who's stupid enough to think that if she keeps him warm during the working week he'll leave his wife for her. It's an empty way of living and I feel sorry for them but I am glad I had the option of sticking it out for a few years to give myself the freedom to make choices. And I do realise that not every one is as lucky as me. Now shall we talk about something else for a while?"

"Sure. Of course we can. I'll go open us a bottle of wine shall I?"

The joint had been more than enough for me but I scurried into the kitchen so that Gabriel wouldn't notice how my cheeks flushed with shame that, until recently, I'd been one of those gullible bimbos he'd described.

I must have been standing in the kitchen for a while, bottle in one hand, corkscrew in the other, before Gabriel came in from the garden, took them both from me and opened the bottle himself.

"Here, let me do that. I'm sorry if I was being smug Ellie."

"Smug and elitist," I said over my shoulder from where I was fetching glasses from the cupboard.

"Sorry, smug and elitist. Don't let's talk about this any more. It's getting cold — let's go into the living room, have this glass of wine, listen to some music, be together — and don't let's talk any more about jobs or money or kids in care or any of that sort of stuff."

He took a big gulp of his wine and then kissed me gently, cupping the back of my head with his hands to hold my face close to his. He tasted like blackberries.

As we lay together that night I tried very hard not to think about anything else but the warmth of his skin against mine.

CHAPTER
TWENTY-FIVE

1947-2007

Jack and Laura never talk about what happened during the war. By the time Jack makes it home the war has been over for months and people are not interested in what went before, only what lies ahead. Britain is in the process of rebuilding itself and does not choose to dwell on the darkness it has dragged itself out of. People are putting their best foot forward, wearing their brightest, shiniest faces to greet a new era.

This suits Jack because he does not want to talk either. Laura sees the physical evidence of what he has been through: his shrunken frame, the sores, the scars — these things speak of the atrocities he has endured — but Jack refuses to tell more than his body testifies to.

Laura does not push for information but concentrates all her efforts on getting her husband well again. She wants to heal his sores, fatten him up, make him strong and fit again. She lies with him at night protecting him with her body, keeping him warm, hoping her presence next to him will comfort him. When he wakes at night shouting and she holds him tight, she asks him what his nightmare was about, but she does not question the answer he always gives.

"It was nothing. I'm fine. I'm home now."

He does not tell her the truth. How in his dreams he is back in the camps, working on the Thai-Burma railway. The death railway. To begin with, hunger had been the biggest problem for him but once his body had eaten itself away in the struggle to stay alive and his stomach had shrunk to nothing he didn't miss eating very much. He had even got used to the way he looked, his skin drawn so tight over his rib cage that he felt his bones might burst through. All the prisoners became skeletal with legs that looked longer than they should because no-one had any thighs or buttocks, just skin stretched over bones. Walking bags of bones. What he never got used to was the constant death. Most days someone lost the fight against starvation or disease and fell dead where they worked or didn't wake up in the morning. Worst of all were those who lost the fight against despair and took their own lives. Jack found the suicides harder to stomach than seeing a man shot or tortured to death and it is the faces of the men who gave up hope that he sees most in his dreams.

The secret of survival in the camps was never to give up hope and never to get ill. If you could work you were still useful and you were left alone. If you became sick — with dysentery or beriberi, which were rife — and could not work hard enough, you were no longer worth feeding and would be beaten or tortured and pushed faster along the road to death. Jack's stroke of luck was that he only became really ill when the end of the war was in sight. He managed to stick it out till VJ day. Just.

He would have been dead if the bombs had been dropped on Hiroshima and Nagasaki any later. As it is, he is barely alive when his camp is liberated and it takes months of nursing in a military hospital before he is in sufficiently good health to make the long journey home.

Kitty does as Laura tells her and does not mention Trevor and her baby sister in front of Jack even though she misses them both terribly. Alone with Laura she asks when are they going home, when can they see Trevor and Sarah again, but all Laura will say is, "Not right now darling".

Eventually Kitty stops asking and forgets about Trevor and Sarah — almost. She gets used to thinking of the strange man who sits in the kitchen, staring for hours at his own hands or his cup and saucer, as her father. She is a stoic little girl — she gets used to most things eventually. Slowly Jack gains a little weight and some of the sores heal although the biggest one, splashed across his thigh like a burn, is ulcerated and stubborn. But his physical health is not the biggest problem — it is Jack's mind that is more damaged. He deals with what he has seen and suffered by shutting down a lot of the time. If he allows himself to think or feel, the nightmares get even worse. He retreats further and further into himself.

Laura's hopes of Jack becoming again the man she married also retreat. Every morning when she wakes she finds Jack asleep on the floor next to the bed.

"I'm sorry love," he says. "I got so used to sleeping on bare boards in the camp I find bed sheets too hot now. It's nothing to do with you, honest."

Eventually she gives up on sharing a bed with him and allows him to have a bedroom of his own so he can sleep on the floor there. She realises there is no chance of her ever having another baby. Jack cannot even bear to have Kitty near him for long — her noise and youth, her stout little energetic body that simply can't stop still — although slowly he grows more used to her, can spend short periods of time playing snakes and ladders or Ludo with her. But he tires quickly and often waves her away before the game is over.

Laura is lonely but she loves Jack fiercely and she works hard to keep home and hearth together. She puts Trevor and Sarah totally out of her mind. Jack's family and her own family and the people of the Rhondda fall into step along side her and keep her secret, never mentioning Trevor and Sarah again. They can all see just how ill Jack is, how weak and disorientated. They do not wish to cause him any more pain. In any event it is an easy secret to keep because Jack rarely leaves the house and he does not welcome visitors.

Eventually Jack is diagnosed with battle anxiety. He finds this curious, since he did not actually see much battle and what haunts him is not the fighting but the faces of the men who died in the camps and the guilt that he survived. Later, much later, the deaths of those in Hiroshima and Nagasaki add to that store of guilt. But all of this Jack keeps to himself. He does not want

262

to spread the infection of what he has been through by sharing it with Laura.

Laura is relieved that Jack has chosen to draw a line under the events of the war. That way, she need not tell him what happened to her either. All she will say is, "It was easier for me. I had Kitty to care for."

Between them they sweep almost four years under the carpet, four long years during which Jack endured more deprivation than should be physically possible and Laura suffered from a grief so large she thought she would sink. She had not expected Trevor to come along and offer her a life raft away from that grief and had been deeply grateful for a second chance at happiness. And in that second chance were sown the seeds of an even greater sadness.

Laura tries very hard over the years not to think of her brief other life. A lot of the time she is successful. She concentrates on looking after Jack, on keeping the house clean and tidy, on putting food on the table. She knows that if she is to have any hope of sleeping at night, of not remembering, she must keep herself constantly on the go, forever busy, so that she does not have the energy to think of her baby or of Trevor. From being a woman who cries a lot, Laura becomes a woman who works a lot instead.

When it becomes clear to her that Jack is never going to get well again she finds herself a job doing the office work for a local fruit and vegetable wholesaler. She has no training, no experience, but gets the job by agreeing to work for a very low wage. At first her duties are limited — answering the telephone, making tea, filing — but she is a hard worker and a fast learner and soon she is more or less running the business, doing the books, sending out invoices, chasing when payment is not made on time. There is no fat in Laura's working day — she does not chat with the other staff or make small talk with the men who drive the delivery lorries and her terse manner earns her no friends — but she is invaluable to the business. As soon as she is certain of her value she asks for a pay rise and gets it. If there is something that needs to be done, Laura gets it done and if there are no invoices to send out or wages to process she will clean the office windows or tidy up the storehouse. She is the last to leave each evening, locking up the office and walking the mile home to tire her body out even more.

She carries on working the minute she gets home, peeling potatoes for the evening meal without even taking her coat off, shouting up the stairs to Kitty to make sure she is doing her homework, checking on Jack who is normally sitting in the chair next to his bed staring out of the window when she gets in.

She numbs herself with physical activity, doesn't dare let herself feel. She pulls up the drawbridge to her heart in an attempt to protect herself. If the worst comes to the worst and she still cannot be sure of sleeping without dreaming she cleans out her kitchen cupboards late at night, scrubbing the surfaces and lining them with fresh white paper.

Sometimes, despite her best efforts, just as she is dropping off to sleep, she thinks she hears a baby cry and the image of her tiny daughter's face swims into her mind. She tries to push it away but by then it is too late and she remembers how Sarah's face would light up in the morning when she went to fetch her from her crib and how she would scoop her up in her arms and take her into their bed. Trevor would smile at the two of them sleepily and budge over so that there was room for Laura to lie by his side and feed their daughter. In a little while Trevor would call for Kitty and lie on his back, bringing his knees up into the air so that Kitty can climb on him and pretend she is riding a horse while Laura finishes feeding Sarah. From time to time he drops his knees, making Kitty fall with a whump onto the bedspread and squeal with laughter.

Over the years Laura learns how to close her mind to this memory, make herself hard and tight so that the memory can't get in. She is determined that Jack will never find out that she did not stay true to him. She knows her betrayal of him will finish him off for good so she locks her other life away where he can't find it. She is aware that by protecting Jack in this way she is also protecting herself against guilt and regret and the pain of lost love; and if in that process she also closes herself off against the daughter she still has, she figures it is a price she has to pay.

When the first letter from Trevor arrives, the sight of his big loopy handwriting on the envelope squeezes her chest with pain; and a sliver of memory — of his big hands around her waist and his smiling eyes looking into hers — pierces her mind, but she does not open the letter. Even though she wants to she cannot bring herself to throw the letter away and instead she hides it in a box beneath her bed.

Jack never makes the journey all the way back to Laura. There is too much of him left behind in the camps of the Far East. He tries as hard as he can and Laura tries every bit as hard to reach out and grab him and bring him safely to shore but she dare not tell him the path her life took when she believed Jack was dead, and he dare not tell her what happened to him when he wished he had been.

Jack was once a big strong man. He would not have survived the camps if he had not been. Some of that strength stays with him for a long time because Kitty is sixteen when he finally dies. When the next letter from Trevor arrives, Laura thinks about opening it, of reading what it is Trevor has been trying to tell her all these years, but she decides not to. *No good can come of that now*, she thinks to herself. *I made my bed and now I've got to lie in it*. She stuffs the letter away in the box with all the others. By the time the eighteenth letter arrives Kitty is married, blissfully happy with one baby already and another on the way. And after the eighteenth letter, no more come.

Laura works even longer hours at the office. Without Jack and Kitty at home to look after, there is not enough work at home to tire her out. Her boss tells her he cannot afford to pay her overtime for the long hours she works but she tells him not to worry, she is glad to do it. She is also glad when Kitty's family expands to the point that Kitty can no longer refuse her mother's offer to help with the housework and the ironing. Laura keeps her daughter's house clean and her never-ending mound of ironing under control. It is Laura's affection that Kitty craves but it is help with the house work that she gets.

It surprises Laura how long she continues to live. She has worked so hard and slept so little that she had expected her body to wear out long before, but day after day dawns and to her irritation she wakes up every morning. She is eventually forced to retire from the fruit and vegetable wholesalers even though her boss' son let her work on till she was well past seventy, right up to the point where he closed the business and sold the land for an enormous profit to a supermarket chain. Thankfully by then it takes less work to wear Laura out and the task of keeping her own house tidy and ironing for her grandchildren is enough to keep her busy. As she gets older it becomes harder to keep the memories out and she often falls asleep or wakes up dreaming of her daughters and her husbands. At the going down of the sun and in the morning she remembers them. She dreams in particular of a day when the four of them went up the mountain to pick wimberries. There was an abundance of fruit that year and they gathered a big basket of them. Kitty played nearby or helped them pick, eating more than she dropped into the basket, and Sarah slept quietly on a blanket. Afterwards they returned home heavy laden and Laura made jam with the fruit, four big jars of shiny, dark-blue sweetness. In this dream Trevor and Jack have merged into the same man and Laura wakes up smiling, feeling that her troubles are finally over because there is only one husband after all not two. And then she wakes up some more and realises she is old and on her own and there are no husbands at all.

From time to time she thinks about getting the letters out from underneath her bed. Sometimes she thinks she will read them and other times she resolves to burn them so that Kitty won't find them after she has gone but she does neither. When she eventually keels over while ironing her tea towels, her final thought is of the letters and she dies annoyed with herself for not having burned them and leaving things tidy for after she has gone.

CHAPTER
TWENTY-SIX

That night at Gabriel's I did not sleep well and by 6 a.m. I was wide awake. I could hear Maud scratching at the kitchen door to be let out. I didn't keep a bathrobe at Gabriel's house so I got dressed quickly and went downstairs to open the door for her. She was pleased to see me and twisted herself round my legs a few times, her fur warm and soft, before dashing out. Maud was a bit of a tart and visited a number of households in the street throughout the day. Often when Gabriel and I were walking to his house we would spot her sitting in the window of one of the neighbours' houses, watching us with disdain as we walked by as if she didn't know us at all.

Since I was up so early anyway I decided I would just go home, leaving Gabriel asleep in bed. I had three more crosswords I needed to deliver and I wanted to get them out of the way by lunchtime so they wouldn't be hanging over my head all weekend, like homework left till Sunday; but in reality I was also still a bit annoyed with Gabriel for being so lucky in life and for being such a self-satisfied prick about it.

I was upstairs with my head in my dog dictionary, finishing off the last few clues, when I heard the door bell. I knew that Trevor was outside gardening and that he couldn't hear the bell from there, so I ran downstairs.

I opened the door to a thickset, grey-haired woman.

"Sorry to bother you love but does Trevor Richards live here?"

"Yes he does. He's out the back in the garden. Do you want me to go get him for you? I'm his granddaughter."

"Is your mother called Sarah?" the woman asked. There was something familiar about her, something I recognised, but I couldn't work out what it was.

"Yes she is. Look I don't want to be rude but do you mind me asking who you are, since you seem to be asking me a fair few questions."

"I expect we'll all have lots of questions before the week's out," the woman said, cryptically. "Give this to your mother for me will you love." She handed me a letter.

"Can I tell her who it's from?"

"Tell her it's from her sister, her sister Kitty. I've put my telephone number on the back of the envelope in case she wants to call me."

As I shut the door behind her I saw Trevor standing at the top of the stairs leading up from the basement kitchen. He looked like he had seen a ghost.

"Grandad?" I asked, my voice quavering, suddenly realising that the familiar thing about the woman had been her Welsh accent. "Who was that? What's this all about?"

"I'm sorry love I've got to talk to your mother first before I can talk to you."

And he turned and made his way back down the stairs.

"Grandad?!" I shouted after him.

"Later love, there'll be time enough later." His voice was weary, resigned.

My mother was out somewhere, not due back till teatime, and I didn't think I could wait that long. My stomach was churning with nerves. My mother had a sister? How could that be? Had my grandfather had an affair he had never told us about?

I sent Gabriel a text, said I was going to spend the evening with my mum and granddad and that I'd give him a ring in the morning. He sent me a two word message back — *ok cool* — which made me feel even more annoyed with him. Why was it so cool that we wouldn't be polishing off a bottle of wine together that night while watching *The X Factor?* I tried to concentrate on finishing the crossword puzzle but questions about the woman who claimed she was my mother's sister fretted their way around my head constantly until finally I heard my mother's key in the lock.

"Yoo hoo. I'm home. Come and get me!"

This is what she always used to shout when I was little and she arrived home. She said it in exactly the same way as she had said it all those years ago.

"Dad? What are you doing up here? You hardly ever sit up here. What's wrong — what's happened? Is Ellie ok?"

I shut my bedroom door at this point. Although whatever Trevor was telling my mother involved me too in some way, I knew it was my mother's news first and foremost. I lay on my bed, watching time judder past on my old clock radio.

After about an hour I heard raised voices in our narrow hallway and then the front door banging shut loudly. Finally Trevor called up to me.

"Your mother's gone for a walk to try to clear her head. Time to tell you now Ellie."

My heart was banging in my chest as I made my way downstairs.

"Don't worry lovely girl," he said when he saw my face. "It's not as bad as all that. Perhaps you'd better read Kitty's letter first."

He handed it to me.

Dear Sarah,
This is a difficult letter to write but I won't forgive myself if I don't get it written.

My mother, Laura, died a few months ago. When I was little I used to dream all the time about a beautiful baby, a little sister, but my mother told me I was being fanciful and eventually the dreams stopped. I used to dream about a man too, a big, strong, handsome man with hands as big as shovels who would whirl me high in the air but Mam told me I had made that up too. After she died and I was clearing out her house I found a box of letters hidden under her bed. They were letters from your father, Trevor. One a year for

272

eighteen years, telling her all about you, how you were getting on in London, what a good child you were and asking her to get in touch. I guess she never replied because the letters were all unopened but they must have been important to her because she kept every one of them.

I don't understand why our parents should have kept us secret from each other all these years. I would like to change that in the years we have ahead. Please contact me if you would like that too. This may sound odd but I feel I have missed you all my life.

Your sister Kitty

I put the letter down on the table carefully. Grabbing my bag I fished around in the bottom of until my hand finally closed around the comfort of a small, cellophane-wrapped box. The discarded remainder of the cigarettes I'd bought when I was waiting for Robert to turn up for the weekend.

"I'm going out to the bench," I announced, "I need a fag."

Trevor left me in peace for all of five minutes, then followed me out and sat down next to me. I was sobbing by the time Trevor finished telling me how it was he had come to live in London, sobbing for Trevor and for my mother whose own mother, my grandmother, hadn't wanted her. Trevor and I sat out in the garden, even though it was getting cold and dark and I smoked a few more cigarettes until finally I heard the front door bang again.

Mum joined us out in the garden, sitting down wearily with a bump in one of the garden chairs.

"I'll get you a cup of tea Mum."

"Never mind a cup of tea. I want a bloody gin and tonic — a really big one."

"I'll get one of those for us all shall I?" Trevor said, making his way hurriedly to the house.

"You ok Mum?" I asked.

"Your grandfather's told you then?"

I nodded.

"He showed me the letter from Kitty. I'm sorry Mum."

I didn't know what else to say. Sorry was a pathetic little word that didn't come close to describing how badly I felt for her.

My mother's voice was flat, almost emotionless.

"I called Kitty on her mobile while I was out. She's staying in a bed and breakfast on Clapham Common. Said she wanted to be near me when I read the letter."

"Bloody hell Mum, you've got a sister."

"I had a mother too until just a few months ago and that's the bit that hurts. That and the fact that Trevor didn't tell me the truth."

"I'm sorry love." Trevor was standing in the doorway of the kitchen, a tray of gin and tonics in his hands. "I thought it was for the best. Thought I was doing the right thing."

"Depriving me of my mother and my sister for sixty years was *not* the right thing to do Dad. I've just found out my whole life has been a lie and I'm not certain I can forgive you for that."

Her voice was hard, flinty, hurt. My grandfather was wounded by the force of her words. He suddenly seemed very old, round shouldered and curled in on himself, defeated by his past. I felt a punch of pity for him but also love, hot and fierce.

"Please believe me Sarah! I really did think I was doing the right thing. I tried to get your mother to acknowledge you — would have told you all about her if she was only willing to do that much — but after Jack came back she wanted nothing more to do with either of us. I thought the best thing to do was to tell you she had died."

"Dad, I know you thought it was for the best, but I feel like you took something from me that I can never get back. If you'd told me about her I could have gone to see her, got to know her. I could have asked her why she didn't want to know me. Perhaps she would have changed her mind. I would have liked to ask her if she thought about me at all over the years, whether she missed me. And now it's too late."

"I wrote to her. She knew where we were. If she had wanted to she could have got in touch. For years I checked the post every morning, hoping there would be a letter from her asking to see you."

"But you didn't give me the chance to try did you Trevor? So you wrote to her once a year? Big deal! Letters would have been easy to ignore. We should have just gone there, made her acknowledge me. If she had seen me she would have changed her mind. What mother wouldn't? If you hadn't kept this secret all these years I might have had a mother."

My grandfather flinched at this, turned his face away as if my mother had slapped him.

There was an edge in his voice when he finally spoke.

"Times were different then Sarah. People didn't deal with issues like they do now. We didn't have counsellors or Oprah. The way people coped with problems was by sweeping them under the carpet, hiding them, keeping a stiff upper lip."

"So I was a problem was I? Something to be hidden under the carpet?"

My mother had jumped up from her seat, was standing over my grandfather, shouting at him. I was reminded of the rows she and I used to have when I was growing up only this time my mother was the one having a teenage tantrum with my grandfather.

"Sarah, you have never been a problem to me. Just a joy all your life."

My mother sat back down suddenly, finally crumpled into tears.

"Oh Dad. I'm sorry. This isn't all about me. You've had to live with this rejection all your life. I don't know how you've coped with it all. Really I don't."

Trevor reached out a hand and ruffled the top of my mother's head. I could see from his face as he looked at his little girl how he had coped. He had coped because he loved her so much that he wanted to spare her this pain.

"Sarah love," he said as he kissed the top of her head, "you were such a wonderful child, *are* such a wonderful woman, that you made it all seem quite easy."

276

My mother stood up again, this time the better to hug my grandfather.

"You've been a great dad. And a great mum too." She took Trevor's hand, pressed the back of it to her lips, holding it there for a few seconds. "Now then, where's that gin and tonic?"

We each took a big gulp of our drinks.

"Crikey Dad. What did you do? Make these for Cliff? I don't think you bothered to even wave the tonic bottle at the gin. Still, it hits the right spot. You don't think I could have a cigarette too do you Ellie?"

I looked at my mother in amazement.

"What?" she said "You think I was young in the sixties and never smoked? Gave up years ago when I was pregnant with you. I think I can risk having one today of all days."

So I handed her a cigarette and she smoked it very proficiently, without coughing or spluttering, and the three of us finished our gin.

My mother stubbed out her cigarette, looked at my grandfather.

"Dad? Can I ask you something?"

"Of course."

My mother's voice was thick with tears. "Why did you let her go Dad?"

"Because Sarah love I didn't have any other choice. And neither did Laura. The moment she found out Jack was alive she turned on her heel and went straight to him. She didn't even have to think about it because she loved him more than she loved me. She always did, even when she believed he was dead. And even though he came back only half the man he used to be, *because* he was only half the man he used to be, she couldn't do anything else but go to him and I couldn't do anything else but step aside."

"Is that why you never got married again?" Mum asked, "Because you were still in love with Laura all this time?"

"Perhaps in the beginning I was. When we first got to London I did hope that somehow she'd find her way back to us. But when she didn't reply to my letters, never once tried to see you again Sarah, I couldn't for the life of me understand how she could do that. Not to you, her own daughter. That helped me to stop loving her."

"So why not get married again? It's not as if you were ever short of admirers!"

"I came close a few times. There was Mrs Murray — do you remember her, used to work in the shoe shop on the High Street? Fine-looking woman. I thought I might want to marry her at some point. And then there was Mrs O'Neill — she came close too — but I never loved them like I loved Laura. Even though I stopped loving her I remembered how it *felt* to love her, how looking at her used to make me feel. And that's no way to start a marriage — knowing from the beginning that you don't love your second spouse as much as you loved your first. Found that little bit of truth out by bitter experience I did."

I had spent too long round lawyers not to realise there was a legal issue here.

"Anyway, you couldn't really have got married again when you were still technically married to Laura. Or were you? Married to her? Once Jack came back. Which marriage was valid?"

"Her marriage to me. Because Jack had been declared dead, our marriage was legal. I divorced her in the end — all done through lawyers — but even then she didn't contact me or ask about your mother."

"And how do you feel now? Now that you know she's dead?" My mother asked this, probing her own hurt like sticking her tongue into a mouth ulcer even though she knew it would be painful.

"I'm sorry Sarah — I know this is all new to you and it's a big shock — but Laura's been dead to me for years. The only effect her death is having on me now is the fact that Kitty has come to find you."

"Are you mad with Kitty about that?"

"Of course not. Kitty was just a little girl. It wasn't her fault. And I loved Kitty like she was my own. I would have brought her with us to London if I had thought that was the right thing to do. You can tell her that if it helps."

My mother yawned. "You can tell her yourself. She's coming round here for lunch tomorrow to meet you both."

CHAPTER
TWENTY-SEVEN

The next morning all I wanted was to see Gabriel. I wanted to pull him fresh from his bed before the day got a hold of him, naked and sleepy and warm, and share with him what I'd just learned about the sacrifices people make for love. I just wanted to be with him, hold him, lay my skin against his and tell him how my grandfather had walked away from the woman he loved so that she could be with someone else and how that woman had walked away from her daughter for the same reason. Telling Gabriel about it would help me make sense of it all somehow and so I ignored our unspoken rules; didn't text or phone him first. I showered quickly, pulled on tracksuit bottoms and a long-sleeved T shirt and made my way over to Gabriel's house. It was still early and if I hurried I would catch him before he woke up.

I picked up some breakfast on my way. There were no chi chi delicatessens or bakeries on the way to Gabriel's so I couldn't turn up with anything fancy like croissants or a pain au raisin. Instead I picked up some thick-sliced, white bread, a packet of butter and a carton of milk. Tea and buttered toast would make Gabriel every bit as happy as a French pastry.

I walked so fast to his house that it almost counted as jogging and all I could think about on the way over was the sleepy smile he would give me when he opened the door. Only there was no need for me to pull Gabriel out of bed that morning because as I turned into the top of his street I could see that he was already very much awake. Not only was he awake but he was standing on his front step, talking to some woman: a tall, lean woman, with dark shiny hair that fell glossily over her shoulders, wearing jeans and black boots and a three-quarter-length black trench coat belted tightly round her waist. She was carrying a big box with a handle on top. I watched as Gabriel took the box from her, walked with her to a car parked right outside his house and put the box carefully and slowly into the boot for her. By this point I had slowed down to a standstill so that I could watch this little scene playing out. And then he kissed her. Not on the mouth but on the cheek, ever so gently, with one hand resting on her arm, the other on the small of her back. I could see from where I was standing that it was a sad kiss, full of regret. I watched a little while longer, saw her get in the car and drive off without looking back. I watched Gabriel watching her drive off. And then I walked the last hundred metres or so to his house so that he would see me before he went back inside.

"Ah Ellie. Didn't expect to see you."

"I know you didn't."

"Do you want to come in?"

"Sure, I've brought us some breakfast."

I followed him into the house. He was barefoot and wearing jeans and a navy shirt left over from his broking days, with double cuffs folded back loosely over his wrists. He probably looked the most sexy I had ever seen him look. Men are never so attractive as when you suddenly see them again through the eyes of another woman. When you are so nauseous with jealousy of that woman you could throw up on the spot.

I handed my plastic bag to Gabriel, said nothing as he set my proffered gifts of bread and butter out on the counter and put the kettle on for tea. There was something different about the house other than the fact that it had recently been visited, more than likely overnight, by the long-haired lovely I had just seen leave. There was something else but I couldn't figure out what it was. And then, as I sat in the kitchen watching Gabriel make toast, it finally dawned on me that things were missing — a small oak box that Gabriel used as a bread bin, a set of three white jugs that normally lived on a shelf above the sink. Finally, with a sudden start, I realised that something else was missing. Maud's food bowls and her little padded sleeping basket, were not on the floor near the kitchen door.

"Where's Maud?"

"Maud Gonne has gone," Gabriel said. "Do you want jam on your toast? Or peanut butter?"

"What do you mean she's gone?"

"Just that. She's gone. Ms Gonne has left the building."

And then it dawned on me that the box I had seen Gabriel put in the car with such care was a cat box.

"Did that woman who was here earlier take her?"

Gabriel stopped rooting through his cupboards for jam and froze. One mention of the woman I had seen him kiss goodbye had stopped him dead in his tracks.

"Yes, but I don't want to talk about her with you, or about Maud ok?" he said coldly.

"Why not?"

He tried hard to hide it but he couldn't. I clearly saw the look of anger and dislike cross over Gabriel's face.

"Because I choose not to Ellie. Because like I told you right at the beginning it is absolutely none of your damn business."

His response, so immediate, so hard, made something inside me grow cold and drop like a stone to lodge in the pit of my stomach but I recovered myself quickly.

"No worries Gabriel, I know the score," I said cheerily, reaching for my bag, "I'll be off when I've finished my toast, let you get on."

"There's no rush." Gabriel's voice was softer now, trying to make up for the harsh way he had spoken to me earlier. "You haven't even told me why you came round."

"No reason," I said, "just fancied some toast."

Now it was my turn to be kissed on the cheek but it didn't have anywhere near the resonance of the kiss I had witnessed earlier. This one was a kiss of relief that a difficult situation, a possible confrontation, had been avoided.

"Well next time you fancy some toast give me a ring beforehand and I'll make sure the kettle's on."

"Will do," I said lightly, struggling to chew my way through a piece of toast that clogged in my mouth like sawdust. I swallowed it down in pieces so big they scratched my throat. All I wanted was to get away from there as soon as I could but not so quickly that I would reveal how hurt I was. I was finally able to scurry out, shouting goodbye over my shoulder a little too loudly and a little too gaily, with toast crumbs still lodged in my teeth.

On the way home I resolved to think nothing further about Gabriel's mystery woman. What was there to think about? Gabriel had a past life he hadn't told me about, one that had turned up to collect the cat she'd left behind in the airing cupboard. So what? I had a past life I hadn't told him about either, one that was responsible for the £10,000 sitting in my current account that I would shortly be using to pay for long haul plane tickets. That had been the deal with me and Gabriel from the outset — ask no questions, get told no lies — and so long as we kept it like that, our pasts would stay exactly where they belonged. In the past. Anyway, I told myself, I didn't have the time or energy to worry about Gabriel's history. I had quite enough on my plate dealing with my grandfather's and the fact that I would soon be having lunch with an aunt that this time yesterday I didn't even know I had.

While Mum made lunch for Kitty, Trevor paced the house like a father in a maternity hospital.

284

"I didn't think I could ever want the toilet so bad or so often. How come nerves affect your waterworks so badly?"

In the end Kitty made it easy for him, holding out her arms as Trevor opened the door and rushing into his tentative embrace.

"I'm a bit too big for you to whirl about your head now aren't I?" she said pushing her face into his chest.

"And I'm a bit too old love," he said, his voice thick in his throat.

"Right. Let's put the kettle on shall we," Kitty said, finding her own way to the kitchen as if she were a regular visitor.

It was odd sitting there with them, drinking tea out of the Shelley cups. My mother and Kitty looked alike in many ways but different in lots of others. Kitty was a lot heavier than my mother and was of a slightly bigger build — but they both had the same heart-shaped face as me and lovely skin. I could see the family resemblance that linked the three of them together — Trevor to my mother, my mother to Kitty — and the way that Trevor's accent thickened when he spoke with Kitty, becoming far more Welsh, lapsing back into south London when he spoke with my mother, just made the links seem stronger.

"The moment I found your letters, Trevor, everything made more sense. Mam was always so distant and wound tight as a spring. She never stopped working, never relaxed. I annoyed her truth be told. She was so different from me — blonde and petite and pretty — and there was I, this big lumbering girl with dark hair and size seven feet who was always hungry. I used to think she was the way she was because of Dad and after he died I thought it was because I reminded her of him. Now I know there was much more to it than that."

My mother leaned over and squeezed Kitty's hand gently.

"I was lucky though," Kitty continued. "I met Stan when I was fourteen and he likes a girl with a bit of gafael."

Sarah looked at her quizzically. "A bit of what?"

"A bit of gafael. Something to get a hold of," Kitty laughed, patting her well padded thigh. "Stan loves me enough for a whole family's worth. We got married when I was seventeen and I've been happy every day since. We've got five wonderful children who've all done really well for themselves: university, careers, everything — I've got photos in my bag for you to see — and I've nine beautiful grandchildren. I've been truly blessed Sarah — honestly — life has been good to me."

Kitty rummaged around in her capacious navy handbag and dug out the photos for us all to see her big, smiling family. Happiness shone out of the photos. My mother looked at the children and at the children's children — studied their faces.

"So these are my . . .?"

"Your nieces and nephews yes." Kitty beamed and she began to rattle off the names of an extended family my mother had never met. Kitty saw the look on her face.

"Sarah love, I'm sorry, I don't mean to push you too hard. We don't have to do all this in one go. We've got a lot of catching up to do you and me, we all of us have, but I'd really like to try if you're willing."

My mother got up from her chair and went over to hug her half sister, trying to kiss her cheek but somehow managing to get her ear instead. They both laughed.

"I'd like that Kitty. I'd like it very much."

"Right then, let's get started. Tell me Trevor, have I made this up? I remember you twirling me above your head, remember that clearly, but did you also used to bring me biscuits?"

"No you didn't make that up. That was me. I used to hide them in different pockets and make you look for them."

"Well there you go then — I knew those things were actual memories." Kitty's hand fluttered at her throat. "It's such a relief after all these years to know that I wasn't hallucinating when I was little. That the things I remembered were real. Mam kept telling me it was all just in my head."

"You were a good little girl Kitty. Good natured and loving. You were chuffed to bits when Sarah was born — never jealous. You used to show her off to everyone. *My baby*, you'd say, *come see my baby*. I was very proud of you."

Kitty looked over at my mum quickly, touching her eyes gently with the tips of her fingers in an effort to keep the tears in.

"I know this sounds soft," she said, "I'm an old-age pensioner for heaven's sake, but it makes me feel awful happy to hear someone say they were proud of me, even if it was sixty odd years ago."

"Well I was proud of you," Trevor handed Kitty his handkerchief, the clean, fresh, ironed one he keeps in the lefthand pocket of his trousers, not the one he uses himself which he keeps in the right. "You were a good girl and it looks like you've turned out to be a good woman too."

Kitty reached over, took Trevor's big hands in hers and rubbed her thumbs gently over his mottled old skin.

"I'm a lucky woman Trevor, that's what I am. I've had a lot of joy in my life and a lot of love too. Mam's life wasn't so joyful and she never let on why."

Trevor got up from the table at this point, making a show of clearing the cups and saucers.

"Yes well, I don't think Laura was the only one not letting on. I didn't tell Sarah the truth either — or you for that matter — and I'm sorry for that. You both deserved better."

Trevor's voice was shaking with emotion. Mum went over to him at the sink where he was pretending to wash dishes and put her arm round his shoulders.

"It's ok Dad. We're all ok. We're just going to have to make up for lost time now, that's all."

Trevor gave a weak little smile. "Heaven knows girls there's been enough of it lost."

288

CHAPTER
TWENTY-EIGHT

Mum and Trevor and Kitty talked for a long time, drinking tea until Trevor said he was tired and went to bed, at which point they moved on to wine. Kitty said she wasn't much of a wine drinker — she preferred a sweet martini and lemonade herself — but after the first glass she seemed to get the hang of it pretty well. It felt weird hearing my mum talk about her life, describing something I was part of to someone who was to all intents and purposes a stranger, but a stranger who also had a major stake in mum's life. I got really uncomfortable when Kitty asked about my dad and how come my mum and he were divorced. It was the first time I'd really heard my mother talk about my father as a woman as opposed to a mother.

"Roy is a good man and he was a great husband but the thing was I never really fancied him very much. When I met him, I liked him so much that I wanted to be with him and I was knocking on a bit — well past 30 — and I wanted to settle down, have kids, the whole shebang — so I kidded myself that I didn't need all that flippy tummy and weak at the knees stuff. But the truth is that's exactly what you do need if you want to stay married."

This was the first time I'd heard this and it made me cringe. Mum had had two big glasses of wine and I thought perhaps she had forgotten I was there but she hadn't.

"Don't go making that face Ellie. Did you think your father and I didn't have sex?"

"To be honest Mum I never really think about it at all. I'd prefer not to if you don't mind."

"Oh don't be such a prude. I'm sure there's nothing I've done that you haven't."

"I'm pretty sure of that too but there are some things that a mother and daughter really shouldn't share."

"Poppycock," she said. She was more drunk than I'd thought. "Anyway I'm talking to my sister not my daughter. You don't have to listen if you don't want to." She waved her empty glass in the general vicinity of the bottle and Kitty filled it up for her.

"OK Mum — you've got a point. But before you get down to telling Kitty what a crap lay Dad was, just remember that Sandra thinks he's God's gift to womankind and can't keep her hands off him."

Mum wrinkled her nose.

"Ah yes. Those two don't seem to have any problem. But that's the thing about sex appeal — it's very personal. Roy and Sandra have got it going on in the bedroom department whereas Roy and I didn't, so we decided to end it while we were still friends and I think we've pulled it off pretty well, wouldn't you say Ellie."

"Speaking as the child of this sexless marriage I can say from experience that you did indeed pull it off and you are both great parents."

"So there you go then." Mum made a floppy, expansive gesture with her hands which illustrated very neatly that she was about as drunk as I'd ever seen her. I checked the label of the wine we were drinking. A 14.5 per cent Cabernet Sauvignon. That explained it.

"Ooh that side of things has always been great for Stan and me." Kitty said. "Even when we rowed terribly, and we did, especially when we were younger, over the most stupid of things, I knew we'd make it up by nightfall because we would want to go to bed together. Sometimes he'd sit on the bottom of the stairs and wait for me to get tired of being angry and I'd just pick him up on the way to bed. Seen us through some rough patches has good sex."

"Oh dear God," I said. "If you two are going to insist on talking about this sort of stuff I'd better have a glass of wine too. A really big one." I got myself a glass, finishing off the bottle. Mum just reached behind her and pulled another one out of a box near the fridge, opening it expertly; even using the special cutting thing for the foil.

Kitty continued. "You know what I always say? I always say if the rocks are in the marriage the rocks are in the bed."

"Isn't that a quote out of some film?" Mum asked.

"It is — out of *Cat on a Hot Tin Roof* with Elizabeth Burton and Paul Newman. Big Mama says it to Maggie the cat, that's the part Elizabeth Burton plays. That's one of my favourite films that is."

"It was a play first actually, written by Tennessee Williams," I said, dredging up some English lit

291

memories, "and he hated that film because it played down the fact that the bloke was meant to be gay."

Kitty looked horrified. "Who, Paul Newman?! Don't be daft gull. Paul Newman wasn't a homosexual. He was married to Joanne Woodward for donkey's years, for heaven's sake!"

"Not Paul Newman himself. The man he's playing in the film."

"Oh well, that's ok then." Kitty looked visibly relieved at having her idol's virile man status restored.

"Anyway," I said, changing the subject, "what exactly does that mean — the rocks in the marriage bit?"

"It means," Kitty said "that if things aren't going well in the bedroom, things won't be going well in the marriage generally."

"Well that's not exactly rocket science is it? It's pretty obvious that if you've got a good sex life chances are you'll have a good marriage. Dad and Sandra are a living, way too public example of that."

"Well you say that," said Kitty, "but girls of my generation didn't know they were entitled to expect a good sex life. Most of them thought it was something unpleasant they had to endure every so often if they wanted a house of their own and kids. And you certainly never spoke about sex or periods or anything like that. You know what my mother said to me the night before I married Stan — other than that I was ruining my life and that I should stay on at school, get an education and get out of the valleys? She said, *Don't be surprised if he wants to lift your nightie tonight.* That was it! That was all the sex education I ever got. I didn't like to tell her he'd been lifting my skirt for months already."

"So I didn't miss out on a detailed sex education then, not knowing Laura?" Mum joked.

"Sarah love — you didn't miss out on much at all."

Mum was getting tired and emotional. "But I did Kitty — I did. I would willingly lay down my life for Ellie and all this time I thought my mother had died young and that it wasn't her fault she wasn't around to love me. And now I find that she actually chose to walk out on me, chose not to be in my life. Made me miss out on you and all your family. And not just me; Ellie missed out too."

Kitty reached for my mother's hands.

"I've thought about that a lot since I found those letters Sarah. And I know what you mean about being willing to die for your kids. But I've got five of them and if I died for one I wouldn't have been around to take care of all the others. Mam had to make a choice. Whichever one she made meant she was going to lose out. Doesn't mean she didn't love you."

Both Kitty and my mother were in tears and I studied Kitty's photos carefully to stop myself joining them. I looked at all the faces of people I didn't know but to whom I was apparently related. We had always been a family of ones. Dad was an only child and then there was Trevor, Mum, me — no cousins, no aunties and uncles, no big family get-togethers — just us — and I had accepted that as being the way it was. Only it wasn't the way it was — over in Wales there was all this kith and kin to which Mum and I belonged; a family.

"Anyway," Kitty said, dabbing away her tears, "there's no reason for either of you to miss out any longer. Me and Stan would love it if you and Ellie would come to visit us in the Rhondda. We'd be ever so proud if you'd come and stay — Trevor too if he fancies it. It's about time you saw where you were born."

Mum looked at me.

"Would you come with me Ellie? I'd really like to go."

"Sure Mum — if you want to go, I'm up for it."

After all, I'd been halfway round the world and back, I could surely manage a little trip down the M4.

The weight of my life shifted in those twenty-four hours. Kitty went back to Wales and daily life carried on as before — my mother and I went to work, Trevor shopped and cooked and gardened, but things were different and we all of us in the house in Clapham felt it. There was a new lightness about Trevor, as if losing the weight of his secret had put a new spring in his step and Mum was delighted to have been discovered by her sister. She and Kitty spoke on the phone at least two or three times a week, starting to stitch each other into the fabric of their lives. Mum knew the names of all Kitty's children and grandchildren: who worked where, who studied what. They hadn't quite got to the point of discussing what they were going to have for dinner and whether they should serve broccoli or Brussels sprouts with that but I did overhear them discussing the best way to get grass stains out of a pair of trousers so that day could not be far off.

294

"What do you find to talk about?" I asked Mum one evening after she'd been on the phone to Kitty for at least 40 minutes.

"Everything and nothing really: one minute we're talking about what's happening on *Coronation Street* and the next we're talking about how finding a sister after all these years makes us view our past lives differently, makes the future look different too. Talking about the small stuff helps us talk about the big stuff."

Gabriel and I on the other hand were very careful to avoid the big stuff altogether, at least as far as the two of us were concerned. We were still seeing each other as often as we had been; we played pool and drank wine, talked about gardening and the application I was working on with Carol for more contact with Cristina while she remained in foster care. We went to the pub with Gina and Paul and had the privilege of being there when Gina (who had never been very good at waiting for something she wanted) suggested after a couple of beers that she and Paul move in together and then flew into an almighty rage when he told her he had no intention of living with her unless she agreed to marry him. When Paul finally got Gina to understand that what he had done was to propose to her, Gabriel and I were there to cheer when she replied "Not now but not never". We talked about Paul and Gina's feelings no problem; we talked about Kitty turning up and the real reason my grandfather and mother had moved to London from Wales; but neither of us mentioned again the mystery woman I had seen collecting Maud, and I stopped myself from saying anything when I saw him absent-mindedly reaching his hand across the sofa to stroke a cat that wasn't there anymore.

When I told him I had decided on Australia as the destination for my next trip and that I was thinking of going towards the end of November all he said was, "Lucky you! It'll be summer there by then."

He enthusiastically pored over maps and guide books with me and helped me fill in visa applications and price up plane tickets but he never once expressed any disappointment that I was going or even asked me how long I would be away.

My mother and Trevor were equally unconcerned that I would shortly be leaving home again.

"You're sure you're ok with me going Mum, what with just having found out about Kitty and everything?"

"Of course I am. You make it sound as if finding out about Kitty is a bad thing but it's one of the best things that's ever happened to me."

"Sounds like another amazing adventure for you love," my grandfather said when I told him about my plans. "Just so long as you don't go until after we've been on our visit to Wales."

Ah yes. The Visit to Wales. Never had a weekend been so discussed. All three of us — me, Mum and Trevor — were going towards the middle of October. Kitty was insisting that we all stay with her at her house but I didn't think I would be able to cope with that much intimacy. Thankfully Sandra had generously offered me the camper van to sleep in if I wanted to, and since this also gave me the option of a not particularly quick getaway, I accepted her offer gratefully. Sandra and Dad were loving the whole Kitty story and every time I went over to visit them they made themselves comfortable on the sofa and waited eagerly for the next instalment, like it really was *Coronation Street*.

"To think," Dad had said when I first told him about it. "I have a sister-in-law I never even knew about."

He'd got a sharp poke in the ribs with an elbow for that one.

We planned to go on the Friday morning and come back on the Monday. I would drive the camper van but Mum and Trevor would go on the train because the camper van was not very comfortable for three on long journeys. The preparations for the trip were numerous — Mum dug out photos of herself and me when we were little to take with us because Kitty had asked to see them, and she bought presents for all the children and grandchildren: a beautiful, dusky rose-pink blouse for Kitty (carefully chosen from Peter Jones of course) and a bottle of whisky for Stan. She selected her favourite clothes to take with her, setting each item aside as it came through the wash and ironing it before laying out colour co-ordinated outfits on the bed in the spare room, like the paper outfits I used to cut carefully out the back of my *Bunty* when I was little. There were a full two weeks to go before we went and I thought the time was going to drag past for Mum, but as things turned out she ended up having other things to think about. We all did.

CHAPTER
TWENTY-NINE

One morning at 4a.m. there was a loud knocking on the front door. All three of us were woken by it but it was Trevor who got to the door first. Cliff was standing there, still in his pyjamas, with a desperate, panicked look on his face.

"Trevor, will you come with me to the house please? It's Joanie. There's something wrong with her."

"You want me to come with you Dad?" Mum asked, but Trevor just shook his head.

"You stay here Sarah. Call an ambulance. Put the kettle on. I don't think we'll be going back to bed today."

He put his big grey overcoat on over his own pyjamas and followed Cliff home.

The ambulance wasn't necessary. Joan had died in her sleep, lying neatly on her side of the bed next to Cliff, with her curlers in her hair. Cliff had woken in the night for some reason and reaching out to touch her had known almost before his hand was on her arm that she was not breathing. He hadn't knocked us up because Joan needed help. It was because he did.

There was a lot to get done after that. Cliff was in too much of a state to organise anything and with his daughter living in Jamaica and Joanie's son in Norfolk, it was Mum and Trevor who took up the responsibility of letting everyone know, organising the funeral and putting a notice in the local paper.

The first thing Trevor did once he was certain that Joan was dead was remove her curlers, very gently, one by one.

"She wouldn't want anyone to see her like that, not in her curlers," he explained when he got home.

A lot of people turned out for Joan's funeral. Not just immediate family and friends but people for whom Joan had cleaned and ironed over the years and most of the Jamaican community of Clapham. They were there to support Cliff because his daughter hadn't been able to get a flight over in time, or at least that's what Cliff said. Even Gabriel was there. I hadn't asked him to come but he just turned up at the church. It was the first time I'd ever seen him in a suit and he looked even more handsome than usual. In the church the white, middle-class families bowed their heads and were respectfully quiet and the big rowdy Jamaican families — grandparents, parents and children — kept up a constant stream of chatter and laughter and chased away the usual sad gloomy silence of a funeral. The older Jamaican ladies kept right on chasing away the shadows throughout the service, punctuating the minister's words with announcements of "Praise Be" and "Halleluia" and "Thank the Lord" which was making Joan's son visibly wince but was lifting the spirits of the rest of us. Cliff had chosen upbeat hymns, happy and tuneful and the Jamaican community sang these loudly and with joy. I had never before been to a funeral at which I had tapped my toes and cried at the same time.

Cliff only managed a short eulogy. He said he was going to miss Joanie terribly and that she should sleep in peace until he came to join her but that in the meantime he'd put a couple of shirts in her coffin to give her something to do while she waited for him. Then, because Cliff had asked her to — Joan being such a fan of Barry McGuigan, — Gina sang "Danny Boy". Her deep soulful voice took hold of the sweet sentimental song by the corners and laid the melody gently over the congregation, like a mother laying a blanket over her baby.

And I shall hear, tho' soft you tread above me
And all my dreams will warm and sweeter be
If you'll not fail to tell me that you love me
I'll simply sleep in peace until you come to me.

As the song came to an end, Cliff lifted his hand ever so slightly and, with the tiniest little wave, said goodbye to Joan. I looked around at the people in the pew with me. Tony with his arm around Beth, Paul watching Gina intently, Mum with her arm linked through Trevor's and Dad and Sandra standing next to them, hand in hand. However many people Kitty might have lined up for us to meet when we got to Wales, I was proud that this little group of people was my family and very glad that Joanie had been one of them. I cried for Joanie then; not just tears of sadness because I would

300

not be seeing her again but tears of thanks that she had been part of my life. And when Gabriel reached over and took my hand, squeezing my fingers ever so gently, I cried a little bit more.

Mum, Sandra and Teresa had made the food for after the service.

"We'll sort all that out for you Cliff," Mum had said. "You've got enough to be getting on with and Joan's son won't be able to organise refreshments from Norfolk."

There were sandwiches and vol au vents and spicy Jamaican patties. Sandra had baked a Victoria sponge and some spiced fruit cake which she had sliced and spread thickly with butter. There was tea, served in Joanie's favourite rose pattern tea set, and whisky and sherry for those who needed something stronger. Although Cliff most certainly needed something stronger he couldn't bring himself to break the habit of half a lifetime and drink in the house. He didn't quite go to the lengths of getting under his car to do some maintenance but he did sit on the low wall outside the house to drink his whisky. Trevor and Clive went out there and kept him company while I helped Mum and Teresa wash the dishes and tidy up.

There's something very therapeutic about getting stuck in and doing the dishes after any of life's big events — christenings, weddings, funerals. I was washing; Teresa and Mum were drying and putting away. There was a feeling of restoring order, of doing something for Joanie that she would want done properly. For once, doing dishes felt like a feminist action — being part of the solidarity of the sisterhood of women that help each other in times of crisis by rolling up their sleeves and doing domestic chores. I washed the rose pattern tea set carefully, scouring the tea stains gently and swilling each cup in warm water before stacking it on the drainer for Mum and Teresa to dry. Joan's tea towels were faded and worn but each and every one of them was impeccably ironed. It made me sad to think that they would not get ironed again.

Margaret, Joan's daughter-in-law, came and stood in the kitchen while we were working. She didn't offer to help but sat down at the little kitchen table and poured herself another sherry. She had obviously had quite a few already.

"Shall I put the kettle on again Margaret? Make us all another cup of tea?" Mum asked tactfully.

"Oh not for me thanks," Margaret said, "I prefer this." She took a long swig of her sherry. The glass she was holding was a crystal sherry glass, very small with a little flower pattern, and with that one gulp it was half empty again.

Mum put the kettle on anyway.

"How is Graham coping?" Teresa asked. "Must have been an awful shock for him."

"He's fine," Margaret answered. She didn't volunteer any more information and to fill the awkward gap in the conversation Mum said: "It was a lovely service wasn't it?"

"Do you think so?" Margaret said haughtily. "Graham and I thought it was wholly inappropriate.

302

I'm not certain Joan would have approved of all those happy-clappy hymns and that young girl singing a secular song like "Danny Boy". The family is Catholic you know."

Mum, Teresa and I all paused for a second before regaining our composure and carrying on with the dishes.

"Oh well," Mum said soothingly. "Joan was married to a Jamaican man after all. I guess over the years their two cultures would have got mixed up together."

Margaret downed the rest of her glass. "No she wasn't," she said curtly.

"No she wasn't what?" Teresa said equally curtly. She had her back to Margaret, ostensibly concentrating very hard on the drying up, but I could tell from the way she stiffened, her shoulders hunched up around her ears that she had lost all patience with Margaret.

"No she wasn't married to Cliff. She and Graham's dad were never divorced. Like I said she was a Catholic and she added sins to her soul every year she lived with Cliff. It's lucky that Graham's father died a few years ago or else there might have been an argument over Joan's estate."

Teresa slowly put her tea towel down on the drainer and turned around to face Margaret.

"An argument over the estate? An argument over the estate?! Have you looked round this house Lady Muck? There isn't an estate to argue over. This house is rented and about the only things of value that Joan possessed are this tea set and that glass you're drinking out of. Marriages aren't always made in church you know.

They're sometimes made when people share a life. Now if you know what's good for you, you'll finish off your sherry, go find your husband and tell him that it's time for you to go. Otherwise I suggest you keep your big mouth shut for the rest of the afternoon."

Margaret got up from the table. She was seething, her face bright red with indignation. She screwed up her face, searching for something cutting to say back but she was too well oiled to think of anything and all she could manage was to reach for her glass one last time. It was already empty. I picked it up from the table and took it to the sink. By the time I'd finished scrubbing Margaret's coral pink lipstick from the rim, Margaret herself was also gone. Less than fifteen minutes later we heard Graham rounding up his boys and saying a polite good bye to Cliff. Then there was the sound of a car engine starting up and the car pulling off.

Now it was Teresa's turn to reach for the sherry.

"Good riddance to bad rubbish," she said as she downed her glass in one.

We finished the last few dishes, wrapped up the left over food in cling film and filled Cliff's fridge. We all knew he wouldn't eat any of it.

"I'll come back in a few days to throw it all out," Mum said.

Cliff looked tired and drained as we left; his face pale even under his dark skin. There were no more ceremonies and speeches to get through, no more people for whom to put on a brave face. Just Cliff on his own in a house empty of Joan. A widower, even if he had never been formally able to marry his wife.

"Do you want to come back with me?" Gabriel asked as we left, catching hold of my hand, "I don't much fancy sleeping on my own tonight. Funerals make me feel awfully . . . well, mortal I suppose."

I knew that what Gabriel was after was the comfort of a nice "do not go gently into that good night" shag but I wasn't offended by that because the idea appealed to me too. I knew that Gabriel and I would not try to make sense of the way we felt about Joan's funeral or of our fear of death by talking because that might involve talking about our feelings but I also knew that we would have poignant, intimate sex, our emotions bruised and close to the surface, and that the sex would make us both feel a lot better. I had a quick word with Mum and Trevor (didn't mention the bit about shagging obviously) and then gladly took the hand that Gabriel offered me for the short walk to his house. I could feel the little row of gardening calluses across his palm and when I lifted his hand to my mouth to kiss it, the tips of his fingers smelled faintly of garlic.

"I know this sounds a bit odd," he said "but I really quite enjoyed Joan's funeral."

I didn't tell him what Margaret had told us. I was pretty certain that Mum and Teresa wouldn't be telling anybody either. If Joan would have worried about being seen in her curlers, she'd be turning in her grave if she thought people had found out she'd been living in sin all these years.

"I enjoyed it too. It's a bummer isn't it that the one party all your family and friends make a real effort to come to is your funeral? Joan would have liked to have been there — if there is such a thing as heaven, Joan is looking down right now and bitching to all the other dead people about who didn't come and that Mum and Teresa have put her tea service away in the wrong place."

The thought of Joan, perched somewhere on a fluffy cloud in the heavens, complete with wings and a harp and peering down at us, made me smile to myself but also made me sad all over again and I found I was blinking back yet more tears.

"Ellie, you ok?"

"I'm fine," I said and then, putting on my best Vinnie Jones stare, "it's been emotional, that's all."

Gabriel saw I was shivering, and put his arm round me as we walked the last few hundred yards to his house. It was getting cold. September had come and would soon be gone and even though all of Clapham was now littered with remembered kisses, I would soon be leaving London and our summer of love really would come to an end. I don't know whether it was that or whether it was the emotion of Joan's funeral and the gentle way that Gabriel had sqeezed my hand in the church but I suddenly turned to Gabriel and asked him on impulse, "Gabriel, you know I'm going to Wales soon with Mum and Trevor to meet Kitty's family? Do you fancy coming with me?"

"Won't that be a bit weird? Me coming with you on a big family discovery trip?"

"What? More weird than it is already! Come with me. It'll be good to have you there and Mum and Trevor will enjoy spending a bit of time with you before I go off to Australia."

"Are you sure?"

"Positive."

"In that case I'll come with you."

CHAPTER
THIRTY

Trevor and Mum took a taxi to Paddington station to catch the train to Wales. This was an event in itself. Trevor thought people who took taxis were guilty of both shameful extravagance and extreme laziness. He thought the same thing of people who used tumble dryers rather than hanging their washing on the line or who bought ready-made mashed potato instead of getting the potato peeler out. Still, Mum insisted.

"Look Dad if we take the Tube we'll have to change trains and that's a lot of effort. Anyway, it won't cost that much."

I knew she would distract his attention when they got to the station so that he wouldn't see how much the fare was. He would get into a bad mood otherwise about wasting money.

Gabriel and I waved the taxi off and then bundled our bags into the camper van.

"I'll drive if you like," Gabriel offered. "I've never driven a camper van before."

I threw him the keys. "Great! Be my guest." I'd driven it plenty of times and knew how temperamental the gear box was.

It was a beautiful October morning, cool and crisp, the sun low in the sky. We crossed the river at Albert Bridge, the pretty ice cream-coloured one that always makes me think of icing and wedding cakes and, as the sun glinted on the water and lit up the whole of London with the hazy amber colour of autumn, I had a rumbling feeling of excitement and expectation in the pit of my stomach like I normally get when I set off travelling. We wound away along the north side of the river, past tall, gracious, eighteenth-century houses with blue plaques and little balconies looking out over the busy Chelsea embankment and on to the river. In no time at all we were on the Talgarth Road and I was pointing out to Gabriel the short stretch of artists' houses with enormous double length windows that I have always liked.

"I think those are my favourite windows in the whole of London," I told him. "The houses are a bit scruffy but the quality of the light inside must be fantastic."

Gabriel was struggling with the gear box and could only look across at the windows quickly.

"Very lovely. Although it must be pretty difficult to concentrate on your painting or sculpting or whatever with the sound of three lanes of traffic tearing past your window 24 hours a day."

"I'm sure when they're standing by their easels surrounded by sunshine that's a minor distraction."

"You don't even know if artists live there any more. This is just next to Baron's Court you know, very swish part of town, probably full of stockbrokers and city traders."

"Listen Gabriel, just go with me on this will you. I like to think that this little stretch is the home of struggling artists, working all day in their garrets and sustained only by their muse and shed-loads of natural light. I'm never going to know for a fact whether I'm wrong so let me indulge myself will you? It's just one of the things I do when I'm on my way to Heathrow."

"But you're not on your way to Heathrow Ellie, not yet anyway. You're on your way to South Wales, the land of your fathers."

"Same difference. We're on the way to Heathrow right this very minute, it's just that today at least I'm not going to the airport."

"Not today maybe but very soon you will be," Gabriel said cheerfully, glancing over at me with a smile on his face. "En route to sunny Australia."

I could see that he was happy, indeed positively delighted, at the fact that I would soon be leaving and the realisation of that stabbed me in the heart.

Neither of us said anything for a while, refusing to have the conversation that hung, heavy and loaded, in the air between us. It was Gabriel who finally broke the silence.

"Did you say you'd made a picnic? I'm starving."

"*I* didn't make a picnic" I corrected him cheerily, "*Trevor* made us a picnic so that we wouldn't spend money at the services. We've got tuna sandwiches, egg and onion sandwiches, apples, crisps, Kit Kats, even a flask of coffee. What would you like?"

"Cup of coffee and a Kit Kat would be great please. I'm not certain it's a good idea to unleash egg and onion sandwiches in here."

"What do you mean? Egg and onion sandwiches are the best. They're my favourites."

I rummaged around in the bag at my feet. Being in charge of a flask was a bit of a novelty for me. Girls who jet off round the world at a moment's notice don't tend to own flasks. Flask possession is for girls who make lists and pack carefully before they go to the Lake District youth hostelling.

I balanced the cup carefully on my lap, poured out the coffee and then topped it up from a miniature bottle of Baileys rather than milk before handing it over to Gabriel.

"What are you doing?" he said, glancing over at me. "It's not even ten o'clock yet!"

"Don't worry. I didn't put much in. Just thought we needed a bit of fortifying before we meet my long-lost family. If you think that's bad, I've got two bottles of wine in my rucksack."

Gabriel took a big swig of the sweet, gently alcoholic coffee.

"Tastes pretty good," he said. "Bit like a girly cocktail but good all the same."

I took a swig straight out of the Baileys bottle.

He shook his head. "You're a little bit wild you know that, don't you?" he said.

"I like to think so."

From the Talgarth Road it was not long before we joined the M4 which would take us all the way to

Wales. Gabriel had got the hang of the gear changing by then and we rumbled along at a steady 60 miles an hour in the inside lane, faster, sleeker vehicles flashing past us in a constant stream. When we got taken over by a big articulated lorry with a sign on it urging people to Eat More Chips, Gabriel started to get a little frustrated.

"Doesn't this thing have any more welly?"

"It's a camper van. What did you expect? An Audi TT?"

I don't know why I said that. I didn't mean to. It was the first fast car that came to my mind. I went cold as soon as the words were out of my mouth and I kept quiet for a while after that. Gabriel had no idea of the bit part that an Audi TT had played in my life and so had no idea that I had unwittingly invited the memory of Robert, and our journey to Brighton together in his wife's fortieth birthday present, to come and sit with us in the rattling little van. I peeped quickly at the memory — the wind in my hair, the wait for Robert in the hotel, the first time he and I made love — and then I folded it up into a little square, opened the window and threw it out.

"You ok Ellie? I'm not really being rude about Sandra's pride and joy you know?"

"I know that. Shall we listen to some music?"

"Cool. I've burned a few new compilation CDs if you want to dig one of those out of my bag."

I chuckled. "Like I said Gabriel: this is a camper van. It's got a radio and a tape player. No means of playing CDs."

I rummaged through the tapes that dad and Sandra kept in the glove compartment.

"Now, would you like Janis Joplin or Fleetwood Mac?"

"Why don't we see what we can find on the radio?" Gabriel said politely.

I fiddled with the tuner and found a station whose reception was acceptable and we listened to hits from the eighties and nineties and people calling in to enter general knowledge quizzes and guess the mystery voice. I went into my travelling trance: a kind of meditative state I am only ever lulled into when I am on some form of transport — a car or bus or plane — where my body relaxes but my mind is set free to pick over the jumble of things rolling around in my head and think them through with a greater degree of lucidity than I can otherwise achieve. I wish I could do this on my own — just sit still quietly somewhere and let my mind wander but I can't. I can't get my body to go into the right kind of physical limbo by myself. I need to be on the move. Perhaps that's why I've always travelled so much.

I settled into my trance and sat there silently while Gabriel concentrated on driving. I stared out of the window as we moved along at a steady pace. It felt like my powers of observation were keener than usual. I could make out the individual cows in the fields and people walking on the bridges over the motorway in high definition. I watched the people in the cars that overtook us: a series of other lives, of people on their way somewhere, one eating a banana, another singing along to whatever music was playing on their stereo, four old people with white hair travelling in silence, a people carrier stuffed full of family; all of them fast asleep except the dad who was driving. Everything I saw seemed more vivid, the colours brighter and bolder, and all the time my mind was whirring, sorting and sifting. Filing. Deciding. In no time at all we were approaching the Severn Bridge and Gabriel was poking me in the leg, telling me to sort out the change to pay for the crossing.

The Severn Bridge reminded me a bit of the Albert Bridge we had crossed about three hours earlier — another suspension bridge but bigger this time and more modern, with lots more cars. The water of the Severn estuary was the colour of milk chocolate, murky and rolling gently and the camper van made a little whump noise at regular intervals as we crossed over the sections of the bridge. I wondered idly whether we would survive if the bridge were to collapse and the camper van and all the other cars on the bridge were suddenly plunged into the water, but before I could make up my mind we were over the other side and paying a hefty fee just to get into Wales. We passed a sign welcoming us to Wales and I stirred myself out of my travelling trance and began to feel nervous about the meeting that lay ahead.

I fished out the directions that Kitty had sent us and began to look out for road signs. We came off the M4 onto another busy dual carriageway for a while and the scenery around us slowly began to change. Hills appeared either side of us. By the time the dual

314

carriageway had dwindled to a single lane, the hills had grown into full-blown mountains with rows of houses, packed tightly together, rising in crazy steep lines up their sides.

"We must be getting close," Gabriel said.

"How do you know?"

"Look over there," he pointed to the roundabout ahead of us. Draped over one of the signs on the roundabout was a big white sheet, on which someone had painted in big, black, wonky letters

Trevor, Sarah, Ellie and Gabriel Welcome to Wales!

I clapped my hand over my mouth. "Omigod" I said through my fingers.

"There's a welcome in the hillsides for you," Gabriel said, in a cod Welsh accent.

We came off the main road, took some twists and turns along impossibly narrow streets of terraced houses and found Kitty's house. It wasn't difficult. It was strung with multi-coloured bunting and there was another Welcome sign fluttering from the top window.

"There's lovely," Gabriel said in his terrible Welsh accent again.

"Shut up Gabriel," I snapped. "I need a moment to think about how to handle this."

"Too late," he said, parking up. "Kitty and your mother are at the door waiting for us."

Apart from the bunting, Kitty's house was like all the other houses in the terraced street, two windows upstairs, one window and a door downstairs, like the kind of houses I used to draw when I was a child. There was no front garden and the front door opened straight out on to the street which was where Mum and Kitty were stood waiting for us, pink cheeked and excited.

"Hello, hello, welcome," Kitty said, throwing her arms round my neck and hugging me tightly and clumsily, all a fluster. She turned her attention to Gabriel, hugging him just as tight.

"Gabriel. Pleased to meet you. Aren't you lovely and tall? Come in, come in. Everyone's dying to meet you. They're all inside waiting."

I felt nervous, excited and worried, all at once. Like I was about to go and pick up my exam results or dump a boyfriend. My stomach was turning somersaults. I looked over at Mum. She looked every bit as flustered as Kitty but she took my hand and squeezed it hard.

"In you come Ellie. You too Gabriel. There's a lot of people in here waiting to meet you."

The hallway leading to the house was tiny, rows of shoes lined up on the floor and dozens of coats hung up, forcing us to walk into the house in single file. As we entered the living room my overall impression was of a row of smiling strangers in the middle of which was my grandfather, wearing the widest smile of all.

"Ok everyone," Kitty announced. "This is Ellie and Gabriel."

There was a burst of hellos from the row of faces.

"Ellie and Gabriel — this is Stanley and this is Joanne, Amanda, Simon, Ian, Anwen, Darren, Nicholas, Mark, Rhianydd, Samantha, Janine . . ." She carried on with the roll call of names. I had heard them all before, Mum had even drawn up a little family tree for me before we left, trying to explain which ones were Kitty's

316

children and which ones her grandchildren, but I knew I had no chance of remembering which name belonged to which face. It was like one of those long photos they used to take of everyone at school, where there was always one kid who tried to get in the photo twice by starting at one end and then running to the other before the photo was finished, ending up with two blurred faces at either end. Here, every single face was blurred except Trevor's who sat calmly in the middle of it all.

One of the blurred faces sitting closest to Trevor got up and made some space for me to sit down.

"Hello Ellie love. I'm Stanley. Delighted to meet you at last. Sit down by there, next to your grandfather. Do you want a cup of tea?"

Stanley was a small man, barrel-chested with thick glasses and a kind voice, who bore absolutely no resemblance to Paul Newman. I smiled and nodded at him.

"Two sugars please," I said, remembering vaguely that sugary tea is good for shock.

I was grateful for the opportunity to sit down. My legs felt like dead weights and there was a faraway buzzing in my ears, like I was about to faint. I couldn't see Gabriel, wasn't even sure if he had followed me into the living room to face this barrage of new-found family. The room was very hot and noisy, voice after voice piled on top of each other, none of them making any sense. Trevor leaned towards me and whispered in my ear, "Take a deep breath Ellie. A few deep breaths. It certainly helped me when I got here."

Stanley put the cup of tea in my hand. I took some deep breaths. Slowly, things started to come back into focus. I saw Gabriel standing near the doorway, also being presented with a cup of tea. He smiled at me. Trevor kept his hand on my knee. The noise level subsided a bit. I saw that all the faces were turned towards me and that they were all smiling.

Kitty clapped her hands. "Come on everyone. Talk amongst yourselves for a while. Let Ellie and Gabriel drink their tea in peace. They've had a long journey. They'll be addled."

The faces did as they were told and began to talk amongst themselves and the noise level around us rose once more.

CHAPTER
THIRTY-ONE

"You all right love?" Trevor asked, squeezing my knee gently. "Camper van make it ok?"

I nodded, took a sip of the tea.

"I've never seen so many people in one small room before," I whispered to Trevor.

"Neither have I. It's marvellous isn't it?"

I did a double take at Trevor. He was still grinning and I realised that he meant it. He really did think that all these people crammed into one room was a good thing.

"I don't know," I said. "I'm used to being an only child with no cousins. I'm feeling a bit overwhelmed by it all."

"Just sit there and drink your tea, you'll feel better soon."

I took more deep breaths, let the noise just wash over me for a bit. I looked at the faces one by one, began to see from the repetition of heart-shaped faces and smooth, clear skin, which ones were related to Kitty and which ones had married into the family. I watched as Gabriel was suddenly whisked away into the kitchen, Kitty's arm firmly beneath his elbow. The noise level suddenly subsided again as Kitty, Gabriel and my mother emerged from the kitchen, all three of them holding a bottle of Cava in each hand.

"I want us all to drink a toast," Kitty declared over the sound of Gabriel popping corks at top speed. Stanley dished out a wide and varied collection of glasses and he and my mother began to pour out Cava for everyone. It took a full five minutes before they all had a glass in their hand and Kitty continued: "A toast to family."

"To family!" Trevor's voice was the loudest and clearest of all.

It turned out that bunting was Kitty's favourite party piece. She fished it out of the loft and strung the house with it for every family occasion — weddings, christenings, graduations, even apparently for the annual summer family barbecue. Gabriel told me this when he and I snuck outside, ostensibly to fetch some stuff from our bags in the van, but really because I needed a breath of fresh air and a little bit of peace.

"Family barbecue? Have you seen the size of the garden? There's barely room for the barbecue let alone the family that go with it. How does she manage that then?"

"Probably the same way she's managing this reunion," Gabriel said, "with a big shoehorn."

"How is it possible for there to be so many of them anyway?" I asked. "Everyone seems the same age. Is that natural?"

"Haven't you been listening to your mother the past few weeks? Kitty's got five kids. She had her first when she was 17 and her last when she was 41 and her

320

youngest child is about the same age as her oldest grandchild so yes — some of them are the same age."

"How come you were listening to my mother?"

"I wasn't. But I've just spent the last twenty minutes in the kitchen with them both."

"Twenty minutes? Is that all it was. It seemed like you were gone a lifetime. I hope it wasn't too awful for you."

"Not at all. Kitty's a really good woman. It means a lot to her that you're all here. She just wanted to show off her family — all of you, the old ones and the new."

I looked away. I felt a bit ashamed of myself. Gabriel was right. Kitty was a good woman — very kind and loving — and my mother was clearly enjoying every minute of being with this huge extended family, flitting around the room, bright eyed and chatty — but I was feeling horribly over-faced by the whole thing.

"You're right. It's just that I'm not used to the clamour of so many relatives."

"There's way too many of us isn't there?" A dark haired girl was standing on the door step, smiling. She was small and slight with a heart-shaped face and lovely clear luminous skin. Her hair was cut short and spiky.

"Oh hello." I said. "Didn't see you there. You're —"

"I'm Ceri. Spelt C.E.R.I., pronounced Kerry. Not Cherie or Cherry. Ceri. If you're wondering where I fit in, I'm Kitty and Stan's youngest daughter. Which makes us first cousins. Well half first cousins. Do you want a cigarette?"

I shook my head. "I'm ok thanks."

Ceri took a small tin from the back pocket of her jeans, expertly rolled a cigarette with a single hand, lit it quickly and then came to join Gabriel and me leaning on the back of the van.

"Mam would be tamping mad if she saw me smoking. She warned us all that we were to be on our best behaviour while you were here. Make a good impression."

"You're doing that all right," Gabriel said, ever the gentleman. "Everyone's been really welcoming and friendly."

Ceri shrugged her shoulders ever so slightly. "So far at least. Usually when we all get together there's tears by bedtime."

"What do you mean?" I asked, worried now.

"Don't worry. We're not dysfunctional or anything. Well not that much. It's just that Mam puts such a lot of effort into these family get-togethers she ends up totally knackered and then she tends to get a bit weepy."

"I wouldn't have guessed that," I said. "She makes it all look so effortless."

"Are you kidding? She's been preparing for this for weeks now, running around like a milgi as my dad says. Like a greyhound that is. It's been a right palaver. Don't feel bad or anything — she loves doing it. It's just a lot of work, that's all. And she's so happy to have found Sarah that she wants the whole thing to be perfect for her."

"It is. Perfect that is. And Mum — Sarah — she's happy that Kitty found her. It's just a bit . . ."

"Strange? Weird?"

I nodded. "I guess."

"Strange for us too, but it must be more difficult for you because there's only one of you and there's tons of us. I always wanted to be an only child when I was little. I thought it must be great not always to be one of a crowd."

I smiled at her. "Did you? I always wanted a brother or sister. One at least."

Ceri smiled back at me, ground out her fag under her shoe, pushed the butt down a drain with her toe.

"We'd best get back in. Our mothers will be worrying about us. Once more into the fray, what do you say? You too Gabriel."

She put her arm round my shoulders as we walked back in, just for a second, lightly and quickly. It made me feel warm and included: part of something.

"Anyway Ellie, what's with the wine thing?" Ceri asked. "Since my mother came back from London, she's had my poor dad down Somerfield every whipstitch, fetching her wine to taste. She's been tipsy every night, deciding which Cabernet Sauvignon she was going to buy for today. Me and my sisters have been trying to get Mam off Cinzano for years, she goes up to London once to visit you lot and she comes back thinking she's ruddy Gilly Goolden. Your mother some sort of wine critic or something?"

I could hear Gabriel laughing out loud behind me.

"She likes to think so," I grinned.

By the time we got back in, the Cava bottles were empty and the noise was at an even higher decibel level.

My mother and Kitty were scurrying round the room, handing round trays of little sausages and prawns in batter.

"There you are Ellie love!" Trevor greeted us merrily. "Give us a hand will you. I've said to Kitty I'll go swill these glasses out in the bosh so that the taste of the Cava doesn't spoil the taste of her Cabernet Sauvignon."

Gabriel looked at me quizzically.

"He's going to swill the glasses out in what?"

"In the bosh," I laughed as I followed Trevor out to the kitchen, "it's what he calls the sink."

Imagine you were holding a big paper bag full of lots of balls — ping pong balls, rubber balls, snooker balls — and that all of a sudden the bottom of the bag burst and the balls went everywhere, bouncing and rolling and skittering over the floor.

That's what it felt like being with Kitty and her family — like there were dozens of balls bouncing off the walls and the floor and rolling under your feet — and every one of those balls was talking and laughing. This was a family that laughed a lot and laughed loud. It was absolutely bewildering. Still the chat with Ceri had helped put me at ease and I decided I would get myself a big glass of that Cabernet Sauvignon and take it one relative at a time.

I had not seen Trevor look so happy for ages. I had never heard him sound so Welsh. He'd dumped virtually all trace of London in his accent and was singing away with the rest of Kitty's family. He was talking to two of Kitty's youngest grandsons who were sat at his feet, chins in their hands, listening intently as he told them that when he was younger he used to be a wrestler in the circus in London.

"See these hands boys?" he was saying, holding his hands palm out so that they could be inspected, "see how big they are? I could pick up two men with those hands and hurl them out of the ring so that they bounced on their heads all the way back to their Mams. I had the grip of the Malagmites, I did."

The two boys tentatively measured their own little hands against Trevor's. I could see them working out that this bloke was old now but that with hands that huge and fingers as thick as sausages, he certainly looked like he could once have been a wrestler.

He used to tell me that story too when I was little, only then the circus was in Cardiff not London. I must have been at least 13 before I realised it wasn't true. Come to think of it, I still didn't know who or what the Malagmites were.

Watching him there, surrounded by Kitty's family, recently reunited with his accent, it struck me that this should have been Trevor's life. This is where he belonged, here in these valleys. He should have been with Laura. She had been the love of his life and they would have been married sixty years by the time she died. It would have been a careful, gentle marriage in the early years but once Laura had finally learned to let go of the memory of Jack it would have developed into a great one, loving and kind and romantic because Trevor would have been romantic I was sure of that. They would have had a few more children after Mum and then life would have been one long merry-go-round of school and university and first jobs, followed by weddings and christenings and a gaggle of grandchildren to help look after. Laura would have given up worrying about her weight, even got a bit thick round the middle from sharing too many Raspberry Ruffles with Trevor. They would still have held hands on their way to the shops. He would have been devastated by her death and would miss her dreadfully every single day but, held safe and loved in the middle of his big, busy, laughing family, the life left over would still have been a good one.

Only that wasn't the way Trevor's story had turned out. Jack wasn't dead after all and had found his way home and after that Trevor's life had been wrenched off the path it was following and forced down a different path altogether. One big twist in the tale and the tale became another.

In soap operas, terrible, terrifying things happen to people all the time — daughters bludgeon their fathers to death with a wrench in the garage, women marry mass murderers and find themselves being driven with their family into the canal — and in those soap operas people cry and scream and mourn and tear themselves apart with guilt for a few weeks and then they move on, get over things, chat with their neighbours again in the café or the pub or over the garden fence.

That's not how it is in real life. In real life, it takes people a long time to process the terrible things that happen to them. To work out how they feel. When something seriously bad or sad happens, people concentrate on just getting through the day, putting one foot after the other, getting up in the morning, going to bed at night, surviving. They keep busy because there is usually a lot to do after a life-changing event — a funeral to organise, a house to be cleared, paperwork to sort, people to be told, a new home to be found. Eventually one day, you find that you have moved far enough away from the scalding pain that you can bear to take a look at it and think about how it makes you feel. You don't cry for three weeks and wake up one morning to find you are miraculously all better. It's a far more gradual, boring process than that and it can take a long time.

That's how it must have been for Trevor when Jack turned up and Laura just turned on her heel and left. He would have kept busy, concentrated on moving to London, on his baby daughter, on finding them somewhere to live and a job. He would have saved all his energy, all his thinking, just for coping. And then one day he would have felt strong enough to get the memories of Laura out, to test his feelings, face the pain and realise that he was already out through the other side of it and could start to forget her. And having survived that pain, could he really be blamed for protecting his daughter from it? For killing Laura off so as to explain why she was not in Mum's life? Wasn't that braver than telling her that, through no fault of her own, Laura had been faced with a choice and that the choice she had made had not included Sarah?

We'd had a good life the three of us in the house in Clapham. Trevor had done well by Mum and she had done well by me. If when Mum was little she had known of Laura's rejection she might not have had the same confidence, the same joy for life. And if when she was old enough she had insisted on travelling to Wales only to have Laura close the door in her face; who's to say that that door closing might not have flung her off the good path she was following and onto another, less happy one?

But then I looked up and watched Kitty and my mother. The two of them were standing out in the kitchen having thrust plates of food in people's faces until they were sure everyone had eaten more than they should have and were clearing up together, collecting the last few sandwiches and corned beef pasties and putting them all onto one serving plate so they could wash up the rest. They hadn't stopped smiling or talking the whole time I'd been there, always gravitating back to each other. Kitty and my mother's lives had been lived in such totally different ways yet they were connected by something so fundamental, so essential, that they felt part of the same thing. They felt and acted like sisters even though they had spent sixty years apart. I knew they were going to enjoy being sisters for the rest of their lives but I also knew, without a shadow of doubt, that they had deserved to learn about each other much sooner, however difficult the consequences of that might have been, however well intentioned the reasons for keeping them secret from one another.

Trevor, Mum and me. We all now had a life-changing event to come to terms with and would have to fathom out how it had changed the people we thought we were and how it would affect the people we were going to be. This reunion with Kitty and her family, and with Wales, was going to take some getting used to and it was going to take a while. Right now we were concentrating on getting to know a room full of smiling strangers in a house wrapped in bunting.

I was relieved that in the space of the summer I had already managed to process and file Robert away. If I wanted to, I could pull his file out of the cabinet and look at it but it didn't hurt any more. Not at all.

Gabriel was one of the main reasons I had been able to do that. Gabriel who right then was busy working the room, chatting to my cousins, sidling up to me every now and again just to check I was ok. Gabriel with his long legs and his gardener's tan. Gabriel who had always kept his distance from me and who had a beautiful, dark-haired former girlfriend who was none of my business. Gabriel who seemed glad that our summer of love was drawing to a close.

Eventually, the party wound to an end and parents gathered up their children, husbands and wives collected each other and the house slowly drained of people. I was surprised to find out that only Kitty, Stanley and Ceri actually lived there.

"All the rest left home long since," Kitty said. "Ceri's the last one to go."

"And the one that's hung around the longest," Stanley teased. "Twenty-four and still living at home! I keep telling her it's time she flies the nest and stops putting the kibosh on her mother and me having some time to ourselves."

"Oi Dad, you and Mam get plenty of time to yourselves! I'm round at Jamie's most of the time and anyway since when did having a houseful stop you having time to yourselves? You managed to make five babies no bother."

Kitty and Stanley grinned at their last-born fondly and then at each other.

"As you can see Sarah," Stanley said "Ceri is not only our youngest child she is also the most chopsy. Got a bell in every tooth she has. And if there's some cause to support, Ceri will be there supporting it. She's the Red in our spare bed and she's got the T shirt to prove it — CND, Socialist Workers Party, anti-vivisectionists, she's got the lot. She was even a vegetarian for a while but she missed her Mam's cooked dinners too much."

Ceri was pouting. "Don't do this Dad!"

"Do what?"

"Take the piss out of the things I believe in. You always do it. It's really unfair."

"I'm sorry love but it's just so easy to wind you up. Anyway, it's getting late and it's time for you to be getting yourself round to Jamie's this evening. Sarah needs your room tonight."

"Oh dear Ceri. I hope I'm not putting you out too much." My mother looked horrified that she was turfing Ceri out of her bedroom.

"Don't be daft," Ceri said. "I'm going to meet Jamie down the pub and then we're going to get a Chinese take away and watch telly until we fall asleep on the sofa."

"That's all right then dear. I don't need to feel bad then." My mother looked relieved.

"Not at all. I hope you get a good night's sleep everyone. I'll be over in the morning for my breakfast."

She banged the door behind her as she left.

Trevor looked absolutely done in by this stage, the early morning start, the journey and a good few glasses of Kitty's Cabernet Sauvignon having taken their toll.

"If you don't mind girls," he said, getting wearily to his feet, "I'm going to turn in now and get into the bathroom first. Age before beauty and all that."

Trevor kissed me and then my mother and then finally Kitty. He shook hands with Stanley and Gabriel and started to make his way upstairs but before he left the room he turned back and looked again at Kitty.

"I'm ever so glad you found us love. Goodnight."

CHAPTER
THIRTY-TWO

After the heat of so many bodies crammed into Kitty and Stan's little terraced house, the camper van seemed dark and uninviting. It took a while for Gabriel and I to fish out our sleeping bags which were cold and slippery and to settle down on the two narrow little sleeping spaces the seating of the van provided. I hugged my knees into my chest in an effort to warm up.

"That doesn't work you know Ellie."

"Doesn't it? It always works for me, eventually."

"Well it sort of works I suppose but it keeps you cold longer. What you're meant to do is push your feet down as far into the sleeping bag as they'll go and totally relax. That way you'll warm up the air in the sleeping bag that much faster."

"Trouble is I'm too cold to undo my knees from my chest," I said, my teeth chattering.

"I'd get in there with you if there was room."

"I'd insist you did if there was."

"Look, imagine you're on a beach, a beautiful sandy beach and the sun is beating down and you're curling your toes in the sand."

"I can't," I said grumpily, "I'm too cold."

"Just try it for a bit."

I did as Gabriel suggested: pretended I was on a beach and stretched my legs out in front of me.

"That's it," Gabriel said. "The sand is like white powder and the sun is hot and there's not a cloud in the sky. The sea is crystal clear and is lapping gently on the shore —"

"Stop!" I said, holding the palm of my hand out in front of me like a policeman.

"Why? What's wrong?"

"Your clichéd travel agents' description of the seaside is making me need a wee."

"Well if you do need a wee, you'll either have to wake up Kitty and Stanley or just go twti down outside in the street." "Hey," I giggled. "Who's been teaching you Welsh?"

"I heard Kitty saying it to one of her grandkids earlier. I think it sounds sweet."

"G'night Gabriel. Thanks for being here."

By the time I had warmed up I was already asleep.

In the morning when we woke up the insides of the van windows were foggy with condensation. Someone was tapping on the window. I struggled out of my sleeping bag, wiped a clear space in the condensation with the heel of my hand. Ceri was standing outside with two mugs of tea.

"Here you go," she said, as I opened the door and she handed me in the two mugs, "Two sugars in each. Dad says that's how you take it although I have to say I thought you Londoners would be more health conscious than that and think that white sugar is evil.

Still, you'll need it to help you get going for the day ahead."

"Why?" I asked "are we going anywhere in the day ahead?"

"You bet," she said. "We're going to Cardiff. Dad and Gabriel are going with Trevor to see Wales play New Zealand and you and I are going to have a proper catch up. I asked Mam if she wanted to come with us but she says she wants to have some time 'alone' with Sarah."

Ceri put little inverted commas round the word alone with her fingers as she said it.

"Looks like we've got ourselves a plan," I said, taking a big sip of my tea. It was strong and very sweet. Refreshing. Ceri went back into the house.

"Gabriel?" I asked, poking the bottom of his sleeping bag with my foot, "did you know you were going to a rugby match?"

The sleeping bag shook its head.

"Do you want to go to a rugby match?"

The sleeping bag nodded its head.

"That's ok then." I sat up a bit to finish off my tea.

We travelled down to Cardiff together by train. Not a big sleek 125 like the one my mother and grandfather would have taken from Paddington but a little three-carriage train that stopped dozens of times as it wound its way down the valley and was stuffed with men wearing red rugby shirts as if they were the ones who would be playing, and women and teenage girls on a shopping mission. It wasn't long before we'd left the valleys and arrived in the city centre.

"It's not that far is it?" I said wonderingly to Ceri.

Ceri sighed.

"It might feel like it but the Rhondda really isn't the back end of beyond, you know. It's not like they show us on the telly — poor unemployed miners who still haven't got over the collapse of the miners' strike yet, and gangs of kids with drug problems all huddling together in the shadow of the dark gloomy hills getting pregnant while it pours down with rain. We do have a bit of that mind, but there are loads of us who've got decent jobs and running water and Sky television and everything."

There was a tangible buzz of excitement as we approached the Millennium Stadium. It looked like a giant flying saucer that had landed right in the middle of the city, its enormous white spikes rising above the hotels, shops and apartment blocks, dominating the sky line; modern and majestic. A river of men and boys and women too, flowed towards it. There were lots of red shirts in that river, and plastic daffodils and Welsh flags and red and green jesters' hats with bells on, but also lots of black shirts and New Zealand flags mixed in. We passed stalls selling more flags and scarves, red and black, and small fleets of burger vans. The smell of fried onions scented the air. There was a feeling of enormous energy and emotion as the crowds of people babbled and roared towards the stadium. This crowd was not just on its way to watch a game; it was on its way to do battle. Trevor's

face was so flushed with excitement I caught a flash
of the little boy he must once have been in there
somewhere.

Ceri and I escorted them to their gate, watching and
waving as the river plunged into the stadium.

"Right then," she said, "I thought we'd go down to
the Bay. It'll be quieter down there. I'm going to look
out for a cab for us. It's not that far but it would take
too long to walk."

There seemed to be a lot of people dressed in red
shirts still drinking in the pubs and bars around the
stadium.

"Aren't all these people going to be late?" I asked.

Ceri looked into the windows of the pub we were
passing and smiled.

"Not everyone can get a ticket for the match or
afford one either. Lots of people just come down to
Cardiff to watch it on the telly in the pub. Be part of
the action that way. The people who've been to the
match will be in the pubs again afterwards. An
international day can be a very long day."

"Does that cause trouble?" I asked, "between the two
lots of fans?"

"Not really. Rugby's not like football. There might be
a little bit of argy-bargy but not much, even less with
New Zealand fans. They've got a lot of sheep there
too."

Suddenly she saw a cab with its light on and hailed
it. It pulled up at the kerb for us and we got in. Within
five minutes we were being dropped off at Cardiff Bay.

"This doesn't look like Wales at all," I said as we climbed out, "it's like being down at the harbour front in Toronto or Boston or somewhere."

We were looking out over a flat expanse of calm water, around which curved modern apartment blocks and a small parade of trendy bars, shops and restaurants. Parents and children were walking along the waterfront, eating ice cream, and I could see a line of people queuing to get on a ferry across to the other side of the harbour. Sea gulls whirled and screeched over head. The place had a jaunty, holiday, seaside feel to it.

"Where are we?" I asked Ceri.

"This used to be the docks area — Tiger Bay — where coal and steel and stuff were brought to be transported elsewhere by sea. Now it's had a ton of money spent on it to bring in tourists and they've put in a barrage to stop the tide and keep the water looking nice. I wasn't awfully keen on that to begin with — I was worried about all the birds that used to feed on the mud flats when the tide went out — but they built them feeding grounds elsewhere so I was ok with it after that. It's still a working docks though, over that way. See that old red brick building there — that's the Pierhead building which used to be the headquarters for the Bute Dock Company and that glass block there, that's the Welsh Assembly debating chamber that Richard Rogers designed. And that modern building over that way, the one that looks like it's got a sail on the top — that's the St David's hotel. Five star and very swanky."

"You know an awful lot about this area."

"Oh I bring all our visitors down to the docks, show off about Cardiff a bit, do my tour of the *Doctor Who* filming locations. Pisses me off that no-one mentions that it was coal and steel from the valleys that helped build these docks in the first place, but I always make sure I point it out."

"What's that behind us?" I pointed to an enormous bronze building, like a hunched up armadillo, with huge letters inscribed on it.

"That's the Millennium Arts Centre. You've got all sorts of concerts going on in there — opera, classical, musicals — the lot."

"What's it say on it?"

"It says 'In these stones horizons sing' and in Welsh 'Creu gwir fel gwydr o ffwrnais awen' which means 'Creating truth like glass from the furnace of inspiration'. Aren't those lovely words? Loads of meaning stuffed into just a short sentence and they sound nice too."

"I've noticed lots of Welsh, on signs and things. Is there much call for that? I didn't think that many people spoke Welsh any more."

Ceri grimaced at me, clenching her fists together. She looked really pissed off.

"God. It really annoys me when people say things like that. Tons of people speak Welsh and more and more learn it every year." She cocked her head at me. "Sarah says you've done loads of travelling. Tell me — when you go off to other places do you bother reading

338

up about them or do you just rely on what you've seen on the telly when you go there too?"

"Woah! Steady on. I didn't mean to offend you, I've been to Majorca. I know about Majorcan Catalan versus Castilian, so I do know something about minority languages."

"See there you go again. I mean I'm glad I don't have a total Philistine for a cousin but for the people of Wales, Welsh isn't a minority language. It's our language, the main thing that makes us different from England. You'll be telling me next that you walked into a pub in North Wales once and that everyone suddenly switched from speaking English to Welsh."

"Does that happen then? That sounds awfully rude?" I was teasing her by now but she was too wound up to realise. She twisted her face even more, banging the heel of her hand against her forehead in frustration.

"No. It doesn't. It's an urban myth. People come here, English people mostly, and expect people in Wales to be speaking English, then get all annoyed when they hear them speaking Welsh. If you go into a bar in Spain or France you expect people to be speaking Spanish or French don't you?"

I nodded quickly, not wanting to annoy her further.

"Well then, it's exactly the same in Wales, people speak Welsh in pubs, especially in North Wales where there are more Welsh speakers. Why should we be expected to speak English just so that visitors can listen in to conversations that are nothing to do with them?"

"I don't think you should be expected to do that at all. It wasn't actually me who mentioned the pub in

North Wales thing you know. I've never even been to North Wales."

Ceri looked a bit bashful. "Oh yes. Sorry about that. I do tend to go off on one a bit about this. It just really gets on my nerves when people don't respect different cultures and expect everyone to be just like them."

"No worries. I understand. Language of the oppressor and all that."

Ceri grinned at me. "Yeah well I'm sorry anyway. Like my dad says, I'm too mouthy and I've got no tact. Can we go get something to drink now? I'm gagging for a frothy coffee."

We made our way towards the bronze armadillo where there was a modern café restaurant with tables and chairs outside and a couple of buskers with a violin and flute. We ordered lattes and after a while the waiter brought us over a thick, white mug each, full of steaming milk and a thick sprinkling of chocolate powder on top.

We sat there for a while in silence, drinking our frothy coffee and listening to the buskers who were very good.

Eventually Ceri finished her coffee and put her mug down.

"What do you think our mothers are talking about?" she asked.

"Based on the stuff they've been talking about on the phone I reckon they're working their way through a discussion about who makes the best shortbread biscuits, Tesco Finest or M & S, what they should make us for dinner tonight and do they think their mother felt bad about what she did."

"You're probably right. They seem to be coping with it all ok though don't they? At least my mother is. Is yours?"

"I think so. In fact I think she's more than coping. I think she's really enjoying the whole thing. She's found a real connection with Kitty. Makes me think there's something in that saying that blood is thicker than water."

"Too right there. After Mam found those letters absolutely nothing was going to stop her from getting in touch with Sarah. Dad kept telling her that it might be better to let sleeping dogs lie and that a lot of water had gone under the bridge and a long list of other sayings but she was having none of it. She was going to London to find Sarah and that was that. End of. She had every intention of staying up there until she found her. Dad was lucky Trevor was still at the same address else he might have had to put up with my cooking for weeks. You've no idea how determined Mam was. Do you know how many nights she'd spent away from my dad before she came to London?"

She looked up at me. I was obviously expected to respond to this question even though I had no absolutely no idea of the answer. I shook my head.

Ceri held up two fingers.

"Two, two nights in her whole life ever. One night in hospital for when she had each of my two oldest sisters. After that, she said she had the hang of it thanks very much and she had my two brothers and me at home because she couldn't bear to be away from Dad. I couldn't believe it when she told me she'd booked herself a bed and breakfast and she was going up to London on her own. Wouldn't let my dad go with her or anything. Bought herself a mobile. It was like she was on a mission. Honestly, she was scary."

I felt a twist of affection for Kitty, remembering how I'd opened the door to her, little realising how much courage it had taken her to get there.

"I guess finding out you've got a sister after all those years would make you pretty determined," I said.

"It wasn't just that Ellie. You would have to have met my Nan to know what made Mam so determined. Nan was an awfully difficult woman to spend time with. She never sat down. She was always on the move, always working and she made you feel guilty if you didn't keep as busy as she was. Everything was a job to my nan, including us grandchildren. I don't think she ever enjoyed spending time with us; she just wanted to get the work we created over and done with. She used to drive Mam to distraction. All she wanted was for Nan to sit down and just enjoy things. She'd throw these big family parties to celebrate everything and anything — honestly, we've even had Halloween parties the last few years for the kids — but Nan wasn't capable of just enjoying stuff. She'd be whisking the cup out of your hand before you'd finished drinking just so she could go and wash it up and she plumped up the cushions on the settee every time one of us went for a wee. None of us knew then why Nan needed to keep herself so busy.

Finding Sarah is helping Mam to put everything into perspective."

"You know what Ceri? Up until we came here for this visit, I hadn't really thought about how anyone else was affected by this. I was only bothered about Trevor and my mum. Meeting everyone, spending time with you all, I'm beginning to understand how selfish that was and that we're not the only ones who're involved."

"It's funny. I might not be alive if it hadn't been for nan's past."

"What do you mean? None of us would be here if our grandparents hadn't been here first." Suddenly it dawned on me. "I wouldn't be here if your nan — our grandmother — hadn't been here first."

Ceri smiled at me.

"I don't mean like that, although I suppose that bit's true too. I mean that my mother had such a lonely childhood with Nan being the way she was and her dad ill and then dying. You know she used to say to my nan that she thought she could remember having a baby sister and my nan used to say that it was all in her head and that she was remembering a dream or something. Anyway, Mam always felt that something was missing and then when she met Dad and got married all she ever wanted was to stay married for ever and to have a house full of kids and non-stop chaos. I think if she hadn't felt that way she would never have made it to baby number five. As it was my nan almost dispossessed her when she told her she was having me. Apparently it's indecent to have a baby at 41."

"Don't say that. Tons of women have babies when they're older than 41 nowadays."

"Nowadays they do but in the Rhondda women are usually gearing themselves up to be grandmothers by that age. Well Mam did — Joanne had a baby just before I came along so my nephew Mark is older than me!"

"I've got to confess I find it a bit difficult to keep on top of who's who."

"Don't worry, Jamie does too. He tends to keep away from family parties if I let him get away with it, says he's allergic to bunting. Gabriel doesn't seem to mind though — he was right in there yesterday, chatting away to everyone. My mother reckons that's a skill that is. Have you been going out long?"

I counted on my fingers.

"About three or four months I think. Not long. But it'll be coming to an end soon because I'm leaving for Australia next month."

"What do you want to do that for? Gabriel's gorgeous, almost as stonking as Jamie. There'd be no way I'd leave someone like him behind just to go hang out on the other side of the world. And haven't you got a good job in London, helping with child abuse cases or something? What kind of job are you going to do over there? Work in a bar? Anyway, shall we order a sandwich? I'm starving."

As Ceri pored over the menu I thought about what she had said. I thought about the life I would be leaving behind me in Clapham and what I might expect to find when I arrived in Australia. I thought about how glad I was that Gabriel had come with me to Wales and how good it had felt when we first walked into the chaos of Kitty's front room and he had gently tugged my shirt free from my jeans so that he could put the flat of his hand, warm and reassuring, against the bare skin of my back. And I knew that if I was to take my leave of him lightly I was going to have to do it sooner rather than later.

"Right then," Ceri announced. "I'm going to have the feta cheese and red pepper baguette with a side order of chips. What about you?"

"I'll have the same thanks. I've always been a fan of double carbohydrate."

"Well you'll fit in just fine with this family then, I'll go up and order and by the time we've finished those and had a wander round it'll be time for us to get back into town and meet the boys to get the train home."

CHAPTER
THIRTY-THREE

The next day my mother announced that she wanted to visit Laura's grave. I thought my grandfather would try to dissuade her, would see this as misplaced and unnecessary sentimentality, but he did not. Far from it. It turned out that Trevor's parents were buried in the same cemetery as Laura and that he wanted to pay them a visit.

Kitty decided not to come with us. She said she had the Sunday dinner to see to. Given that she was expecting at least fifteen people this was probably not just an excuse. She seemed to have been cooking or cleaning or peeling veg practically the whole time we'd been there. The house already smelled deliciously of roasting meat.

"I'm doing two meats today see — beef and pork — because there's so many of us. Got the beef in already and when that's done, I'll put the roast potatoes in at the same time as the pork. Yorkshire puddings'll go in last."

I found myself unexpectedly looking forward to lunch, not just for the feast that Kitty was preparing but also for the family that would gather round the table. Although still big, this gathering was going to be far smaller than the one with bunting when we'd arrived. I enjoyed Ceri's spiky, challenging company and I knew that with her fairly constant politico chatter she would keep the conversation flowing and that I'd learn even more about what made this big noisy family tick. Also her Jamie was coming and I was looking forward to finding out what exactly the definition of stonking was. It seemed like I was getting into the swing of this whole Waltonesque experience and when Gina sent me a text which said *Have you run from the hills yet?* I could send her one back which said truthfully, *Hills are alive with the sound of lots of people. I'm liking them.*

Kitty drew us a little map of where Laura's grave was and explained to Gabriel how to find the cemetery.

"It's pretty simple love," she said. "Just keep going straight up the valley and you'll see signs for it after a while."

All four of us got in the camper van, Trevor in the front with Gabriel and me and Mum in the back, slip-sliding around on top of the sleeping bags. We followed Kitty's directions and headed straight up the valley. It was another glorious autumn morning, the sun still low in the sky, making us squint as we peered out the windows of the camper van. The leaves of the trees that lined the road were turning copper and gold and the low sun shone through them, giving the trees a sort of fiery glow like in the adverts for Ready Brek. Rising high above the road the grassy hills were still mostly green but covered in places with bracken the colour of rust.

347

"I can't get over how beautiful it is," Trevor said. "It used to be all pit heads and slag heaps and now look at it! I'm sorry that with the pits closed there's fewer jobs but I'm ever so glad that our boys don't work underground anymore and breathe dust. My valley really is green now. And orange too, at the moment."

I could see Trevor's face in the wing mirror of the camper van. He seemed very calm and content. At home with himself. After a while he told Gabriel that the cemetery was not far away now and, sure enough, soon after that we saw a sign telling us to turn off to the right. The camper van made its way slowly up a narrow road which rose steeply up the hillside. The entrance to the cemetery was about a third of the way up and although we could have driven in, we parked up in the car park outside. It did not seem respectful to take a bright orange camper van into a cemetery.

As we walked in I was immediately hit by that sombre, sad nostalgia you get in churches and graveyards. You walk slower, talk quieter, feel small and insignificant next to the reminders all around you of those that have already lived and gone. The graves in this cemetery were dug into the side of the hill, row upon row of them looking out over the valley, like the tiered seats in the Millennium Stadium. Beneath us we could see the road that wound along the bottom of the valley, lined on both sides by streets of terraced houses, laid in straight lines along the lower parts of the hills. If we looked straight across we could see the hill which formed the other side of the valley, a replica of the one we were standing on, reaching high into the pale blue autumn sky which was streaked with white cloud. It was warm for October, the air moist and languid. It was incredibly beautiful.

Mum fiddled with the little map that Kitty had drawn for her and pointed to the far end of the cemetery.

"It's over there somewhere," she said quietly.

Trevor held out his arm to Mum and she took it gratefully. Together, they walked slowly through the rows of graves. Gabriel and I kept a short distance behind them. After a while, Trevor stopped and the four of us gathered round two headstones. One was dedicated to Jack Harris: the other to his wife, Laura.

Nobody said anything for a while, we just stood huddled together looking at the graves. They were graves same as all the others in this beautiful cemetery but the woman who lay beneath this headstone had a secret she'd taken with her all the way there.

Finally, Trevor spoke.

"Sarah, let me tell you a bit about your mother. Things I should have told you before now. She was the prettiest woman I ever laid eyes on — have ever laid eyes on since. Just looking at her was joyful. From the moment I saw her I wanted to be by her side always. She didn't think she would be able to love again but she did. Make no mistake — your mother really loved me — and she loved you too. So much, so very much. She used to smell your hair all the time and rub her cheek against your baby cheek, so soft and innocent. And when she put you into your cot she used to make this clicking noise with her tongue that used to comfort you and send you right off to sleep. When we moved to London I used to try to make the same noise. At first it didn't work as well as when Laura did it but you got used to me in the end."

My mother was crying by now, big heaving silent sobs that shook through her shoulders. Trevor took her in his arms, held her tight. I felt that Gabriel should not be part of this family scene but as I lifted my head I saw that he had already moved away and was standing a little distance down the path.

"I'm sorry Sarah. You two should not have met this way. I should have done things differently. I wish I had. If I had my time over, I would."

Mum didn't say anything, just turned her head deeper into Trevor's shoulder. They stood like that together for a long while.

Eventually, Trevor disentangled himself gently and rummaged around in a big plastic bag he'd brought with him.

"I brought something for Laura," he said. "Something for you to plant on her grave."

Out of the bag Trevor produced a trowel and two small, scruffy-looking plants, brown and withered. He saw the look of concern on my mother's face and smiled gently.

"Don't worry love. These are strawberry plants, summer fruiting. Your mother was very fond of strawberries. With any luck if the weather's not too snowy they'll do ok over winter and will produce fruit next summer. Laura would have liked that."

I watched as Trevor knelt down next to Laura's grave and instructed my mother on how to plant out strawberry plants.

"You've got to be careful with strawberry plants. Too low in the ground and the growing crown will rot, too high and the roots dry out. They need lots of water, strawberries do and there's no shortage of that up here but they also need a fair bit of sun which is not so certain. This variety is called Cambridge Favourite. Very reliable but we're planting them a bit late, should have been in by early September really."

When they were done, Trevor got up slowly, one hand pressed to the small of his back.

"I'm definitely getting older," he said ruefully and then in a gentler tone of voice, "May you rest in peace Laura. I really hope you do."

My grandfather collected up his plastic bag.

"I'm going to leave you here for a while now Sarah. I've got a grave I need to tidy up a bit. It's just over there." He pointed in the direction of a grave a few rows away. "It's the grave of John and Elen Richards, my parents. I'd best get back in their good books. I figure I might be seeing them again sometime soon. You can come and join me later if you'd like — you too Ellie — but I'd like some time alone with them first, make the grave look a bit more respectable."

I went to join Gabriel and we walked slowly back along the path together. Behind us Trevor was standing at one graveside, my mother at another. My heart felt heavy with loss and sadness and missed opportunity. If just one or two things had been different, so would all our lives have been.

We walked out the gates of the cemetery, past the camper van. We walked for a little while, knowing without discussing it that we both needed to put some distance between ourselves and the graveyard, and made our way towards a weathered wooden bench perched high on the hillside.

"You feeling all right Ellie?" Gabriel asked as we sat down.

"Ok I guess, considering how many of the dead people back there I'm related to."

Gabriel smiled at me, took my hand and squeezed it gently.

"John and Elen Richards. Laura Harris. It's weird that my great grandparents are buried so close to my grandmother. You know, even if none of this had happened I still wouldn't have met Trevor's parents because they both died before even Mum was born. I suppose they still live on in a way, in us. I'm even named after my great-grandmother. Elen."

"I didn't know that," Gabriel said, "I thought your name was Ellie."

"There's lots of things you don't know about me Gabriel. There's lots of things I don't know about you either."

Gabriel didn't say anything, just kept hold of my hand. We sat there for a while in silence. The sun was shining and there was still a little bit of warmth in it but the leaves beneath our feet were wet and brown, already starting to rot down, and they clung damply to the soles of our shoes and the hems of our jeans. I could smell the smoke of coal fires in the air. Winter would be here before too long. I glanced over at Gabriel. He looked comfortable sitting here on this hillside, dressed in jeans and big heavy boots with a thick fleece, a washed-out red colour which suited him, making him look even more handsome. His hair was a bit longer than usual and I wanted to run my hand over it like I so often had before, feel the soft prickles part against my palm, but I held back.

"You know what Gabriel? I've been doing a lot of thinking this weekend, well these past few weeks if I'm honest."

I felt Gabriel flinch next to me. He started to pull his hand away from mine, then thought better of it and left it where it was but the connection between us was already broken and his hand suddenly felt awkward and stiff in mine, like it no longer belonged there. I knew he didn't want to hold my hand any more so I gently removed it, thrust it deep in the pocket of my jacket.

He didn't say anything and I could sense that he didn't want me to start this conversation, hoped that if he didn't reply I might not carry on. But I had made my mind up and even though I knew this was going to be a difficult conversation I was determined to push on.

"Anyway, this is what I've been thinking. I've been thinking that I don't want to go off travelling, not any more."

Suddenly I had Gabriel's attention.

"I've got some money that I didn't expect to get, quite a lot of money in fact, and I've decided that rather than use it to go to Australia I want to stay on at Collins & Co and use that money to do the course I need to qualify as a solicitor. Just part-time to begin with because the money I've got won't pay for everything and I need to carry on working while I study. I want to be a childcare solicitor, like Emma, and help children be with the right family, even if that turns out to not be the family they started off with."

Gabriel opened his mouth, started to say something. I put my finger to his lips and shushed him,

"Don't say anything. I haven't finished yet."

"Go on then," he said, looking away from me, down at his feet, picking leaves off the bottom of his jeans.

I was gabbling by now, keen to get out what I needed to say,

"The thing is, I was wondering, now that I've decided to stay, whether maybe you want to move this relationship forward? Because if you do, I do too. Only if we *are* going to do that, I need you to break your no-kiss-and-tell rule. I need to know who that woman was who took Maud away and about all the women before her. And what sort of childhood you had and what used to make you laugh your head off when you were little and what used to keep you awake at night. What still keeps you awake at night. Whether you might like to have kids some day."

Gabriel said nothing, no reassuring nods of the head, no quiet little "hmms" to let me know he was listening. I struggled on.

"I need to know all that sort of stuff. And I need you to know the same sort of stuff about me, including how

I got this money for my law exams — which, looking back, I'm not that proud about, but which I can't pretend didn't happen. If you and I are going to have any chance going forward, you need to know everything that's gone on in my life — good and bad, even if you like me less when you do, because all of that makes me who I am and has led me here, to sitting on this hillside with you, right now. I don't want us to have secrets. I've learned this weekend that secrets make people lose out on stuff: love mostly, and family. What do you say? Want to carry on making hay?"

Gabriel still didn't say anything for a while. Finally he looked at me, but not straight on, just out of the corners of his eyes.

"Look Ellie, I always thought you and me were just having a fling. Gina told me at the beginning that you wouldn't stick around for long, that it wasn't your style and that you always packed your bag eventually."

I bit my lip. It was the answer I'd expected and the one I'd prepared myself for but it still hurt to hear it out loud.

"I thought we were only travelling on this bus together for a few stops, I never thought we were going to the end of the line."

"Fair enough," I shrugged my shoulders, sadness rising up from my toes and filling my chest with lead. "That's what I thought too, to start with, but I changed my mind and I was hoping you might have too."

"I'm sorry Ellie, I'm not explaining this properly."

Gabriel turned towards me, grabbed hold of my knees and pulled them towards him so that our knees were touching. He fished in the pockets of my jacket, dug out my hands and clasped them tight in both of his.

"Lots of times I've wanted to ask you how come you ended up living back at home in Clapham or why some things suddenly made you go all sad and withdrawn but I've stopped myself from doing that because there wasn't any point. I thought any day now you'd be letting me know that you'd booked your plane ticket and had fixed a date to go. That's what I thought you were building up to tell me when we drove past Heathrow on the way here and that's what I thought you were about to tell me now."

"That *was* what I thought I was going to do. I'm sorry if I've got you here under false pretences. I didn't mean to mislead you. I just changed my mind that's all."

I tried to pull my hands away from Gabriel's but he held them even tighter.

"Ellie — you idiot — listen to me. I've kept my distance from you because I thought you would be moving on again soon. I've not told you personal stuff about me or my past or how I feel about you because I didn't want to share that with someone I was only spending a short time with. I haven't even introduced you to my parents or my sister and you wouldn't believe how much they've been nagging me for weeks to take you up to Suffolk to meet them, but I just didn't think there was any point getting into all of that with someone who wasn't going to be around for long."

356

Gabriel paused for breath. "But if it looks like we're going to be staying on this bus together a bit longer, I guess I can start letting you in now."

He kissed me then, a kiss which started off gently and then turned firm and passionate. Finally we broke away and, with my hand held warm and safe in his, we sat side by side, looking out over the russet beauty of the Rhondda valley in autumn, its houses and cars and roads laid out beneath us, tiny as a game of Monopoly. On the brink of a new start and with old stories to tell.

Finally Gabriel broke our silence.

"You know Ellie, about these kiss-and-tell stories. It's going to take me a little while to get through them all. Not that I'm bragging or anything but well, I've done my fair share of kissing in my time. But Sofia — that's the name of the woman who came to collect Maud that morning — she was her cat really and she always said she'd come back for her just as soon as she got a garden — Sofia's story is going to take the most telling. It started off a happy story but it ended up a sad one and I still feel bad about parts of it. We lived together for such a long time and I loved her. I really did. But I never loved her quite enough to marry her and she knew that, deep down, and in the end she found someone else who *did* love her that much. And then I was sorry that person wasn't me, even though today's the first day I've ever actually said that out loud. Anyway, I suppose what I'm trying to say is that in some parts of the Sofia story I won't come out of it looking that good and that I don't really know how to begin. But for the record, just in case you've gone off me by the time I get through it all, I want you to know that I think you'll walk those lawyer exams and become an absolutely brilliant childcare solicitor and that I'm very glad, so very, very glad, you've decided to stay. You ok with all that?"

I nodded. I was just fine with all that. And I knew exactly where I would begin my story when the time came to tell it. I would begin at the beginning.

For a long time I lived with my mother and grandfather in a tall terraced house in Clapham.

Also available in ISIS Large Print:

Legacy

Tamara McKinley

Following in the pioneering footsteps of the women who have gone before her, Ruby and her new husband James brave a long and treacherous journey to start their new life together. However, they soon discover that there are many more dangers than just those that meet the eye. When James is tempted away by the gold rush, Ruby must join forces with the Aborigine girl Kumali and learn to adapt, if they're going to survive.

Meanwhile there are other new arrivals to Australian shores: a Tahitian with a mysterious past, a naïve young schoolmistress, and an English aristocrat, all unaware that their destinies are irrevocably intertwined. As fortunes are made and lives are lost, many secrets will be uncovered. But those torn apart by feuds, greed, hatred and circumstance, will ultimately find they have to unite under the same flag . . .

ISBN 978-0-7531-8540-7 (hb)
ISBN 978-0-7531-8541-4 (pb)

Miss Buncle's Book

D. E. Stevenson

The scene of this entertaining story is laid in a charming English village. The plot centres round Miss Barbara Buncle, a maiden lady who was obliged to write a book because — as she naively explained — her dividends were so poor.

Unfortunately, Miss Buncle had no imagination, so she wrote about her friends — quite kindly and truthfully, of course, for she was a benevolent and veracious soul. The reactions of her friends to Miss Buncle's book, however, were a little surprising, and the far-reaching and unexpected results of its publication caused quite a stir.

ISBN 978-0-7531-8552-0 (hb)
ISBN 978-0-7531-8553-7 (pb)